MW01231241

THE ENEMY OF MY ENEMY

RICHARD CALDWELL

CHAPTER 1

Yana walked with a steady, somewhat brisk, pace along Constitution Hill, the path that leads from the shopping district, thru the garden park toward Buckingham Palace. She pushed the baby carriage easily over the gently sloping stone pavement that wound thru the trees and radiantly green, grassy, meadows. Hundreds of tourists ambled along in the same direction while some sat idly on blankets and lawn chairs in the uncharacteristically brilliant, morning, sun. Since it was Sunday, the "Changing of the Guard" ceremony wouldn't start for another hour, but already the crowd was beginning to build. Yana had attended the ritual each Sunday for the past three weeks and knew the precise timing and routine followed by the New Guard and the Regimental Band as they moved from Victoria Barracks, up High Street, onto Castle Hill and into the forecourt of Buckingham Palace.

She knew the crowd would be thick around the front of the Queen Victoria Memorial statue and between each of the three front gates of the palace. It was important that she positions herself in a good spot in front of the winged statue and close to the path along which the New Guard would be marching as they proceeded to the palace gate. She wanted to be at the front of the crowd and as close to the procession as the horseback mounted police would allow. Although it was only mid-morning, the temp was already starting to climb. London, all of England for that matter, was in the middle of a major heat wave. There had been reports of infants and the elderly dying from heat stress.

Yana's husband, Nizar, walked with her, just slightly ahead and to her right. They had immigrated from their home in Syria shortly after being married three years ago. Nizar was a software developer and worked at the London branch of HP. He was tall and, Yana thought, very handsome. As always, his beard was neatly trimmed and his coal black hair, sporting a razor-sharp part, was always carefully combed. Nizar was immaculately dressed in a white, button-up, Ralph Lauren shirt, perfectly creased, black, slacks and cap toe Alan Edmond shoes. Yana didn't know how he managed to look well-groomed even when he first woke up in the morning, but she loved it. Nizar was selected for his position after working remotely, as an independent contractor, for the firm before they were married. Thanks to his job with an international business they came to the United Kingdom on a work visa rather than having to go thru the normal vetting process required of refugees. That process was longer, more in-depth, and fraught with the dangerous possibility of the Brits uncovering stains from their or their family's past; and there were plenty of stains. As they walked, Yana reflected on her and Nizar's relatively brief courtship and subsequent marriage. They were introduced by a mutual friend who later became what they referred to as their benefactor. She truly enjoyed Nizar's quick and biting wit and his knowledge and insight into a wide range of topics in addition to those relating to computers.

Most importantly, she appreciated his willingness to talk with her, not just at her, like so many, really all, other men in her country. He would actually listen to her and seek out her opinion especially when it involved politics or social functions. Make no mistake, he was still the unquestionable ruler of the house and perfectly willing, and adept, at handing out the occasional slap to her face. He had even whipped her with his belt, or the cane he kept above the door frame in their bedroom when she did something to displease him. She didn't mind though. That was an integral part of their religion and the laws and culture that was established around it. All of her friends and every other Syrian family that she knew of behaved the same. It's who they were. However, the one passion that she and Nizar shared so completely, the bond that made them emotionally inseparable, was an all-consuming, white-hot, burning hatred for Shiites, Christians, all things western, and of course Jews. She wanted to vomit every time she had to ride a bus, or buy groceries, or anything else that brought her into contact with the infidel whores with their bare heads and exposed, lily-white, flesh. Like her peers, Yana had lost her figure immediately after Nour was born. It didn't matter. She had nothing but contempt for the obsession that western bitches had for their bodies.

Their daughter, Nour, fidgeted a little bit but did not cry as they walked like the scores of other young families heading toward the ceremony. Nour was almost six months old and was beautiful in every way. She had lost her baby hair a few weeks after she was born but was now growing the same deep black, almost blue, hair of her father. Yana had rubbed scented olive oil on it before they left their apartment and it glistened whenever the sun's rays sneaked thru openings in the carriage cover. Yana and Nizar had purchased the carriage at Harrods almost two months before Nour was born. Its top and sides sported the bright red and blue design of the British flag, the Union Jack. Everything at Harrods was ridiculously expensive, and this thing had cost a small fortune, but it didn't matter. They were spending money their benefactor had sent expressly for the purpose of getting settled into London's Kensington community. Even in their relatively modest flat, that required a substantial amount of money. Their benefactor didn't seem the least bit concerned about how much money they spent on clothes, their flat, or anything else they might need. Well, Yana thought, that wasn't exactly true. He was careful to warn them not to be too ostentatious. Both she and Nizar respectfully heeded his warning. The carriage had large, spoked, wheels with thin solid rubber tires mounted on flexible strips of aluminum one of which curved upward and one downward. This design served as a spring and mitigated bouncing when pushing the carriage over rough surfaces like the cobblestones on the older, quaint, streets sprinkled around London; all of Europe for that matter. The actual body of the carriage was quite large, almost a meter long and standing almost a meter high at the edge. It had a folding top that could be opened, or closed completely, to protect its precious cargo from the sun or rain. Right now, Yana had it halfway open, so Nour didn't get a sunburn, yet which allowed the tourists and others to see the baby and make the obligatory "gooche goo" sounds that adults found so charming. Nour lay on a fitted mattress with two small pillows wedged between her tiny body and the sides of the carriage. Underneath the mattress were ten, one-kilo blocks of Czechoslovakian Semtex.

Leighann bounced down the stairs from the upper deck of the bright red "Hop On Hop Off" bus when it stopped at the corner of Palace Street and Birdcage walk. She and Heather got off the bus and studied the map they received when they purchased tickets for the day-long bus tour. They had arrived in London the day before to begin a twelve-day Globus tour of England, Wales, Ireland, and Scotland. The tour was a reward they had given themselves after graduating from the University of Alabama at Birmingham, UAB. Leighann and Heather had both finished their Bachelor of Science Nursing, BSN, degrees and were waiting to take their nursing board exam in July. Leighann wasn't worried, she had studied her ass off for the last four years and had managed to graduate with a 3.25 GPA. Heather had partied like a rock star and seldom cracked a book, yet the little bitch still ended up with a 3.5.

Leighann and Heather teased one another mercilessly, but woe to the person who said anything even remotely derogatory about one to the other. They were BFFs and when not in class, or on separate dates, were virtually inseparable. They had been randomly assigned as dormitory roommates in their Freshman year and had hit it off from the get-go. Leighann had been born and raised in Chatsworth, Georgia and instantly tagged as "Hillbilly" by Heather even though she was from an equally rural community east of Montgomery, Alabama.

Both girls were attractive, actually quite pretty. They were both slim with athletic, beach volleyball looking bodies. Leighann had short brown hair highlighted by streaks of what she called "sun bleached" blonde. Heather's was equally short, straight as a board, and cut in what Heather thought was the cutest bob she had ever seen. They had decided to go on this tour of the U.K. and Ireland the summer after their Junior year while on a five-day visit to Cancun. A couple of those days were still a bit foggy, and they had decided that one visit to Senior Frogs was enough for a lifetime. It was some-time during that extended party, and under the influence of either Mexican weed, tequila, or both that they had gotten a bit more phys-ical with their friendship. Neither girl considered themselves any-where near the gay side of town, but things happened and had done so a couple more times after a bottle of wine and nothing on TV.

They had worked their butts off during the summer, after returning from Cancun, and on weekends and some nights during school to save up the money for this trip. It wasn't outra-geously expensive, but neither of their families was rolling in cash. Leighann's dad did slip her $300 in cash when he drove them to the Atlanta airport. "You girls go out for fish and chips on us," he said as he helped unload their suitcase from the trunk of his Nissan. Leighann's eyes moistened at the memory of his gesture. She loved her parents and truly appreciated the sacrifices they had made for her during the last twenty-two years.

Leighann had applied for a job at Grady Hospital in the bowels of Atlanta, just north of I-75. She had been conditionally hired, and would also receive a $5000 sign on bonus, pending she passed her state Nursing Board exams. Heather had accepted a similar offer from Erlanger Hospital in Chattanooga. Grady is what is generally known as a "safety net hospital" since it admitted and treated anyone, regardless of their ability to pay. It also had one of the busiest, and most experienced, emergency departments in the country. Gunshot wounds, stabbings, attempted suicides, and heart attacks were routine. The saying among healthcare professionals was "if you have an emergency go to Grady, get stabilized, then get the hell out of there." Hi-octane was precisely the environment that suited Leighann. She thrived on the adrenalin rush and the controlled chaos found in an emergency department.

Most importantly, she honestly, truly, wanted to help people, especially what she considered the downtrodden dregs of society. And there were plenty of those to go around in that part of Atlanta. Leighann would never touch a patient.

The girls were met at London's Heathrow airport the day before by a Globus Tours representative and transferred to the Millennium Gloucester hotel in South Kensington. They were scheduled to check out tomorrow morning and begin their tour. The first stop would be Stonehenge. However, today was what Globus referred to as a "day at leisure." They planned to see as much of London as humanly possible despite their raging jet lag and mutual exhaustion. After talking to the Concierge at the hotel, they had decided to purchase a 24-hour pass on the Hop on Hop off bus tour. There were three routes on the tour, and they could get off at any one of almost sixty stops and wander around. Top of their list was the Tower of London, Piccadilly Circus, and especially Buckingham Palace for the changing of the guard. The Concierge had explained that, since it was Sunday, the ceremony would begin when the Guard was assembled at 10:30 and begin their march to the front gates of Buckingham Palace. They would arrive there around 11:00. He cautioned the girls that because it was a weekend, there would be a huge crowd and that they should get there at least by 9:30. He went on to say that with so many people jockeying for a place to watch that it would be hard to see the entire procession and posting of the guard, but their best option would be to stand near the east gate and as close to the road as the mounted police would allow. He also warned them that the place would be swarming with pickpockets and they should keep their purse strap around their neck and shoulder and in front of their bodies.

Leighann kept running over the Consigner's instructions as they followed the crowd from the bus stop, along Grosvenor Place and around to the front of the Palace. It was only a little past nine but the area in front of the Palace, and on the front of the Victoria Memorial, was already eight or ten people deep. There were three or four police on huge, beautiful, horses moving back and forth along the spur road, working to keep the crowd behind a movable, wooden, barrier and out of the path the Guard would be taking. Now and then the police would have to stop and single out an overly aggressive tourist to warn them to "take your cell phone" back behind the barrier. One of the police was a no-nonsense female who didn't hesitate to move her horse "up close and personal" virtually pushing an errant onlooker back into the crowd. The crowd was a mixture of Asian, Caucasian of some sort, and a sprinkling of Indian, Pakistani, or from one of the middle eastern, Hijab wearing, regions. It was heavy on Asian and Caucasian and virtually devoid of blacks. Leighann had never seen so many selfie sticks in her life. Of course, hers and Heather's added to that number.

The crowd, more like a mob by now, was constantly shifting as people exchanged one standing spot for another to get to where they thought would give them the best vantage point. Leighann and Heather took advantage of the movement and eventually found themselves pressing against the top rail of the wooden barrier. Across the street, directly in front of them, was an equally large, but more concentrated, crowd clustered around the Victoria Memorial monument. There was an odd, but not unpleasant, assortment of smells wafting up from the swarm of tourists. A mixture of sweat, garlic, *nuoc mam*, and horse shit. The palace mounted police didn't bother putting poop catchers on their steeds. A cleaning crew always came by after the ceremony, but in the meantime, pedestrian beware.

Yana and Nizar walked thru the gate at the end of Constitution Hill and entered the street leading to the front of the palace. Based on their previous visits they had decided that Yana would find a spot for herself, Nour, and the baby carriage in the front of the palace on what would be the left-hand side of the band as the procession marched toward the east gate. She wasn't concerned about being near the street. She was perfectly content to be in the middle of the crowd. Nizar would fall in with the viewers clamoring for spots on the Memorial. In Nour's diaper bag, that he was carrying was four, two kilo, blocks of Semtex. As with the explosives in the baby carriage, a blasting cap was inserted in each block. Each cap had a short length of detonation cord linking its top to the top of the next cap. The last block of Semtex in the chain had an additional cap wired to a disposable cell phone. Packed around the sides of the blocks in Nour's bag, and in the baby carriage, were hundreds of three quarter inch nuts and one-inch bolts.

Nizar had been astounded, during their earlier visits, at the almost total lack of security surrounding the ceremony. Sure, there were four mounted police, but they seemed only intent on keeping the crowd behind the barriers and the paths clear for the procession. There were also several; he had counted five, soldiers patrolling along the path who were intently watching the horde of cell phone camera-clicking tourists. Nizar knew they were there to stop anyone who started attacking bystanders with a gun or knife or like the lone lunatic who went after a guard at Notre Dame with a hammer. They shot him, like a dog, not fifty feet from the front door of the church. Regardless, no one stopped any of the tourists who were pulling their suitcases or carrying backpacks to the ceremony. This was especially strange on the heels of the rock concert bombing in Manchester and the AK-47 slaughter at the London Eye. The Brits were an arrogant, overly assured breed who seemed hell-bent to take whatever was dealt out and still "carry on."

At precisely 10:30 a Sergeant gave the command to "fall in" and the Royal Band and New Guard assembled into military formation at Wellington Barracks. After being inspected by a Captain of the Queens Guard, they began their march out of the barracks courtyard towards Buckingham Palace. Each member's left foot hit the ground with every beat of the bass drum as they moved forward with a perfectly synchronized thirty-inch step. There were a couple of new members of the band taking part for the first time today, but they have practiced the formation and the marching hundreds of times. They would make no mistakes.

A few minutes before 11:00 a.m. the procession makes a right turn from Birdcage Walk and begins moving along the street between the Palace and the Victoria Memorial. As usual, the crowds on either side of the road began to clamor for a look at the band. They jostled one another as they adjusted their positions to take photos or cell phone videos. Overall, however, the crowd is very well behaved and are careful not to step past the barrier and into the street. Of course, the presence of the mounted police and their constant admonitions "mind the path" keep the tourist horde from getting out of control.

On the north side of the Palace, on the far side of Constitution Hill, just outside of the park gate a man wearing a New York Yankees baseball cap stands behind a tall, concrete, fence column. There is a sign on the column warning those entering the area in front of the Palace to "beware of pickpockets." As the Drum Major leading the procession makes a "column right," the man takes out a cell phone and begins entering, +44 20 7730, then slowly, also to the sound of the bass drum, 4, 4, 6. The man steps behind the concrete column and presses 9.

Yana and Nizar never heard their phones ring. The speed of sound, at sea level, is roughly 343 meters per second. The explosive velocity of Semtex is 8,700 meters per second or over 25 times the speed of sound. They, baby Nour, and everyone around them were dead long before the ring of their cell phone reached where their ears would have been milliseconds before. The twin, synchronized, explosions sent the nuts and bolts packed around the Semtex into the crowd with more force than rounds from an AK-47. The results were beyond devastating.

Leighann and Heather had been able to work their way right up to the street barrier and had a perfect view of the band and guard as they marched in front of the Palace. They died instantly.

The Horse Guard nudged Billy, the huge, chestnut brown, Arabian, up to the entrance of the center gate where he usually waited for the band to pass. From here he could keep the crowd behind the barriers and out of the street leading into the closed gate. The heat and humidity were getting close to unbearable, and Billy didn't like that one bit. He snorted and plopped his hooves ever so slightly but enough to let the guard know that he was getting impatient. It was already getting quite warm, and they were both ready to start moving again. The blast came from his right and blew the guard out of his saddle. His booted foot caught itself in the saddle's left stirrup which caused what remained of his mangled body to hang like a grotesque rag-doll from Billy's left flank. Billy attempted to run but only moved a few, agonizing, steps before he staggered and fell among the dead and dying. His painful bellows mingled with the screams and could be heard mournfully blocks away.

Despite the tremendous force of the twin blasts, and their proximity to the front of the Palace, none of the glass in its windows was shattered, unlike other nearby buildings. The Palace window panes had long ago been replaced with one-half inch, bulletproof, plexiglass which was capable of stopping a would-be sniper round. The concussion did cause structural damage to the window casings, but the windows held and prevented shards of glass, and body parts, from being hurled inside the Palace.

The man with the Yankees cap slipped from behind the fence column and joined the howling crowd stampeding away from the Palace. Those fleeing toward the park jammed into the gate leading to Constitution Hill. The man knew the police would be searching every square inch of every public area anywhere near the Palace and slipped his cell phone back into his pocket. He would remove its SIM card, wipe it clean, and toss it into a trash can once he reached the train station in the next block.

CHAPTER 2

Abdulla smiled as he watched the BBC coverage of the attack from his suite in the Hermitage Hotel in Monte Carlo. He always felt a tingly, physical, thrill, and more than a little satisfaction, anytime Jews or crusaders were slaughtered by, well anyone, but especially Jihadists. He didn't truly understand why, since he didn't conform to anywhere near the letter of the law as it related to Islam and he had no personal hatred for Jews or infidels. It was almost as if ingrained in his DNA. As he had done for the past five years, Abdulla had come to Monaco to watch the Grand Prix and to preen around the casinos and discos with his always beautiful, always young, and expendable "catch of the day." He had shipped his Lamborghini Aventador Coupe to Monte Carlo; he wasn't about to be out shown by the scores of other, thirty-something, multi-millionaires in town at the same time, and for the same reason. These displays of grossly excessive wealth and testosterone had become something of a ritual with his crowd, and he loved it. Abdulla smiled at the BBC broadcast showing the images of carnage and mayhem. Censors had removed most of the gore from the news footage, but the terrified screams and utter panic was obvious and felt in an odd, perverse, sort of way, pleasing to his senses.

Abdulla was from Qatar, the first-born son of an unbeliev-ably wealthy family. His father, a sheik, had parlayed a substantial inheritance into an enormous, diversified, fortune. Following in his father's footsteps, and heeding the advice of British investment advisors, Abdulla had grown his family's wealth even more. Despite his overly extravagant lifestyle, he was a shrewd and cunning businessman. As with most of Qatar's elite, the core of his family money had its origin in the oil and nature gas fields of the relatively tiny peninsula. Were it not for having what is generally considered one of the three largest reserves of natural gas, and oil, on the planet, Qatar would be dirt poor, more appropriately "sand poor." Compared to its neighbors, it had no other natural resources; nothing to mine and virtually no arable land. Historically, Qatar had the reputation throughout the Arabian countries for breeding camels and not much else. Thanks be to Allah, and the internal combustion engine, those days were long gone. Today Qatar boasted the highest per capita income in the world and Abdulla was at the top of the heap.

Abdulla's family had sent him to an all-male, military academy in Switzerland for his secondary education. At first, he felt entirely out of place among the other students in his Freshman class even though the majority were also transplants from other European and Middle Eastern countries. Thanks to the school's academic demands, and intermural soccer, he soon made friends and found himself bonding closely with a bookish, religious extremist, from Saudi Arabia. It was here that Abdulla began to develop a love and appreciation for math and science. It was also the time when his religious and political views, shaped by what some would consider peculiar perversions, began to meld and his aspirations for power and control started to emerge.

Almost every weekend he and his friend, Saad Al Talal, had stayed awake late at night reading the Quran, dissecting every line of every Sura, and discussing the various aspects of Sharia law. Although he didn't consider himself to be an Islamic fundamentalist, much less an extremist, Abdulla's beliefs were being fashioned, not so much from Saad's feverous rantings, but because of his thoughtful examination of Islam and his blossoming penchant for violence and power. Abdulla found himself enamored by the concept of a regional, even global, caliphate. While lying in bed, waiting for sleep to bring the intensely vivid dreams he experienced almost every night, he would sometimes imagine himself as the Caliph. The undisputed ruler of all the territory and all the inhabitants of the caliphate. His fantasy included infidel slaves and meting out brutal penalties for breaking even minor laws. Crowds would part as he walked among them. Men and women alike would cease talking, or whatever they were doing, and bow in his presence. He would be recognized and revered wherever he went. In time, his fantasies began to consume him.

Like Abdulla, and all the students at the academy for that matter, Saad, or rather his family, was incredibly wealthy. He could also trace his royal heritage back for hundreds of years, not just the last several, petroleum-dependent decades. Saad's family always projected a conservative appearance publicly, both politically and with their Islamic beliefs. However, privately they regularly funneled considerable amounts of cash, maintained in untraceable offshore accounts, to extremist groups in various parts of the world. Although they received the lion's share, this funding wasn't always limited to Islamic terrorists. In years past, family money had even found its way to the Irish Republican Army and a violently radical group, Aum Shinrikyo, in Japan. Politically, the family maintained the appearance of being closely allied with the United States and the European Union. In reality, they detested the thought of any association, much less support of, these infidels. Without knowing he was doing so, Saad continually injected this hatred, and contempt, into Abdulla's subconscious thoughts and beliefs. More importantly, he exposed Abdulla to the subtle art of deception; deliberately projecting one image while being, in some cases, the total and complete opposite.

Abdulla's friendship with Saad lasted and grew, the entire time they were at the academy. At the end of their Sophomore year, Abdulla traveled to Riyadh with Saad to visit with him and his family during the vacation period separating the school class year.

Abdulla was amazed at the opulence of Saad's family estate. Abdulla's family home in Qatar was lavish but seemed squalid compared to the palatial extravagance Saad had grown up in. It was during this visit that Abdulla began to develop his passion for driving and exotic cars. On his sixteenth birthday, Saad's father had given him a Ferrari; a red, 570 HP, 458 Italia. It was staggeringly beautiful and looked like it was breaking speed limits just sitting in its garage bay. The problem was there wasn't anywhere in Riyadh where its beauty, power, and speed could be truly appreciated. Saad longed for the day when he could take it to the UK, Germany or Austria, and scream down the speed limitless sections of the Autobahn. Every single day, during their vacation time together, Saad and Abdulla would venture out to one of the long stretches of desert highway, driving faster and faster each day, trying to get a feel for the nuances of the Italia's gears, steering, and sheer power.

They took turns driving and were careful to demonstrate, one to the other, their skill and daring behind the wheel while at the same time showing respect for the car and to Saad's father's trust. They would also take along a couple of the AK-47's that Saad's father kept in his Riyadh estate. After arriving at a remote site along highway 40, which eventually led to the holy city of Mecca, they would fire hundreds of rounds at rock targets, lizards, or hapless sand snakes that happened to be at the wrong place at the wrong time. Once they had spooked a pair of Arabian Oryx when they started to fire. Abdulla had started to aim at the fleeing animals, but Saad reached out and pushed up the barrel. He admonished Abdulla for even thinking about killing one of the graceful beasts. He laughingly warned, "don't even think about it. Not only is the Oryx nearly extinct, but it's also the national symbol of, and one of the few animals in, your pitiful little country."

Abdulla chuckled then shot back a comment about Saad's compassion for a wild goat but at the same time his willingness to chop off some reprobate's head for screwing another guys wife. Then on a somber note, he told Saad that he had never seen a public execution. Saad told him that public executions were no longer announced in advance but that he would see if one was to be scheduled during Abdulla's visit. Then, somewhat offhandedly, he remarked: "if not we will arrange for one."

Two days later Saad informed Abdulla that an illegal Iraqi immigrant had been caught trying to bring heroin into the country from a boat docked in a port in Jiddah on the Red Sea. He had been convicted of smuggling and sentenced to death. The execution was to be carried out on Friday, and Saad's father had agreed to escort he and Abdulla to the event. For the rest of that week, Abdulla's mind raced with a mixture of anxiety, anticipation, and emotions he had never experienced before. He hardly slept Thursday night and when he did his dreams were even more vivid and violently intense than they usually were, and that was almost beyond comprehension.

Abdulla and Saad were awakened at the first light of dawn Friday morning by one of the hordes of male servants who were constantly flitting around the estate. They dressed and joined Saad's father for the morning prayer and then a breakfast of boiled eggs, cheese, pastries and strong Turkish coffee. The condemned drug smuggler wasn't fed breakfast. He hadn't been given anything to eat or drink since sundown the day before. His guards didn't want him pissing all over himself later this morning.

Around 0800 a huge Saudi, wearing a black suit, a thin black tie, and a dazzling white shirt, picked Saad, his father, and Abdulla up in a Mercedes S600 Maybach and drove them to Deera Square in central Riyadh.

When they arrived, they were met by two local police officers and some unidentified prison official who opened the car door and escorted them to an area near the center of the square. There was a small crowd all of whom stopped talking and parted to the left and right as their group walked forward. They stopped a few meters from what Abdulla noticed was a square, grated, metal drain sunk into the intricately patterned stone pavement. At 0900 the prisoner, a dark, smallish, man blindfolded and wearing a white jumpsuit, with his hands tied behind his back, was led out of a parked van by two police escorts. They stopped a few feet from the drain and waited as a man carrying a gleaming, curved, sword, called a sulthan, approached from a building bordering the square. Saad's father said his name was Muhammad Saad al-Beshi, who was widely known as Saudi Arabia's leading executioner.

When al-Beshi was in front of the prisoner, he ordered him to get on his knees and to recite the Shahada. The prisoner mumbled "there is no God but God. Muhammad is the messenger of God." With that, al-Beshi, getting a signal from the prison official, raised the sword and with one blindingly swift stroke severed the prisoner's head which dropped and rolled about a meter on the gently sloping paving stones. The prisoner's headless body slumped forward, blood spurting wildly from its neck onto the pavement and flowing toward the drain. As they made their way back to the waiting Mercedes, Saad turned to Abdulla and, as he slapped him on his shoulder, said, "and that my friend is how Sharia law is handed down in our country."

On their way back to the estate Saad's father told Abdulla that the prisoner would have been sedated and that his head would be sewn back on his body before being publicly hung on a pole as a warning to other would be smugglers. "It's a surprisingly effective deterrent" he noted with a chuckle. That night, Abdulla began to hear the voice.

After graduating from the Swiss academy, Abdulla began his freshman year at the University of Paris-Sud or as it is better known, Paris XI. He and his parent's money had been courted by several prestigious institutions including Cambridge. But Abdulla had chosen Paris XI for its reputation as being one of the top 100 universities in the world, for its outstanding math and economics programs, and its unmatched, multi-cultural environment. Its nearly 30,000 students represented over 130 nationalities. However, and almost equally important, was the fact that Paris XI was in Paris. Abdulla had grown to love the French culture and especially Paris. He had also developed an appreciation for French cuisine, red wine, and an occasional line of Columbian cocaine. Vices which, although strictly forbidden in his culture, he succeeded in working to his advantage with the crowd he was starting to entertain.

In addition to Arabic, Abdulla spoke English, which was the formal language of the Swiss academy, and almost perfect French. Even native Parisians had difficulty discerning a foreign accent during casual conversation.

Abdulla earned his Bachelor's degree, with honors, in three years and immediately enrolled in the EMIN, Master Course in Economics and Management of Network Industries. He completed this course of study and was awarded a Master's degree in two years as recommended by the university. Although his academic performance was outstanding, it was his thesis that garnered the most attention, both praise and disdain. Its title was *The strategic use of terror to change national social, political, and economic direction.*

Abdulla received his Master's degree in September, and following his graduation, attended by the immediate members of his family and Saad, his father presented him with the keys to what would become his most prized possession, the Lamborghini Aventador. More importantly, that night, at a lavish celebration dinner at the Le Meurice restaurant, he formally asked Abdulla to come to work in the company office in Abu Dhabi. Abdulla was overcome with a mixture of joy and excitement. He accepted immediately asking only that he be allowed to take a few weeks off to allow he and Saad to drive his new car around Europe and the UK. His father put his arm around Abdulla and told him "Of course my son, we will begin arranging your office immediately. Let's plan for you to begin in early December."

Before they departed, Saad told Abdulla some people were in Paris for a petroleum export meeting, that he wanted him to meet. The next day they took a taxi from the hotel to the Musee d'Orsay. From there they hailed another taxi. Saad directed the driver to take them to a small Italian restaurant in the heart of the fourteenth district, Montparnasse. When Abdulla asked, "why the cloak and dagger," Saad told him "from this point forward, you must think of yourself as the fox who is chased by hounds and always cover your tracks." Inside the restaurant, they were escorted to a small dining room near the back which was roped off and marked as "reserved." Three Middle Eastern men, dressed in top of the line, casual, western attire, greeted Saad. Speaking French, they were introduced as Messieurs Gray, Black, and Brown. The man identified as Mr. Black said "In the future, after we have earned one another's trust, we will share our true identities. But for now, it is better for us, and you, to remain somewhat anonymous." Abdulla's face reflected his confusion. Saad touched his shoulder and said "I feel your concern. In due time, you will learn what all of this is about, and your questions will be answered. In the meantime, please, play along and trust me as your friend."

Without looking at a menu, or asking for anyone's preference, Mr. Black ordered the fish of the day which was served with a house specialty salad, pasta, and Tiramisu, another house specialty. Abdulla thought it would have been nice to have a glass of Barolo, but again, without asking, Mr. Black ordered San Pellegrino sparkling water for the table. Abdulla felt it best to "do as the Romans do" and to follow the leads of his Muslim hosts. Over lunch the men shared mostly small talk but, as Abdulla observed, took what appeared to be well-scripted turns casually asking about his education, political views, and, eventually, perceptions on Arab unity. Not once did they ask about his family, Islam, or politics in general. He would later learn they knew more about him, his background, and his business than most of his family and, except for Saad, all his friends.

After serving the Tiramisu, the head waiter closed the door to the room, and no one interrupted their conversation for almost two hours. Finally, Mr. Black stood up and said, "thank you for meeting with us my brother. Over the next few days, as the two of you race around Central Europe, Saad will enlighten you as to who we are and your opportunity to, perhaps, take a leadership role in our organization." Then, briefly slipping into Arabic he said *"ma' al-salamah"* to which Abdulla intoned *"fi aman Allah."* With that, Messieurs Gray, Black, and Brown, without looking back, walked out the door.

After the men had gone, Abdulla looked at Saad and demanded, "OK my friend, who were they and what was all this about?" Saad smiled and said, "let's go back to the hotel, and I will tell you everything while we finish packing what few things we are going to be able to squeeze into the trunk of your new toy."

Saad turned away all of Abdulla's questions, and refused further discussion, during the taxi ride back to the hotel. However, after they were in Abdulla's suite, he opened up. Saad explained that in the late 70's two very rich, and regionally very influential, men were discussing their concern for the future of Saudi Arabia, the countries surrounding it, their culture, and their collective role in world politics. They realized that, at least for the foreseeable future, they could exercise considerable force by controlling their share of the world's supply of natural gas and petroleum.

However, they also realized that the countries of the Middle East were at best ununited and constantly at war with one another and threatening the stability of the entire region. And things were getting worse since Mohammad Reza Pahlavi, the Shah of Iran, had been deposed. To insert some degree of influence into the political direction of the region, and to focus the rest of the world's attention of other matters, they formed a small, and extremely exclusive, ultra-rich, association which came to be known as, MA, the "*maharib alsamt*," or silent warrior.

Membership in this secret, shadowy organization, was blatantly exclusive and by "need-based" invitation only. Its officers included business executives and royalty from Jordan, the United Arab Emirates, Oman, Kuwait, and Saudi Arabia. Abdulla's graduate thesis had caught the attention of one of the MA officers who suggested that he may be a candidate for a position vacated by a recently deceased member from Bahrain. Saad's brown, almost black, eyes locked fiercely onto Abdulla's, and his entire demeanor changed when he mentioned the former member. He didn't come right out and say it, at the time, but Abdulla got the distinct impression that he hadn't died from what one might consider "natural" causes. Saad went on to explain that Abdulla, and his family, had been vetted extensively weeks before their lunch meeting had been arranged. Saad smiled and said that by now the MA knew more about him than his mother did.

The next day, Abdulla and Saad left Paris after morning prayers and breakfast. Abdulla squeezed the wheel of the Aventador until his hands started to cramp. He imagined that his knuckles were ready to burst out of the lambskin driving gloves that his graduate academic advisor had given him for graduation. He usually had no qualms about driving in Paris traffic, but the thought of doing so in a new E350,000 Lamborghini made for a spike in his stress "titer."

They followed the N4 out of town and by the time they merged with the A26, in the Champagne region, he had begun to calm down. They would meander thru Nancy and then stop for the night in the university town of Strasbourg near the German border.

As they traveled, Saad talked incessantly about MA. He explained that its role, albeit continually evolving, was to develop a strategy for the unification of Arab countries, the expansion of Islam, and ultimately a regional Caliphate governed by Sharia laws. MA didn't actively engage in any overt actions or activities which might draw attention to its members or for that matter its very existence. Instead, it used its intelligence resources and vast monetary reserves to fund, what most of the world considered, radical, ordinarily violent, factions and military groups like certain segments of Al-Qaeda, the Mujahideen, and Hezbollah. They had nothing to do with ISIS which they considered being little more than rabid animals. They quietly sat back and watched as that group annihilated itself with its savagery and poorly focused war with the United States and Russia.

The MA's tentacles reached deep into the Middle East, the entire Islamic world for that matter, yet its demand for secrecy and practice of working only behind the scenes had kept its existence out of the spotlight. There might be rumors floating around the intelligence communities, but to date, no one had infiltrated its ranks or had any real evidence of the MA's existence. This success was due, in no small part, to the manner in which potential members were identified and subsequently nominated, their rigorous vetting process, communication methods, and of course their practice of posing as friends and allies to their sworn enemies.

Abdulla and Saad drove to Strasbourg then over the next two weeks headed north, screaming up the German Autobahn stopping in Heidelberg and then heading north to Frankfurt. They thoroughly enjoyed the blend of medieval and ultra-modern architecture, the forested countryside, and German hospitality. But Abdulla was absolutely thrilled by the raw power and responsiveness of the Aventador. He also relished in the admiring looks they got as they crept thru city streets or flew by a BMW or Mercedes on stretches of open road.

Each night, during and after dinner, they talked of little else than MA and the vision of Middle Eastern unification, and domination. Abdulla was becoming more and more excited about his potential role in the organization. But it was his fantasies of power and control that, secretly, began to dominate his every waking moment and ravaged his increasingly intense dreams. They seemed to last all night; or until the voice jarred him awake, his heart pounding and screams uncontrollably erupting from his lungs.

After visiting Berlin, they drove south to Munich, crossed another, now deserted border station, and headed into Austria. The Austrian Alps were staggeringly beautiful. Not since their days at the Swiss academy had they seen anything so captivating. The highway was well built and meticulously maintained but required one hundred percent of the driver's attention. It looped back and forth on itself as it climbed up the towering mountains of Southern Germany, then dropping thru the Brenner Pass in Austria before heading toward Verona in Northern Italy.

There were countless bridges built onto, not into, the sheer face of mountain after mountain. They jutted out into space with only a winding guardrail separating the, blessedly light, traffic from valley floors that appeared to be a kilometer below. They spent the night in Verona and then drove south to Florence. They wandered around the city soaking up its history and indulging in local cuisine but found themselves uncomfortably surrounded by hordes of tourists. It was worse than Paris. Not only that, Abdulla and Saad did not exactly blend in physically with the other visitors.

On two occasions they noticed they were attracting small bands of Gypsies begging for money and, they rightfully suspected, looking for an opportunity to steal their watch or cell phone or snatch their wallet. To Abdulla, they were like annoying gnats at a picnic.

From Florence, they drove west until then picked up the highway which followed the breathtakingly beautiful Mediterranean coast. Their destination, where they would remain for several days, was Nice with its goose egg sized pebble beaches. It was only a short drive from Nice west to Cannes or east to Monaco and what would become their favorite hangout, Monte Carlo.

It was during their stay in Nice, at the Westminster Hotel, when after returning from dinner, and what had become a nightly trip to the casino, they were shocked to find "Mr. Black" waiting for them in the living room of their suite. Mr. Black explained to Abdulla that his real name was Khalid bin Salman and that he too was from Saudi Arabia. He had been born in Al Kharj, outside Riyadh, had received his Doctor of Civil Law degree from Oxford

University. He now lived in Dubai where he, officially, worked as an advisor to the Federal National Council or FNC.

In reality, he reported directly to the Vice President, and functioned as an operations officer, and recruiter, for the MA. The reason for this clandestine visit was to extend an offer to Abdulla to become an official, and active, member of the MA. Abdulla was elated and could barely contain his raging excitement. He reached forward, took Khalid's hand, and kissed the ring on his index finger. What Abdulla did not know was that had he not accepted he would have vanished from the face of the earth. The MA would go to any means to ensure their organization, and its members weren't compromised. Although slow in coming, that knowledge would prove indispensably important in the years to come.

Over the next two hours, Khalid gave a more detailed overview of MA than Saad had been allowed to provide during the recruitment process. He and Saad explained how and when the various factions of the organization would meet; always at a different member's estate or hotel secretly owned by the group and never more than ten members at any one time. They discussed recently instituted communication procedures. Members would use disposable cell phones for initial, or emergency calls to any other member on their restricted "call list." These phones were to be used only once and then immediately destroyed. Khalid detailed how programs operated by the NSA in the United States, and the FSB in Russia monitored every cell phone, and satellite-relayed, conversation on the planet despite vehemently denying doing so. The massive computer arrays located inside Fort Meade, MD continuously scanned communications for keyword patterns in hundreds of languages. Based on increasingly sophisticated algorithms, and their ubiquitous utilization, they could identify potential discussions relating to terrorist or criminal activity. And "who knows what else" quipped Abdulla.

Actually, "we do" replied Saad. "The MA has been able to insert sleeper agents within the CIA, NSA, FBI and virtually every other intelligence agency in the US, the UK, and Russia. China, North Korea and other slant eyes have proven to be more difficult to penetrate." Finally, Khalid went over a short list of code words which he demanded Abdulla memorize on the spot. These were to be used when making an initial call on one of the throwaway phones. Basically, they were to inform the receiver that they should take a previously specified action or to call certain numbers from a secure landline. Around 0200 Khalid said, "that's enough for now, we will talk again in a few weeks" shook hands, and left.

Their postgraduate European vacation had come to an end. It was time, in Saad's case, to begin what passed for work in the Arab world of royalty and for Abdulla to ease into the position his father had waiting for him. Abdulla had arranged to have his Aventador shipped from Nice to a climate-controlled storage facility near Abu Dhabi. He only planned to take it out on special occasions and on what would become an annual pilgrimage to Monte Carlo. A hotel limousine drove them to the ultra-modern, Nice airport where they bid farewell promising to keep in touch and to reunite in Monaco for the Grand Prix in May.

Initially accompanied by his father, Abdulla moved into his office and began to ease into his new role the first week of December. He didn't put on the insufferable airs that generally resulted from positions bestowed by nepotism. In fact, his staff and associates warmed up to him, his wit, and his surprisingly participatory management style almost from day one. It didn't hurt that he was a tireless, energetic, leader often spending twelve to fourteen hours a day at his office or meeting with clients. In July he presented his father, and the parent company Board of Directors, with a plan he had developed to purchase an Austin, Texas startup company. Polymite,

Inc. was barely surviving financially but had applied for a silicon fiber based material, and 3-D production process which Abdulla and his closest technical advisor were convinced would revolutionize the production of materials used in the automotive, aerospace, and a host of other industries. The material produced by Polymite's process was lighter and over twice as strong as carbon fiber.

Even in its earliest stage of development, the 3-D production equipment could turn out sheets of material faster and cheaper than even remotely competitive products. Abdulla and his staff's research had been exhaustive, and his presentation was concise yet thorough. Despite this, there was grave concern from several of the more conservative members of the Board and even his father's body language and nonverbal facial expressions reflected anxiety. After the presentation, and recommendation to proceed with a purchase, there was heated, mostly negative, discussion among the Board. When the time came, Abdulla's father stood up and announced that, regardless of his own misgivings, he was going out on a limb and giving Abdulla permission to proceed with the acquisition.

Within six months, the patent had been approved, initial production begun, and although their marketing campaign had only just started, orders were coming in so fast that the 3-D assembly line was barely able to keep up. Polymite's stock had increased twelvefold adding over a billion Euros to the parent company portfolio. In less than a year Abdulla had gone from "the bosses kid" to the company's rising and brightest star. Abdulla's father and the Board were ecstatic, but their euphoria lasted only a few months. In April of that year, Abdulla's father dropped dead.

There was no sickness or physical conditions that indicated something was wrong. Abdulla's father had just finished having lunch with his wife at a restaurant on the Pearl-Qatar near his office in Doha. He got up from the table, started walking toward the door, and simply fell to the floor. A Doha physician, having lunch at a nearby table, started giving him CPR and continued to do so until paramedics arrived and shocked him, repeatedly, without success, with their defibrillator. Abdulla was at his office in Abu Dhabi when he received the call from his mother. He dropped what he was doing and directed his secretary to charter a plane to fly him immediately to Doha to be with his mother. In accordance with Muslim tradition, family members were already ritually washing his father's body and preparing him for burial.

Saad flew in from Riyadh later that night to be with Abdulla and his family at the funeral. As was the Muslim custom, the body was taken to a family gravesite the day following his death. Abdulla, his younger brother, and four other cousins hoisted the simple wooden coffin on their shoulders and, along with a multitude of friends and family, males in one group, females in another, walked to the open grave and, using hemp ropes lowered it down with the head facing Mecca. Unlike Christian burials, there was no ceremony or discussion at the actual time of burial. Instead, all guests prayed in earnest for Abdulla's father's soul. Following the burial, everyone in attendance returned to what was now Abdulla's estate where, as was their custom, they were served a rather extravagant meal. All guests would stay for the entire day. The Muslim community firmly believed that socializing in this manner helped to ease the loss of their loved one. Saad would remain for the rest of the week.

The month following his father's death, despite his relative youth, Abdulla was formally named President and CEO of the parent company. The vote, by the Board of Directors, was unanimous and without dissension. This was a first for any board level action by the company. And so, it was, having not yet reached his 30th birthday, Abdulla found himself at the reins of the wealthiest, most powerful, private company in Qatar and for that matter most of the Middle East.

CHAPTER 3

On the same day that the Buckingham Palace massacre occurred, North Korea test-fired its latest, most advanced, ICBM, the Hwasong-16; this was the second story on the BBC broadcast that night.

The test flight followed a sub-orbital path which took it over Aomori, Japan and landed in the Pacific Ocean rather than previous targets off the coast in the East Sea. This was a clearly deliberate provocation which could be considered an act of war. As with prior tests, no warning was given to commercial shipping or airlines. Despite continued economic sanctions, and threats of military action, North Korea, or the Democratic People's Republic of Korea (DPRK) as it is officially known, continued its antagonistic quest for nuclear weapons and long-range delivery systems. Intelligence analysts had concluded that the Hwasong-16 now gave the DPRK the ability to strike targets literally anywhere on the planet.

Less than a year earlier they had also tested what they claimed to be, and which appeared to be true, a 5 to 10 megaton fusion bomb. This explosion was significantly more powerful than anything the DPRK had tested in the past and confirmed their development of a "hydrogen" bomb. Government officials from the U.S, South Korea, and Japan expressed unprecedented levels of outrage. China and Russia joined what soon became a world-wide protest. Chang Jong

Nam and his senior military advisors celebrated this achievement and publicly mocked the U.S. and its "puppets." However, this violation and the threat it posed to world peace, and regional financial stability, was so egregious that it appeared China might actually carry out the sanctions it had agreed on.

China was inching closer to establishing itself as the world's largest economic power and the DPRK's "drunken teenager" antics were becoming close to unbearable. The Chinese government was in, what could become, a dangerous, dilemma. Either forcefully restrain one of their few allies, albeit one that was fast becoming more of a political parasite than a military asset. Or stand by as the U.S. and South Korea finally unleashed their technologically superior "dogs of war" on the clearly out of control dictatorship. The U.S. was already in its second year of expanding the deployment of a Terminal High Altitude Area Defense (THAAD) missile interceptor system in response to the DPRK's actions. Chinese leaders had repeatedly called for a halt to this deployment but knew this wasn't going to happen, especially as long as North Korea continued to rattle its nuclear sword. It was an election year in the U.S. and eliminating the DPRK nuclear weapons threat was the number one priority for both Democrats and Republicans.

The sitting U.S. president had proven to be just a point shy of crazy himself and little better, if at all, than the fat guy with a silly haircut in Pyongyang. This made the situation all the more perilous. Even before the H-bomb test, the U.S. had positioned a third carrier strike force in the Western Pacific. The Nimitz, Carl Vinson, and Ronald Reagan carrier groups had conducted exercises with the South Korean military and the Japanese self-defense forces or JSDF. The H-bomb and Hwasong-16 tests had placed them on a wartime footing, and state of readiness, that was unprecedented during what was normally considered peacetime.

Days before the Hwasong-16 test, likely based on spy satellite images of the suspected launch site, the U.S. Airforce had deployed four additional B-1b bombers from Ellsworth Air Force Base, South Dakota to Andersen Air Force Base, Guam. These joined the aging, but still extremely lethal B-52's, and two B-2 stealth bombers that were already on site. This assemblage of air power, coupled with an undisclosed number of Ohio and Virginia class submarines patrolling the DPRK coast, represented the largest, and certainly deadliest, concentration of nuclear weapons in post-cold war history. Despite a constant barrage of speculative chatter from Fox, CNN, and other news channels, most of the world had no idea of just how dangerous the situation really was. Russian, Chinese, and U.S. intelligence agencies knew exactly how grim things had become.

CHAPTER 4

Abdulla awoke with a sleep choked scream in his throat, his entire body shaking and sweat soaking the sheets despite the air conditioning being at its lowest setting. First his dreams, and then the voice. Louder than ever before and now telling him, commanding, what he must do.

"What's the matter," whimpered the stunning "arm candy" curled up next to him. Despite being wide awake, he couldn't remember her name. "You must go!" he barked, only glancing in her direction, as he got out of bed and started dressing. "Did I do something wrong?" she asked as she sat up in the bed. "Now!" was his only reply as he slipped on his shoes and started toward the suite's living room. The aspiring model, a twentyish blonde, slipped on her dress, grabbed her shoes and purse, and walked barefoot out the door, dramatically slamming it as she left.

Abdulla paid no attention to the childish display of drama. He stood at the living room window, looking out at the street that in just few days would be filled with million-euro racecars screaming around the world's most famous Grand Prix circuit. Abdulla wasn't looking at anything in particular, he just stared, unfocused, unhearing, and with no sensation of time, as the voice raged inside his head. Images from the Buckingham Palace news broadcast and the DPRK situation swept aside his consciousness, and he stumbled backward more falling than sitting on the living room couch. Then it hit him. He had an epiphany. In one fell swoop, without any conscious thought, he had a plan. He knew exactly what he had to do and when he had to do it.

Abdulla picked up the telephone from the desk next to the window and dialed the number for Saad's suite on the floor above him. Saad had arrived two days before. Since their pilgrimage to Monte Carlo had become an annual event he, like Abdulla, had reserved the same suite for the next five years. A feat that cost each of them a small fortune.

Saad answered after four rings. Knowing who was at the other end of the line, he said "Do you have any idea what time it is? I suspect not, so I will save you the trouble of looking at the clock. It's barely 0500. I trust you aren't calling to chat about the race." Abdulla blurted, "Saad, we need to talk right away. I had a vision, an unbelievable revelation." Saad replied, "Abdulla my friend, was that vision, in any way, influenced or caused by a white powdery substance?" Abdulla replied, "No! This is serious, and time is critical. We need to talk now. Get dressed and come to my suite; I will order breakfast from room service." Saad said, "Ok, I will be there shortly, but I doubt that anyone is in the kitchen at this time of the morning. You know, this is Monte Carlo."

Twenty minutes later Saad tapped on the door which Abdulla opened almost immediately. "Marhabann, my friend, you must have been looking thru the peephole. Are you expecting the police?" Saad asked, only half-jokingly. Abdulla shot back, "come in, come in, Saad, spare me the barbs and put on your serious face." Saad sat down on the couch and, as requested, assumed a somber demeanor. Abdulla pulled the chair from an office desk and sat down directly in front of Saad. Leaning forward slightly, and staring straight into Saad's eyes, said "last night I was watching the late news on the BBC.

They showed live coverage of the martyr's attack at Buckingham Palace. The carnage was amazing. Then they had an in-depth report on the North Korean ICBM test and the hair-trigger situation that continues to grow in Asia. Apparently, the images from these two stories put some kind of time bomb in my subconsciousness. When I went to bed and eventually fell asleep," Abdulla couldn't resist an impish smile, "I had a vision much like Muhammad must have had. And the voice came again. This time it was as loud and as clear as you would be if you were speaking right now."

Saad didn't dare interrupt. He knew when Abdulla was on a rant it was best to let him say what he had to say and then, and only then, ask questions or attempt to interject some point. "When I awoke this morning, I had a plan. I knew exactly, down to the most minute detail, what I, no what we, must do. The time is now to bring about the Caliphate and we, you and I and the MA, have been chosen to be Allah's instruments for this long-awaited mission."

Saad had never seen anyone, much less Abdulla, so spiritually emotional and, quite frankly, inspiring. Just then a knock at the door jolted Abdulla back into a calmer state of mind, and he got up, opened the door, and let a room service waiter in to deliver a breakfast cart. As he was doing so, Saad pondered the soliloquy Abdulla had presented over the last several minutes. They moved to the round table in the living room, Abdulla poured steaming coffee from the carafe on the cart, and they began to eat from the selection of rolls and fruit. As they ate, Saad spoke up, saying "how do you propose bringing about such a massive change? As we have discussed hundreds of times, no single country in the Arab world has the military might necessary to even challenge Israel, much less the U.S. or Russia. And I don't see the Arab countries ever uniting, or at least not in my lifetime. All we seem to do is run around in all directions, waving some flag that we have made up, and occasionally blowing up a rival mosque or a flock of French tourists."

Abdulla sat down his coffee cup, smiled ever so slightly, and said "you're correct, and that that is exactly the quandary that my Allah inspired, plan will resolve. We will become the catalyst in the process that will bring about the destruction of the infidel's civilization. Well, not a catalyst in the literal definition of the term. We will play an active role. However, we will do so behind the scenes, pulling the strings of the marionettes who do have the power. The power to bring about their own annihilation.

Then, and only then, we will step out from behind the curtains, take center stage, and establish a true, and lasting, world order. The global Caliphate our people have been seeking since marauding Mongols killed our last Caliph in Baghdad in 1258. The time has come Saad."

For the next hour, Abdulla talked almost without stopping, explaining his epiphany and the plan that had emerged from his vision. As he spoke, new and additional details of his strategy began to develop, spilling out like water from an overflowing cup. Although he described his dreams and the visions, Abdulla made a concerted effort not to mention the voice until he had finished his, increasingly descriptive, narrative. Then he sat back in his chair, and with an even more intense, almost maniacal, look in his eyes said "Saad, last night, and many, many times before, like the messenger Muhammad, I have been visited by the archangel Gabriel. It was he who told me what I must do. And it was he who revealed this plan. And Saad, it is he who, even now, shows me the path we must take and the most minute details of what will be required for its execution."

Saad listened but could not speak. His mind was ablaze with thoughts, concerns about Abdulla's sanity conflicting with his sheer brilliance. Then Abdulla continued saying, "We must request an urgent meeting of the Sovereign Council of the MA. It's important that we present this plan to them and request the funds necessary for its execution.

As you know, it is an election year in the U.S. and the timing of the three attacks I described is crucial. Saad, I know that I did not have to present this vision to you at this time. I could have called the MA Chair myself and included you, or not, at the discretion of the Sovereign Council. However, you are the closest, dearest, and most trusted friend that I have or ever expect to have, and I wanted to give you the opportunity to play a leadership role in what could be the greatest event in the history of Islam."

"Or its utter destruction," Saad thought to himself but stood up and said, "well my brother, what are we waiting for?"

Using his disposable cell phone, Abdulla called one of the Saudi Arabia numbers that he had been instructed to memorize. The call was answered on the third ring by a male voice saying, "restaurant Le Paz." Abdulla replied, "*as-salam alaykum*, this is Mr. Blue, I would like to make reservations for six in the Crown Room at the earliest available date." The person at the other end of the line said, "of course Mr. Blue, let me check our reservation schedule. Could you please call me back in two hours?"

Abdulla said that he would do so and ended the call. He knew that the "Coordinator" had verified his cover name and under-stood that requesting reservations for six in the Crown Room was, in reality, a coded request to meet with the Sovereign Council at a location of the MA Chair's choosing. He also knew the Coordinator had immediately started the task of contacting the MA Chair and arranging the meeting.

The disposable cell phones and coded conversations may have seemed like overkill, but their use succeeded in keeping the NSA and other snoops from knowing who they were and what they were doing. Abdulla would call back at the prescribed time and most likely given a date, time, and location for the requested meeting. At the end of that call, he would destroy his cell phone and purchase a replacement.

CHAPTER 5

Two days later, flying economy as instructed, Abdulla was on his way to an estate near Muscat in Oman. Abdulla was met, at what passed for an airport in Muscat, by an ominous looking character wearing immaculate white cotton kundalini pants and a traditional white thobe. Introducing himself simply as Tarig, the man took Abdulla's bag and directed him to a BMW that was sitting in a no parking zone near the airport terminal entrance. Tarig opened the rear passenger door and motioned for Abdulla to get in, he then closed the door, opened the trunk, and put Abdulla's bag inside. After leaving the airport, Tarig drove, talking only when Abdulla asked a direct question, northeast towards the Gulf of Oman and, as Abdulla would later learn, the Al Alam Palace.

An hour later they arrived at the entrance of a walled estate located on a cliff overlooking the ocean. Tarig opened the gate of the entrance using one of the remote buttons in the BMW. Once inside, Abdulla noticed another gated wall in front of them. As the front entrance gate closed, they parked in an area shaded by multiple date palms and covered with flat paving stones. There were three other vehicles, another BMW, a Mercedes, and a Hummer neatly parked near their BMW.

Tarig got out and unlocked Abdulla's door with his remote. Abdulla noticed that his door had been locked after trying, unsuccessfully, to open it himself once they had stopped. As Abdulla was getting out of the car, the gate on the inner wall opened. A white Bentley drove out and pulled behind the BMW. Without speaking, Tarig opened the rear passenger door and again motioned for Abdulla to get in. Turning to Tarig Abdulla said, "my bags?" From inside the Bentley, a voice said, "your bags will be delivered to you shortly, please get in and I will explain." Abdulla got into the back seat of the Bentley and saw that Khalid was sitting on the driver side of the rear seat. Tarig closed the door and the driver, another brutish looking fellow, began driving slowly toward the inner gate.

Khalid said, "I hope you can appreciate our precautions and the need for the utmost in security. After the word leaked that MA had played a supporting role in the Twin Towers attack our members became, shall we say, a bit paranoid about protecting their anonymity and security." Khalid smiled as he continued, saying "I hope that you don't have anything embarrassing in your bags. They are being searched at this very moment but only for weapons or explosives. You could have a kilo of cocaine and a Jewish hooker in your bag, and we wouldn't care, but no guns or knives."

Ahead loomed a huge, two-story, stucco and marble house. A circular driveway curved around immaculately groomed strips of grass and date palms and passed in front of a spectacular, glassed, entrance. A long, blue tiled, reflecting pool, with four gently spurting fountains, lay in front of the house.

As they neared the entrance, Khalid said "given the sense of urgency you expressed when you called, and the fact that the members of our Sovereign Council are extremely busy men, there will be no delay in your presentation. Please be prepared to address the council at 2000 tonight. You will have one hour, no more, to make your pitch. I will come to get you at 1930 and show you to what you will find to be a unique conference room.

When they arrived at the main entrance yet another, large, male servant opened Abdulla's door. Without introducing himself, the man said "welcome, I trust you had a pleasant journey. Come this way, and I will show you to your quarters." Abdulla followed the man across a courtyard and down a short hallway to an ornate doorway. The man opened the door and motioned for Abdulla to go inside. The room turned out to be more like a hotel suite. It had a living room with a couch, a table and four chairs, a writing desk, a full-size refrigerator, and microwave. In the center of the huge adjoining bedroom was a king size bed covered with various sized pillows and brightly colored, linen, sheets. The man told Abdulla, should he wish to eat before his meeting, the refrigerator was stocked with a selection of juices, water, and dinner dishes.

Abdulla noticed that this man, and Tarig, had an almost imperceptible bulge on the left-hand side of his thobe. He correctly assumed that the ban on weapons did not extend to the working staff. Still, without an introduction, the man bid Abdulla goodbye and left. A few minutes later there was a knock at the door. Abdulla opened the door and found his bags sitting in the center of the hall. Whoever had delivered them was nowhere in sight.

Abdulla carried his bags inside and unpacked the clothes he planned to wear that evening. He then went to the refrigerator, got out a bottle of Perrier and a plate of previously prepared flatbread, rice, curried chicken, and green peas. He heated the plate in the microwave and then sat down at the table to eat and mentally go over his presentation.

Abdulla was no stranger to corporate meetings or public speaking and planned, as he always did, to follow the advice of the late Edward R. Murrow, the brilliant, chain-smoking, American news commentator from the 50's. "Tell em what you're gonna tell em, tell em, then tell em what you told em." Essentially, he had to communicate his plan to accomplish a 1400-year-old Muslim objective, the people, money, and equipment required to accomplish it, and to do so in an hour-long presentation. Despite the gravity, and potentially historical implications of what he was going to say, Abdulla wasn't the least bit nervous; after all, like Elwood Blues, he was "on a mission from God."

Khalid arrived at Abdulla's room promptly at 1930. The two walked out into the courtyard, thru a vine-covered archway, and into another, long hall with several doors on each side. Khalid opened the first door on his left, and they both entered with Khalid leading the way. The room reminded Abdulla of a typical business conference room. There was a long table in the center and a whiteboard mounted on the far wall. A projector was installed in the ceiling over the center of the table, and there was a small table and desktop computer next to the wall near the whiteboard. Oddly there were only two chairs in the room, one at each end of the table. As was the Islamic custom, no photos or paintings hung on the walls. Seeing the puzzled look on Abdulla's face, Khalid said "the members of the Sovereign Council will not be in the room when you make your presentation. They will view, and hear you from another room via a closed-circuit television system. As I said earlier, the MA goes to great lengths to protect the identity of its members and especially its executives. We realize these meetings could be conducted using Skype or some similar internet-based conference tool but, as you well know, they can easily be hacked. We don't want the NSA to tap into our business anymore than they already have."

Motioning toward the chair at the near end of the table, Khalid explained, "I will be sitting here and will serve as your audience. That will make it at least a little less awkward. The CCTV system allows for a two-way conversation, so the council members can ask questions or make comments at any time. You will notice that their voices will be software enhanced such that they cannot be recognized. All in the name of security." Khalid sat down in the chair at the end of the table and Abdulla walked to the other end but did not sit down. He would stand during his entire presentation. Abdulla noticed a large clock mounted on the wall at the end of the room. He realized it was there to remind him how much time he had left to speak. It was 1855. At 1859 Khalid said, "members of the MA Sovereign Council, may I present Abdulla Amer Al-Badri." Following that terse introduction and looking toward Khalid at the end of the table, Abdulla began.

"*Masa' alkhayr*, my brothers, thank you for allowing me to appear before you this evening. I am here to present, what you will find to be, the most earth-shaking plan ever conceived by modern Muslims. For that reason, combined with the Sovereign Council's presentation time constraints, I am going to skip the traditional opening rhetoric and empty platitudes and immediately get to the crux of my plan.

As you well know, the Islamic world has long envisioned the establishment of a caliphate which would unite all Muslim countries under the leadership of a single, supreme, caliph; the undisputed religious, and political, successor to the prophet Muhammad. Ultimately this caliphate would also allow us to subjugate the infidels and either enslave or destroy them and their corrupt governments. That, my brothers, is our ultimate objective. However, we are also painfully aware that our current, and previous, governments have never been able to coalesce, to present a single, united, economic or military front from which to leverage our power. In fact, we have allowed what is becoming an endless horde of infidels to, in effect, invade our sacred lands. Like ants, the Americans are all over Iraq, the Russians effectively destroyed Afghanistan, and the Indians continuously threaten our friends in Pakistan."

"I know what you are thinking, thanks to the courage, and selfless sacrifices, of our blessed martyrs we have, over the years, struck back. But I am here to tell you what we all know, deep within our hearts. Each one of those attacks has been in vain. Even the destruction of the twin towers, or the most recent bombing at Buckingham Palace, have been little more than temporary irritants to our enemies. Why? Because these, and the overwhelming majority of all our attacks were conducted without a unified plan of attack and without making any demands of any kind on our enemies.

I am here to usher in a new strategy. We will unleash a series of perfectly timed, coordinated, and extremely violent attacks at the very heart of "The Great Satan." These attacks will initiate a chain reaction that will bring about the utter destruction of the three superpower governments. When that happens, our Islamic caliphate will, like the legendary phoenix of Greek Mythology, rise from the ashes and take its rightful place as "the," not "a" world leader."

The pitch of Abdulla's voice had crept up, and he became more and more animated as he consciously worked his unseen audience. He focused intently on Khalid as he repeatedly stepped back and forth at his end of the conference table. From some hidden speaker the, somewhat metallic, voice of one of the Council members spoke out. "Abdulla, you have made it quite clear that number one, terrorist strikes are, for all intents and purposes, ineffective in terms of accomplishing religious, social, or political objectives. And number two, the Arab states do not possess the military might necessary to bring about large-scale destruction to our enemies. Pray tell, what exactly is your plan and how will it succeed where our others have, so famously, failed?" Abdulla stopped pacing and with just a hint of a smile looked straight at Khalid and replied; "this plan will succeed because it is not mine, it is Allah's."

"At the risk of sounding like one of those deranged souls you see ranting on the streets in Paris or Dubai, I will share visions that I have had, and continue to have. At first, these came to me during dreams at night and included only vague images and instructions from the voice of someone whom I could not picture or identify. Over time, and I am talking about the last several weeks, the voice and images went from misty to a level of unbelievably vivid clarity. Finally, the night before I called to request this meeting, I could identify, without a doubt, the source of the voice. It was the archangel, Gabriel!

I, like our prophet Muhammad, was given instructions, the plan you are about to hear, directly from an angel of God. I could not see his face, or discern his physical features, but I could feel the energy he radiated in every cell of my body. His voice was pure and resonated so powerfully that my lungs seemed to vibrate, and I thought my head would surely explode from the pressure within it. I will start with a high-level summary of the plan I was given and then work down into some of the details of what we must do to accomplish the angel's instructions."

"There are two dynamics currently at play that we must exploit. First is the fact that this is an election year in the United States. This also dictates our timeline. I was given specific instructions to execute our final, and most brazen, attack on what the Americans refer to as Inauguration Day. This will occur on January 20th of next year. To be even more specific, the newly elected president will be sworn in at 1200 on that day. It is critical that we initiate our final attack at that exact time.

The second dynamic and the most vital component of this plan is the situation on the Korean peninsula. The DPRK is acting like the video you may have seen of a monkey with an AK-47. Except their AK-47 is their newest ICBMs and nuclear warheads.

They seem poised, like that monkey, to start shooting these things in every direction. Actually, they will target a couple of large cities in the United States and most likely Tokyo. They will probably not launch anything into South Korea. They think, and rightfully so, that with the Americans out of the way they can use their massive arsenal of conventional weapons and simply roll over Seoul and force South Korea to its knees in a matter of days.

On the other hand, the Americans are set to launch preemptive strikes on Pyongyang, and military and industrial targets in the DPRK, literally, at a moment's notice. The only thing that is holding them back is their fear of retaliation from the Chinese. The Russians are sitting on the sidelines ready to attack whoever appears to be the winner once the Chinese and Americans go to war. Their objective is to crush the survivor, thus becoming the undisputed superpower. However, the Americans and Chinese are keenly aware of this strategy and will launch preemptive strikes against the Russians when the nuclear balloon goes up. That my brothers is when we step in."

"As I briefly mentioned previously, our strategy will be to launch three horrific attacks against the United States. These will be conducted in November, and December of this year, and then the Inauguration Day attack I talked about a few minutes ago.

Each of these strikes will be preceded by a series of demands broadcast via, open channel, communication satellite to the Whitehouse and South Korea from what will appear to be the DPRK. In reality, they will come from us, the MA. We will hack our way into the satellite communication network and will spoof the source of our signal. We will demand that the U.S. immediately lift all sanctions against the DPRK, withdraw its forces from the Korean Peninsula, and accept the DPRK as a nuclear power in its own right. The Americans will readily believe the demands came from North Korea and will repeat their, long-standing policy of not dealing with terrorists regardless of the outcome. Since they will not be a recipient of the hacked messages, the North Koreans will not know their true content. But they will continue their insanely belligerent posturing and will most likely follow them with additional threats if the demands are not met. The DPRK will take credit, again via our spoofed messages, after each attack and will make threats of even greater violence if the Americans do not, to use a popular metaphor, "bend-a-knee."

The American public will respond with unprecedented fear and outrage following the first attack. Despite their different ideologies, the overwhelming majority of both Republicans and Democrats are already demanding that the U.S. take a more forceful stance against the DPRK. There are a vocal few on the far left that believe a peaceful, laissez-faire policy is the best and should be the only, approach to dealing with Chang Jong Nam and his band of crazies. However, they are a minority who will be ignored by even the most liberal American government official. Our second attack will strike fear into the very heartland of America, especially its overwhelming Christian community. Everyday citizens will be frothing at the mouth and ready to take up arms themselves. South Korean citizens living and working in the United States will begin to feel the same suspicions and prejudices that our Arab brothers and sisters have suffered since the Twin Towers were destroyed.

Our third, and according to my vision the final attack will essentially "pull the nuclear trigger." The U.S. will vaporize Pyongyang, using submarine-launched cruise missiles, to "cut the head off the snake." This will be followed by wave after wave of conventional, and tactical nuclear, strikes against military targets, chemical weapon plants, petroleum distribution facilities, and any other infrastructure which could even remotely support wartime operations."

In a room, located on a different wing of the house, seven men sat at a long wooden table, one at the head and three on each side. There was a rank order within the MA Sovereign Council, but no one outside this room knew what it was.

On a wall, at one end of the room, was a 65" HDTV which was connected to the camera in the conference room Abdulla was using. Abdulla's image and the sound of his voice were as clear as it would be if he were in the room with his remote audience. In the center of the table was a conference microphone which allowed the men to communicate to Abdulla at the press of a button. Otherwise, their conversations were private.

Looking one by one at his associates, the man sitting at the head of the table said "I can't tell if he is a genius or a raving lunatic. But when I start to lean toward the latter, I consider how The Prophet may have sounded to skeptics after he was also visited by the archangel Gabriel." At that time, one of the men pressed the microphone button and spoke. "I must say, Abdulla Amer Al-Badri, you make a convincing, albeit frightening case. However, I am curious about some of the details. For example, you haven't told us, specifically, what kind of attacks or the dates, other than a month, or when you were directed to carry them out."

Continuing to look sternly at Khalid, and the camera, Abdulla responded to the statement. "And that sir is by design. If I may be so bold, I suggest that the less you know, the more likely our strategy will be to succeed. Regardless of how sophisticated, or painful the interrogation methods may be, if one of you should be arrested, or fall into the hands of our enemies, you can't confess information that you don't know. I intended to give you a high-level overview of the operation but not enough information to derail it in the event of an intelligence compromise. This approach will protect both our strategy and each of you. Besides, those were the instructions the angel gave me."

The Sovereign Council members looked at one another, and then the man at the head of the table pressed the microphone button and said, "that sounds like a wise approach Abdulla Amer Al-Badri, please proceed with your presentation." Abdulla resumed speaking, picking up where he had left off before the comments from the council.

"Within hours, perhaps less, following the destruction of Pyongyang, the Chinese will initiate the nuclear response they, like the Americans and Russians, have been planning for decades. Their targets will include major U.S. and Russian cities and virtually all military sites. Their WWIII nuclear strategies do not include a losing scenario. They have one-seventh of the world's population, over a billion people. The combined population of the U.S. and Russia is less than half that. As such the Chinese can afford to lose a few hundred million and still have a sufficient number of screaming yellow infidels left over to rule the planet. And that is their postwar objective.

Of course, the Russians and Americans have no intention of letting this happen. The instant their spy satellites, and the powerful new ground-based radar in South Korea and Japan detect an ICBM launch they will unleash their nuclear arsenals on China and one another. European and Asian countries are also most likely on a secondary target list. Their cities may be spared, but their military installations will be destroyed by the Russians. When these dominoes begin to fall, Israel, out of fear for their survival as a nation, will use their nuclear weapons to utterly destroy Tehran. This will put a screeching halt to the Iranian nuclear weapons program.

Due to their dependence on our natural gas and oil reserves, none of the Persian Gulf countries will be touched. The superpowers will assume that, especially with Iran out of the way, our governments are so fragmented that we cannot mount a united military response. They will consider us, or rather our natural resources, to be figs on a tree, ready to be plucked by the winner of their nuclear brawl. And this is precisely the situation we have been waiting for and which was prophesied by the archangel Gabriel. We will announce the creation of the Caliphate and the establishment of a new, Islamic, world order.

Currently, there are nearly two billion Muslims or roughly twenty-eight percent of the world population. That non-Muslim population will be drastically reduced twenty-four hours after the first mushroom cloud pops up over Pyongyang. My brothers, we have less than ten months to secretly begin, and complete plans for the unification of the Persian Gulf states, Egypt, and Turkey. These are the heart and soul of Islam. We must be prepared to take our rightful, God-given, place on the world's throne when, as the Americans say, "the smoke clears."

I must defer the planning for this task, and its associated political maneuvering, to you. My role is to personally oversee the formation and arming of the three strike forces and the counterintelligence units that will carry out the attacks. Once prepared, I will oversee the operational details and personally direct each strike."

Once again, the man at the head of the table pressed the button on the conference microphone. Abdulla, you have succeeded in painting a terrifying, yet cunning and plausible, scenario. However, I need the answers to a few questions to help me process, and better understand, what you are telling us.

Let's assume I believe you aren't totally delusional. That the archangel truly is the source of your visions. That these things will come to pass if we follow your advice, and that we can form an Islamic alliance and the long-awaited, caliphate. Who do you foresee becoming our Caliph? Also, what resources, regarding men and equipment, will you require to stage these attacks?"

Abdulla's back straightened and his face lost all expression as he stared thru Khalid and toward what he thought was the lens on the CCTV camera. "With your permission, I will answer the second question first. It is critical that all the equipment we will use be manufactured in North Korea and smuggled into the United States. This must include the DPRK version of Semtex. American C-4 and Czechoslovakian Semtex contain chemical markers that will allow the FBI to easily, and quickly, identify their country of origin from residue collected at the scene of each attack. Trust me; the Americans will go over every square centimeter of the ground and inspect every surviving scrap of evidence at each site. Even the clothing worn by our martyrs must be manufactured in North Korea. For our plan to succeed, it is imperative that all evidence point directly at the DPRK.

Frankly, I am concerned that our teams will be made up of only men from the middle east. I suspect that the Americans will even analyze the DNA from the blood and bone fragments, and that will be all that remains, from each site. Given enough time they would eventually discover that our soldiers were not Asian. However, the FBI will run out of time after the third attack.

I am sorry for the slight digression, now back to your question. We will need five, shoulder-fired surface-to-air missiles, SAMs. The DPRK has a relatively new model, designated by the U.S. Department of Defense as the SA-20, which reportedly has a range of 5 to 7 miles. These missiles have an upgraded warhead that is twice as powerful as the American Stinger weapon system. They have sold some of these to Taliban rebels who have used them on at least one occasion to shoot down an American F-16 in Afghanistan. The DPRK is, in the best of times, a cash-strapped nation and the expanded economic sanctions imposed by the U.S. and its allies has driven it to become a major source of arms on the black market.

This also allows the DPRK to field test their newest weapons in a real, combat, environment. This situation will work to our advantage as well. In addition to being able to purchase the necessary SA-20's, we can train our SAM team on how to use them while appearing to support our Taliban brothers in their never-ending struggle. We get the weapons, we get the training, and we look like heroes. We can expect to spend about fifty thousand euros to purchase the SA-20's.

Then we must train and equip the SAM team, all our teams for that matter, get them into the U.S., and cover all expenses for the next ten months. As an important side note, all our equipment purchases must be conducted using Bitcoins. This digital currency is untraceable and is, in fact, the preferred method of payment by those dealing in drugs and weapons on the black market. We will also need a minimum of two hundred and fifty kilos of DPRK Semtex and the blasting caps and detonation cord necessary to make five martyr vests and six vehicle bombs.

Before you ask, I could explain why we will need five vests but doing so would expose you to details which, as we discussed, is best you don't know. Finally, on our equipment list, we must purchase a 120mm mortar. This weapon must be equipped with a GPS tracking and aiming computer capable of dropping its projectiles within three meters of designated coordinates. It's ironic that the DPRK, and others, use a GPS system, developed and deployed by the U.S., to aim their own weapons at the Americans. They can thank President Bill Clinton for this technological gift. Before 1990 the U.S. intentionally degraded civilian GPS accuracy. They feared it would be used exactly as we intend to use it. In May 2000 President Clinton, in between Oval Office dalliances, curtailed the use of what they referred to as Selective Availability. Today, civilian accuracy is equal to that of the military.

According to my calculations, we will require ten high explosive rounds for the mortar and a two-man crew to deploy it. A well-trained mortar team should be able to get ten rounds in the air before the first one strikes its target. When I initially conceived this attack scenario, I realized that the combined weight of the weapon, and its ordinance, would be well over 200 kilos. This fact, plus the need to transport the mortar, set it up, and then begin the firing sequence without being discovered presented what appeared to be an insurmountable problem. Then, during one of my many dream visions, I was given a simple, yet brilliant, solution.

We will obtain a large, nondescript, panel truck. Its bed will have walls, but it will not have a roof. We will mount the mortar, and its GPS aiming computer, in the center of the bed such that it is shielded from view yet can still fire thru the open top. At the appropriate time, our mortar team will drive the truck to a predetermined location that is within range of its target. We can easily obtain the GPS coordinates of our target by using a cell phone while posing as a tourist. These coordinates will be accurate to within 3 meters; more than sufficient for our purpose."

Abdulla paused, poured a glass of water from a carafe sitting on his end of the conference table, and took a sip. The water moistened his mouth and the action of pouring it gave him a few seconds to rehash the summary of his presentation. He continued.

"That, my brothers, is a very high-level overview of the equipment we will require. As you well know, the most critical component of any military action, especially as clandestine as this one, are the people who will carry it out. As I mentioned, we will need three attack teams. Five men for the SAM mission, five for a purely suicide attack, and two for the truck-mounted mortar. It should go without saying that these warriors must be totally devoted to our cause. They must also speak perfect English, be capable of working independently for months at a time, and able to blend into various American cultures and social settings.

Equally, if not more, important, they must be willing and able to sacrifice themselves in the name of Islam. We will also need the services of experts who can hack into DPRK computer and communication systems. I respectfully request that Khalid and Saad be allowed to work with me and to head up the recruitment, training, and insertion of these teams." When he heard Abdulla make this request, Khalid's face gave only the slightest trace of surprise. Otherwise, he remained still, displaying no emotion.

"My brothers," Abdulla said, again looking at Khalid, "we must begin recruitment, and detailed planning, immediately. We are on an extremely tight, and strict, timeline. Our plan has a lot of "moving parts," and we have a great deal to coordinate and accomplish. The future of the Islamic Caliphate and our rightful role as true world leaders are in our hands." Once again Abdulla paused and took another sip of water. As he returned his gaze toward Khalid and the CCTV camera his body seemed to relax as if he were shedding some invisible, incredibly heavy, weight around his neck and shoulders. His face was hauntingly serene, and it appears he was looking no longer at the camera but something, somewhere, not in the distance but in the future. He took a deep breath, spread his hands in front of him, slightly apart with the palms up and said, "and now I will answer your first question."

"Who do I foresee becoming our first Caliph? This was not for me to predict nor was it any man's prophesy. It is Allah's will, as directed by the archangel Gabriel that at the proper time I Abdulla Amer Al-Badri will be granted the title, of Caliph of the Arabian Caliphate. I am a true successor to the prophet Muhammad. I am destined to dissolve all the governments of the earth and replace them with a single, everlasting, Islamic nation. Those who refuse to submit will be either enslaved or destroyed at my discretion. Today, the fate of the Persian Gulf countries, all of Islam for that matter, is in your hands. With that my brothers, I conclude my presentation and respectfully request you approve the funds and manpower necessary for the three missions I have described. I also request that you direct Khalid and Saad to assume subordinate roles, and for the foreseeable future, to report directly to me in support of these operations. Thank you, I am humbly honored that you have allowed me to present this extremely important matter." Standing at the head of the conference table, Abdulla clasped his hands together and bowed respectfully.

The man at the head of the table in the other room pressed the button on the conference speaker microphone and said "it was an honor Abdulla Amer Al-Badri. Please have a seat and relax while we discuss what you have shared with us." The man muted the microphone and looked solemnly at the men on his left and right. "As we have noted, we are either dealing with a madman or a prophet. Either way, his proposal can work to our advantage. If he is mad, his attacks will instill absolute terror into the hearts of the infidel Americans. If he is truly a messenger of God, and we can turn our enemies one against the other, we may at long last see the beginning of Muslim world order.

As you know my brothers, the Sovereign Council of the MA isn't a democracy. As in the past, I will make the final decision concerning our approval of Abdulla's plan. However, also as in the past, I seek your counsel before doing so." First looking to the man sitting on his left, he worked his way around the conference table, asking his associates for their feedback and suggestions. The consensus was that Abdulla's claims of visions and commands from the archangel Gabriel walked a thin line between fanatical and divine inspiration. Each man also agreed, perhaps subliminally swayed by the chairman's previous comments, there was much to be gained by proceeding with the plan. After the last man, sitting on the chairman's immediate right had spoken, there was a brief period of open discussion. Then the man at the head of the table, once again, keyed the microphone.

"Abdulla Amer Al-Badri, the Sovereign Council of the *maharib alsamt*, agree that your visions may indeed be a gift from Allah and your plan, if properly executed, will well serve the goals of Islam. This said we will fully fund the equipment and manpower necessary to accomplish tactics you have laid before us. As of this moment, Khalid and Saad are assigned as your subordinates for the duration of this operation and until such time that you release them from that service. Khalid will arrange the initial, and subsequent, transfer of funds and weapon procurement. He is quite adroit with these matters. Go now and *barak Allah fik*."

CHAPTER 6

The next morning, Abdulla and Khalid met for breakfast in one of the estate's smaller, more intimate, dining rooms. After exchanging the usual morning pleasantries, they helped themselves to steaming cups of coffee from a silver carafe brought by a male servant. Another servant brought a large platter of fruit, eggs, and bread then left the room, closing the door behind him.

When they were alone, Abdulla said "Khalid, as you have heard, we have no time to lose. I will arrange for you and me to meet with Saad before the end of this week. I need to bring Saad up to speed on the plan and then share the details of each action with both of you. We have much to do, and as you have learned, the fuse is short and burning." Abdulla and Khalid chuckled at the dark humor buried in the last statement.

After they had finished breakfast, they poured more coffee, and Abdulla called Saad on his disposable cell phone. "Saad, we have been awarded the contract. Please plan on meeting me at 1200 tomorrow at the Al Hubara restaurant. And don't worry, I will pick up the tab." When he had terminated the call, Abdulla told Khalid, "as you might suspect, that was a prearranged, coded, message. Saad will now meet us the day after tomorrow, at 1800, at the Aziza Lebanese restaurant. You have taught me well Khalid. From this point forward, the security of our mission must be first and foremost in everything we do. I randomly chose the Aziza restaurant, and Doha, to make sure our initial meeting place was not under surveillance or monitored in any manner."

For the next hour, Abdulla and Khalid discussed the finer points of what they needed to do over the next several days and weeks. They also reviewed the division of labor necessary to accomplish the tasks that would be shared between the two of them and Saad. Then, looking at his Rolex, Abdulla said "It's time for me to go to the airport. I will see you on Thursday at the Aziza." Abdulla, stood, shook Khalid's hand and clapped him on his shoulder. He then turned and walked to the front entrance of the estate where Tarig stood, waiting for him, next to an idling BMW.

The Aziza restaurant was located on the third floor of the Marriott Marquis Hotel City Center on Omar Al Mukhtar Street in Doha. Taking the stairs, rather than an elevator, Abdulla arrived at the restaurant a few minutes early and waited in the small, front entrance, foyer. Khalid walked thru the door promptly at 1800. The two shook hands and idly chatted about their temporary accommodations and an upcoming soccer game in Oman.

At 1817 a smiling Saad strolled thru the door and joined his companions. Abdulla signaled a waiter who escorted them to a reserved table near the back of the restaurant. Abdulla ordered a bottle of Perrier, and when the waiter left to get the water, said "we will not discuss our plans here. After dinner, we will go to a suite here in the hotel that I reserved just today for that purpose. For now, let's enjoy dinner and one another's company." Later, when Khalid excused himself to go to the toilet, Abdulla would chastise Saad and use his tardiness as an example of what they, and the warriors who would soon be part of their group, must not do. Putting on his sternest expression, Abdulla said, "Saad, it is imperative that we, and each member of each team, be punctual in every action associated with this mission. As we will discuss later tonight, there are many, seemingly independent, components of our plan. However, like the works in an old-fashioned clock, they must function as one. Their synchronized timing is beyond important; it is critical to the success of our effort. One builds upon the other. As such, the failure of one could destroy the others. For at least the next eleven months we must put aside the age-old Arab concept of "better late than never." Looking downright sheepish Saad replied, "I am sorry Abdulla, it will not happen again."

For the next hour, the three men enjoyed the lavishly prepared Lebanese dishes, and impeccable service, for which the Aziza was famous. After they had finished their dessert and coffee, Abdulla using cash, paid the check and left a tip that was generous enough to appease the wait staff but not so large as to bring attention to their visit. They then took an elevator to a business suite located on the forty-second floor. The room had a spectacular view of Doha and the nearby ocean.

The view was wasted on the three men who, following Abdulla's lead, got down to business as soon as they walked thru the door. Sitting around an unadorned coffee table, Abdulla began their discussion saying "there is an old saying. Three men can keep a secret but only if two of them are dead. No other mortals know the details of what I am about to tell you. For the sake of Islam, we must keep it that way." To bring Saad up to speed, Abdulla then described his visions, the directives he had been given by the archangel Gabriel, their goal of establishing a worldwide Islamic caliphate, and their strategy for doing so.

He basically condensed his hour-long presentation to Khalid and the MA into a ten-minute overview. He then proceeded by saying "now I must share the details of our attacks and what you, we, must do to achieve our objective. To protect our mission, I purposely did not go into this level of detail with the MA.

Our first strike will be on the day before the American Thanksgiving holiday. This is one of their most heavily traveled days of the year. Literally, every flight on every airline will be booked to capacity. I have selected five major airports which have publicly assessable areas, streets, cemeteries, parking lots, etc., near their busiest runways. These airports are in, or on the outskirts of Jackson, Mississippi, Chicago, Atlanta, Dallas, and Denver.

During the first week of November, our computer hackers will send a series of messages to the Americans and South Koreans. These messages will direct the Americans to immediately lift all sanctions that have been imposed on the DPRK. They will also be directed to withdraw all U.S. forces from the Korean peninsula and Japan. We will use the normal, blithering, mad dog, rhetoric which has become a DPRK trademark. We will conclude each message with a threat to destroy the U.S., and their allies unless the demands are met within two weeks. As usual, these demands will be ignored, and the crazy American president will respond with his own empty threats.

Well in advance of these communications, we will quietly integrate one of our warriors into one of the multicultural communities within each city. We can use the sleeper cell assets we already have in place if we are certain they are up to this mission. If not, we can use one of the many men currently being vetted for immigration. Regardless of the source, we must be one hundred percent confident that these, and all the soldiers tagged for this mission, can accomplish their assigned task. They must also be willing to martyr themselves at its completion. As the MA has done in the past, we can add some degree of assurance by reminding each one that we have a close eye on their relatives, or other loved ones, in their home countries. This practice always seems to work.

Between 1030 and 1045, depending on the airport location, local weather, and traffic conditions, each man will drive a rented pick-up truck to a predetermined location near the main take-off runway. Under the front seat of each truck will be five kilos of Semtex. The Semtex will be wired to a "dead man" apparatus that, once activated, will detonate the explosive the instant pressure is released on the switch. This will ensure that even if the driver is killed or wounded before completing the last phase of his mission, the explosion will still erase his identity. It will also inflict damage and cause even more terror.

However, this is not even close to our main objective. In the bed of the truck, hidden under an inconspicuous tarp or similar disguise, will be an armed and ready SA-20 surface to air missile, better known as a SAM. Each soldier will have scouted out the public areas near the target runway at his designated airport. He will select a location that is within the target acquisition range of the SA-20 and which affords him an unobstructed view of aircraft as they are taking off.

At that time of the year, those airports will be launching planes every ten to fifteen minutes. During the window between 1100 and 1130, he will select one of the planes as it moves down the runway toward the liftoff location. By the time the plane nears the end of the runway, it will be traveling between 240 and 280 kilometers per hour. At this point, the pilot will use its elevators to "pitch-up" its nose thus increasing its lift. When this happens, the aircraft will leave the ground.

It is at that moment, and for the next few seconds, the plane is most vulnerable. For all intents and purposes, it is a sitting duck. It will be moving fast enough, and have sufficient altitude, to ensure its total destruction in the event of a crash. All passenger jets are capable of flying and landing, with only one engine. But taking off, especially at this point with only one engine is another matter. It's not impossible, but the odds are stacked against survival. The SA-20's fire a heat-seeking missile which, in their case, is capable of acquiring its target as it moves toward or away from its launch position. The SA-20 warhead is also extremely powerful. More so than the U.S. Stinger or NATO versions.

Our soldier will arm his weapon and begin tracking the plane as it moves toward the lift off location. The SA-20 will sense the heat signature of the plane's engine, acquire the target, and the instant the plane is airborne our man will release the missile. These things travel at over twice the speed of sound after they leave the launch tube. It will fly straight up and into the engine's exhaust before exploding.

Since the SA-20 will be launched from less than two kilometers away, the plane will only be a few hundred meters in the air when its engine, one half of its thrust, and its supporting wing, is destroyed. The pilot will not be able to react in time to take any action that would save the plane; not that he could at this juncture. Debris and body parts will be all that is left. I might add, unlike previous models, the propellant in the SA-20's missile is virtually smokeless. Even if the pilot, or passengers, were looking out the plane's windows, they would never see the missile when it was fired or as it approached its target. It would be like looking for a bullet fired from a rifle.

As soon as our soldier has fired his missile, he must leave. No time to lounge around and gloat or marvel at his victory. He is to calmly place the SA-20 launch tube on the bed of the truck and then drive to the closest hospital. He will pull up to the emergency room entrance and go to meet Allah by detonating the Semtex sitting underneath his seat. The Americans will have a hard time choking down their turkey and dressing dinner the next day. This may well be their last Thanksgiving.

Once the attack occurs at the second airport, it will take less than an hour for the American Federal Aviation Administration, FAA, to recognize a pattern and shut down all civilian flights over U.S. airspace. Following 9/11 they refined this process and included it in every airport's disaster plan. For this reason, we will ensure that the attacks, at each of our five target airports, occur between 1100 and 1130 central time. It will be hard to imagine the panic, outrage, and abject terror that our actions will bring about. The entire countries' commercial airline industry will be shut down. Slammed to the ground.

We will exacerbate the situation when we send another set of DPRK spoofed messages saying, in effect, "we warned you, and the worst is yet to come." I am sure the North Koreans have some gobbly gook way of saying that. No pun intended." The three men snickered at Abdulla's verbal sleight of hand and its "gook" reference. Then Abdulla continued. "As you can well imagine, the Americans will be frothing at the mouth. Even the most liberal, faint of heart pacifists, will be out for Korean blood. However, as bad as our airline passenger slaughter will be, our next attack will be even more horrendous and even more egregious to the Christian Crusaders.

In December, we must ramp up our psychological warfare efforts. We will send another set of messages touting the DPRK's ability to strike at will. The communications will reiterate the previously stated demands and will add new, outrageous, requirements to pay the North for damages suffered during the Korean conflict in the 1950's. Communications will also make light of the five airline disasters.

For years the North Koreans have transmitted amateurish videos depicting nuclear strikes on Washington D.C. or the destruction of U.S. aircraft carriers. We will take a similar approach with some of our propaganda. The Americans will assume it is more theatrics from the DPRK. This round of misinformation will begin on Thanksgiving, the day after the planes have fallen from the sky. However, preparation for our second attack must start immediately. I will discuss each of our roles, and assignments, once I have shared the next two scenarios.

At the same time, we are positioning our soldiers for the airline attacks we will do the same for our second, December, strikes. As I mentioned, this attack, rather series of attacks, will be even more horrendous. We will be going for their Christian jugular which will instill unbelievable fear throughout the country and especially in what the Americans refer to as the "bible belt."

Each year, on Christmas Eve, almost every large Protestant church in the U.S. holds what they refer to as a "candlelight service." These are always jam-packed with "twice a year" Christians, those who attend services only on Christmas and Easter. The services are always held in the early evening. This is when it is dark enough to for the symbolic use of candles when they sing their last hymn, *Silent Night*, yet early enough to let them get home and take photos of their little brats in front of a pine tree.

As with the airports, I have selected five churches in five different, relatively large, multicultural, cities, Lansing, Michigan, Columbia, South Carolina, Oklahoma City, Oklahoma, Nashville, Tennessee, and Jacksonville, Florida. These are not the so-called, mega-churches that have gained notoriety over the years. However, they are large Protestant and Catholic institutions that will still pack in a couple of thousand worshipers the night before they celebrate the prophet Jesus' birth.

Six months before December 24th, our soon to be martyrs will begin their infiltration into the local community. As before, we should attempt to draw upon existing sleeper cell assets where available and who are reliable and dedicated to our cause. We must also ensure that each of these assets thinks they will be carrying out a solo mission. We can't afford any conspiracy rumors to start should one of our people be arrested or go off the deep end. Once we have identified the individual, in each city, who will carry out the task I am about to describe, they must begin to attend Sunday morning services at the targeted church. They will do so as inconspicuously as possible but enough to allow their fellow churchgoers to eventually recognize them and become accustomed to their presence.

They should have a well-rehearsed cover story which explains their struggle getting into the U.S. and their subsequent conversion to Christianity. However, they must not oversell their plight. The last thing we can afford is a do-gooder article in a local paper or personal interest story on the six o'clock news. I realize that attending Christian worship services contradicts the Quran and would normally be considered an act punishable by death. But since we are on a quest, in the name of Allah, we have already been forgiven for these transactions.

Our martyrs must make an effort to establish a church-going routine. They must dress in a manner that will allow them to blend in with the congregation, never bring attention to themselves. And remember, they should have at least one set of clothes, pants, shirt, shoes, underwear, everything must have been manufactured in North Korea. They should try to always sit in more or less the same spot, preferably on the aisle and near the center of the church.

And now the undercover *piece de resistance*. We will open a checking account for each man using a common Korean surname. Each Sunday, when the offering plate is passed around, our man will slip in a check for $25.00. Not too much, not too little. Just enough to add to the deception. By December, our team will have blended into the Christian church woodwork. Just another smiling face in the congregation.

On December 24th, our team will, to paraphrase one of their yuletide carols, "don our gay apparel." But rather than a gaudy, Christmas, sweater, they will put on their specially designed suicide vest with its ten kilos of Semtex and a few hundred steel ball bearings. As before, the vest will be configured to use our standard "dead man" detonator.

The service will begin with the choir, attendants, and the pastor marching down the center aisle toward the pulpit. Once they are at their assigned locations at the front of the church, an associate pastor will mumble an opening prayer and direct the congregation to be seated. The director will then have the choir stand and will lead them in the opening hymn. After the hymn, the pastor will take center stage and, depending on the denomination of the church, read a passage from the Christian bible or have a previously selected family read a scripture while lighting the Christmas advent candle.

It's almost time now. Once this ritual is completed, the pastor will direct the congregation to rise and sing one of their cherished Christmas hymns. While the people are getting up from their seats and opening their hymnals, our soldier will step into the aisle and begin walking toward the front of the church. As he is standing up, he will press the trigger button to arm the detonation switch. The people in his immediate vicinity will see him stand and start walking up the aisle but will not pay much attention to him. Most will think that their nice new member just picked an awkward time to go to the bathroom.

After taking just a few steps, which should position him near the center front of the church, he will release the button on the switch and "boom," another horrific North Korean attack in the American heartland. Just imagine the reaction when this happens not once, not twice, but five times in five different cities on Christmas Eve. Although perhaps not as dramatic, from a pure terror perspective, this will easily top the twin towers and the airline missile strike. Unadulterated hate and outrage will gush from the Americans. And they will not have their precious second amendment to absorb any blame. It will all be directed toward the North Koreans and the failure of the U.S. government to do anything to have prevented such carnage.

The Americans are good at waiting until after a disaster occurs before they take any action. The idea of preventative measures seems like an alien concept to them. But wait! We have one more stake to drive thru the American's heart. This will be the one that triggers the beginning of the end.

As you well know, this is a presidential election year in the U.S. For the past six months the Democrats and Republicans have been spending millions of dollars touting their various contenders for this office. They have held debate after useless debate. As always, their election will be on the first Tuesday of November. From our perspective and for our mission, that date, and the winner of the vote for that matter, is irrelevant. It only sets the stage for what is to come.

Our final blow will occur on their president's inauguration day, the twentieth of January. This ceremony happens at noon in front of the U.S. Capitol Building in Washington, D.C. At that time the President, the President-elect, members of Congress, Supreme Court Justices, and everybody that is anybody will be gathered around a stage near the front of the Capitol. The U.S. Marines call this a "target rich environment."

As you might expect, security for the inauguration will be beyond tight. The Secret Service will be swarming like flies on honey. They even go so far as to seal up the manhole covers on Pennsylvania

Avenue. They don't want any armed sewer rats to pop up during the inaugural parade to the White House. Ground, and air, security will be virtually impenetrable within a three-mile radius of the actual inauguration site. But notice my use of the word virtual. Allah has shown me a few chinks in their armor.

Every day, there are thousands of cellphone camera-clicking tourists in Washington, D.C. They flock to the monuments and museums like Muslims to Mecca. The Capitol Building is no exception. In fact, it is one of their most popular tourist attractions. Although there are cameras everywhere, grounds security is surprisingly light. This lack of security is the first chink.

Every four years the inauguration stage is constructed in the exact same location. This location is certainly no secret since the event is televised, literally, all over the world. We know, within less than a meter, the spot where the podium will be placed. In early December, before the stage construction begins and before our Christmas Eve attack, both members of what will be a two-man team will join the crowds of tourists around the Capitol Building. Using the GPS on their cell phones, they will record the coordinates of what will be the stage location. Each man will do this independently and then compare the results to minimize the possibility of user error.

In early January, our assault team will take possession of a 120mm DPRK mortar, ten rounds of high explosive ammunition and propellant charges. These rounds will be fitted with proximity fuses that will cause them to explode in the air immediately above their targets. An air burst increases their lethality, against human ground targets, up to ten times more than standard contact fuses. They will also receive a relatively new targeting computer which attaches directly to the mortar. This computer will use the previously collected GPS coordinates, its firing location GPS coordinates, wind speed, elevation, and ambient temperature to calculate a trajectory which can lob a mortar round to within a meter of its target.

The latest DPRK M-45 mortar has a range of over 8,000 meters. By presetting the fuses and propellant charges, our team will be able to get ten rounds in the air in less than forty seconds. Shortly after receiving the mortar, we will obtain a flatbed truck whose sides are eight feet tall and with an open top. This configuration will allow us to secure the mortar's base plate to the truck's bed and hide the assembled weapon, and ammunition, from prying eyes. We will cover the top with a removable tarp just in case Secret Service helicopters, or surveillance drones, are in the area and get curious.

Two hours before the inauguration ceremony, our team will drive down Martin Luther King Jr. Avenue South East and park in the deserted lot near the United Black Fund building. This will be our primary launch site, but we will identify fall back positions in the event the team determines this site proves unacceptable that morning. Any location within an eight-kilometer radius of the Capitol Building will work. The targeting computer, using its built-in GPS is capable of continuously plotting a firing position. Regardless of its final location, our team must be in within range and parked no later than 1150. They will then remove the canvas cover, arm each of the ten mortar rounds, and prepare to drop the first projectile down the tube.

As is tradition, the actual swearing-in ceremony begins promptly at 1200 eastern time. Standing at a podium at the front of the Capitol building, the Chief Justice of the U.S. Supreme Court will administer the oath of office to the president-elect. They will be surrounded by members of Congress, various dignitaries and heads of state from around the world, the President and Vice President's family, and other straphangers.

The Secret Service will be swarming within and around the crowd. The area in front, and on each side, of the podium will be shielded with panels of bulletproof glass to protect the presidential entourage from sniper fire. However, and here is another one of those armor chinks, there is no overhead protection of any kind.

When the President-elect and Chief Justice are in position, there will be an opening prayer. Thanks to Verizon, our team will be able to watch the beginning of the ceremony on an iPad. At the sound of "amen," the fun begins. One man will drop the first round down the tube. The round slides down the tube and strikes a firing pin, the propellant is ignited, and sends the projectile flying toward the presidential cluster fuck.

In well-practiced moves, this process will be repeated until all nine rounds are in the air before the first round strikes the target. I must note, the Secret Service and the Washington, D.C. police department began deploying their SureSpotter gunfire detection system throughout the city. This system was developed for the U.S. military and initially used in the Vietnam war to detect and locate sniper and mortar fire. When this system detects a loud noise, computer software analyzes its acoustic signature. If the software determines it is gunfire, it will triangulate the source, pinpoint a suspected location within a matter of seconds, and notify the police.

By the time our team fires the last mortar round if not before, the system will have sent an alarm to a central dispatch office. But that's ok. Rounds will already be on their way to the target, and our men will be heading just up the street to their second target, the Savoy Elementary School. They will turn left into the parking lot between the school and the Thurgood Marshall Academy, pull forward fifty meters, and detonate their load of Semtex. It's going to be a dreadful day in the nation's capital. With both the outgoing and newly elected president, most of Congress, and the Joint Chiefs of Staff blown to bits they, whoever "they" is now, will have a tough time determining who's in charge. They will sort out the chain of command by the end of the day, and when they do, and that person gets their hands on the nuclear launch codes, Pyongyang will become little more than a radioactive scar on the Korean peninsula. Allah be praised.

That, my brothers, is our mission, our purpose in life, for the next nine months. From a thirty-thousand-foot perspective, our plans seem straightforward. However, as they say, the devil is in the details. We have scores of tasks which are critical to our success. Although seemingly independent, they build one upon the other and, as the engine in my beloved Aventador must function as one unit. It will be our job, the three of us, to accomplish and then coordinate each piece of this terror mosaic."

For the past hour, Saad and Khalid had sat spellbound, paying rapt attention as Abdulla passionately painted a picture of what, if they succeeded, would be morale-crushing attacks on their mortal enemy. However, like the members of the MA Sovereign Council, deep down inside they nursed concerns about his sanity. Especially his claims to have received instructions directly from the archangel Gabriel. If true, this would make Abdulla, like Muhammad, a prophet, a messenger of God. If untrue, they were listening to a raging madman. And they were about to do his bidding.

Oblivious to their concerns, and without missing a beat, Abdulla continued. "Let's go over our roles. Please listen closely; we cannot commit any of this to writing or share it with anyone outside this room.

Each of us will have designated logistical responsibilities as well as an operational and leadership role for specific attacks. Khalid, based on your previous weapons procurement and intelligence experience I would like you to arrange for and oversee the purchase of the Semtex, the mortar, and its trajectory guidance computer, and the five surface-to-air missiles. You should also acquire DPRK manufactured, silenced, semi-automatic pistols sufficient to arm each of our soldiers. These are to be weapons of last resort. They should only be used, for example with our mortar team, if some neighborhood thug decides to steal their truck or gets a little too curious. You will also assume the role of team leader for the SAM airline attacks. You must schedule and oversee each soldiers training on how to use the SAMs well in advance of their travel to the U.S. The individual cities, and their airports, have already been selected. You will coordinate the insertion of each soldier into the community and provide funds for his living expenses. There are scores of individual tasks associated with each of the three assignments. It is not my intent to micromanage you or your jobs, nor do I have the knowledge and expertise to do so. Each of you is more than capable of running your show or for that matter; the entire mission should something happen to me. I am merely stating dates, times, and responsibilities. The rest will be on our individual shoulders. Just never, ever, forget; the future of Islam depends on our success.

I must ask for forgiveness for the sermonette. I don't mean to give the impression of superiority or sound overly authoritarian. It's just that my passion for this, never before offered opportunity is consuming me. I will apologize in advance for any future displays of zealousness. Now, where was I? Oh yes, Khalid, you have your assignment. Should you have any, and I mean any, questions, or should you need my assistance, do not under any circumstances hesitate to ask.

By the way, Khalid, if something should happen to me, you are to take my place as the Commander of this operation. You must also assume my operational responsibilities or personally designate someone who can. Saad, you are next in line in the event Khalid gets whacked or is incapacitated. Like shit, authority rolls downhill.

Saad, you are by far the most technically savvy of the three of us, and if your pornography collection is any indicator, you can stumble your way into just about any computer system. For that reason, and because you know every geek in the middle east, I want you to head up, what I will call, the phycological warfare component of our mission.

You will select a team to hack into the DPRK, American, and South Korean computer and satellite communication systems. Your team will begin sending the pre and post attack threats we have discussed. It might help to gather up samples of the messages and videos the DPRK has been spewing out the last couple of years. It will take no small amount of skill to duplicate their style of insane rhetoric.

You will also head up the Christmas Eve church massacres. As with the airline attacks, the specific cities and churches have already been selected. Like Khalid, you will recruit your team and help them in their assimilation into their respective communities. This team will be required to interact more closely with their neighbors and church congregations. As such, we must select those with genuinely superior English and American social skills. You will work with Khalid to develop a plan for the delivery of the martyr vests your team will use. I do not see a need for any other weapons. Once they release their detonator triggers, their mission is complete.

I will oversee the mortar attack on the inauguration ceremony. Thanks to the previous administration's lax immigration policy, we already have many suitable personnel assets in the Washington D.C. and surrounding areas. In fact, the place is crawling with Iraqi and Syrian refugees who, over the past few years, have formed their own communities and subcultures. I will have my team rent space in one of those temporary storage facilities with pull down, lockable, doors.

We will preassemble and store our mortar and targeting computer there until the day of the ceremony. That morning our men will back our truck up to the door, load up the mortar, bolt its base plate to the truck bed, and head off to our primary firing location. Naturally, we will practice this routine until we can do it within minutes and without any mechanical hitches.

The fact that we must coordinate three separate, yet related attacks make this overall mission extremely complicated. This is compounded by the need to ensure the men are unaware of the other squads or plans for any actions other than their individual assignment. There are numerous opportunities for error which could cause our mission to unravel completely. It is our collective responsibility to make sure this doesn't happen.

One of our most complex, and dangerous, tasks will be the shipment and storage of weapons and explosives. Khalid will orchestrate their purchase and their transfer from the DPRK to a distribution location in the U.S. He has done this numerous times for various factions in the middle east. He has even arranged for the purchase of explosives for the IRA. I make note of this because even though the task is fraught with danger, we at least have some degree of experience in this area. Getting the stuff on U.S. soil and then clandestinely moving it to eleven locations scattered across the country is another matter altogether. I have high-level plans for doing so. I will devote much of my time to working out the details over the next few days and will share them with each of you once they have jelled a bit.

At this point, we must discuss how we will be communicating in the weeks to come. The use of disposable cellular phones has served us well in the past. However, our need for more frequent, sometimes even daily, detail-laden dialogue makes this medium too cumbersome. Fortunately, we have a solution.

I know both of you have visited sites on the dark web, using Tor, or similar browsers, in the past; Khalid for the purchase of weapons and Saad for his family's questionable financial transactions. There is an ultra-secure, encrypted, email service, Dmail.net, that will fit our needs perfectly. I have taken the liberty of setting up accounts for each of you on the Dmail server. To date, Dmail messages have proven impossible to intercept and decrypt. Dmail is hidden within a video sharing service, somewhat like YouTube, called Dvideo.

The casual user accesses Dvideo and watches, or shares, homemade or pirated movies. However, when a registered Dmail user enters a password, it opens his email account. When you enter a message, the software encrypts it and inserts its bit strings into sections of a video. Message headers on the encrypted message determine its recipients and notifies them that a message is in their Dmail inbox.

The process is reversed when the recipient accesses their mail account. An unregistered user who may happen to view the streaming video would never see the message. Even if they, or government snoops, did they would encounter a 923-bit encryption key that is theoretically impossible to break. I know this is a lot of geek speak, but I threw it in to assure you that our email communications will be secure. Of course, that assumes you don't print the message and leave it laying around for your maid to find."

Abdulla stood up and twisted his body from one side to another then raised his arms in an exaggerated stretching motion. Looking down at the two men he said, "I'm exhausted. That's enough discussion for now. It's time for us to go our separate ways and to start the beginning of the end of Christian domination. Check your Dmail at least every day and err on the side of over communication. We will talk again, one week from today." Walking toward the suite's bedroom, he told Saad and Khalid, "it's time to sleep and to see if the archangel has additional instructions for me."

CHAPTER 7

The Harry S. Truman Building, on C. Street in Washington, D.C., is the headquarters of the United States Department of State. It is a series of interconnected, multistory, buildings sprawling all over what is sometimes referred to as the Foggy Bottom section of the nation's capital. It is easy for visitors and fledgling employees to get lost in its endless string of offices and twisting corridors. David Stakely was not exactly new, but he frequently had to ask directions when walking from one division meeting location to another. He was also still trying to find his way, politically, from his management level position in the Intelligence and Research, INR, division up the organization chart to the Secretary of State.

David was a GS-14 with an undergraduate degree in Political Science from the University of Chicago and an MBA from Northwestern University in Evanston, IL. He was born at Womack Medical Center at Ft. Bragg, NC. Both of his parents were career military officers. Although not unheard of, this was somewhat unusual even for the Army. Like all Army brats, David lived in several states and two other countries before he graduated from high school. As a result, he was exposed to a larger cross-section of cultures, people, and personalities than his civilian peers. Early on he developed an ability to get to know, and to get along with, just about anyone as soon as he met them and to knowledgeably discuss an incredibly wide range of topics. However, because he and his family moved so frequently, he never developed close, and personal, friendships.

Like each of his parents, David was intensely competitive both physically and intellectually. He did well in school, always making A's or B's, and ended up graduating in the top ten percent of his class. Anything less would not have been acceptable in the Stakely family. Slightly above average in height, and with a slim but muscular build, he was often approached by his high school coaches to go out for track or football. However, despite having great hand-eye coordination, and remarkably good, innate, athletic abilities, he didn't have the slightest interest in team sports. He preferred the physical contact, discipline, and one-on-one competition he found in the martial arts. This was not surprising to his father and in fact, perfectly matched his own sports preferences. By the time he was eighteen, David had earned a black belt in Ta Kwon Do.

David served a four-year stint as an officer in the U.S. Army Intelligence and Security Command, INSCOM. After making First Lieutenant, he was assigned to the 501st Military Intelligence Brigade headquartered in Seoul, Korea. This assignment afforded him the chance to work with the South Korean military and to learn at least some of the ends and outs of its politics. By choosing to live in a small apartment off base, he also took advantage of the opportunity to be immersed in the culture and lifestyle of young, up and coming, professional Koreans. He grew to love the cuisine but struggled to learn more than a few dozen words of their language. He considered Korean just short of impossible for a westerner to speak or comprehend. Fortunately, most professional Koreans were relatively fluent in English and relished the chance to engage with Americans.

Most of the older Koreans lived with a nagging fear of an invasion from the north. Until recently, this possibility wasn't top of mind with Koreans who were David's age, and who had not suffered thru war in the 1950's. Recent events were changing all of that. Now, almost all South Koreans woke up every morning wondering if today would be the day.

Shortly after the DPRK test fired its new Hwasong-16 ICBM, a top-secret directive had filtered down to the INR Division. David and the other members of his research group were to begin the development of a treaty to be used with post-war North Korea. Although without explicit wording, the directive spoke volumes about the current administration's intentions. They weren't concerned with, or interested in, reforming the DPRK government or downsizing the military. The majority of each would be eliminated.

The treaty was to be based on unconditional surrender of the north to the U.S. and its allies. Everyone, up and down the State Department chain of command, knew this would never be acceptable to the Chinese or the Russians. It didn't matter how irrational the DPRK leader and his stooges acted or the outcome of an inevitable war. The Chinese would not allow the geographical expansion of South Korea or shared borders with U.S. allies. Any treaty the INR proposed would have to accommodate both the Russians and the Chinese governments, not what remained of the DPRK.

Six weeks ago, David and his team had received a briefing from the INR Director, Jim Phillips, on the contents of the treaty development directive. He acknowledged the near impossibility of developing a pact that would be anywhere near acceptable to all three superpowers. Then he proceeded to remind everyone that they didn't have an option. The President of the United States, POTUS, wanted a document that the Secretary of State, their boss, would have "in his hip pocket" before fireworks began. A deadline for its development had not been stated, only that it was extremely urgent. Based on years of experience, Jim knew this implied there was, in fact, a highly classified target date shared only between the

POTUS and the Secretary. In its absence, Jim directed the group to present him with a draft plan by the end of the month. He then broke the INR group into three, five people, teams. Each team was to develop a draft treaty independently and present to him on the first day of the next month. He would decide which treaty he would take to the Secretary. They had twelve days and, "boys and girls, daylight's burning."

As a GS-14, David was the senior member, and *de facto* leader, of his team. He directed his group to go back to their offices, collect everything they were going to need for the next twelve days, and reconvene in the fourth-floor conference room in thirty minutes; if not sooner.

When David got back to his office, he told Tammy, his Administrative Assistant, that her duty station would also be changing for the next several days. She would be providing any, and all, administrative support he and his team might need. Her first task was to round up a large whiteboard, a supply of dry erase markers and yellow legal pads. David collected his laptop computer and his coffee cup and went back to the conference room which he, and his team, would later refer to as "the pit."

Once the team was assembled, they started discussing the treaty, its ramifications, and the parameters, which David referred to as "the box," surrounding its development. For the first two hours, their discussions went around in circles. Old or existing treaties and several innovative ideas were suggested. Tammy listed each one on the whiteboard. As soon as it was put on the board, each idea was punched full of holes. None of the suggested treaty approaches would be acceptable to all three of the superpowers. Something felt to be good for the Chinese, and the Americans would not be acceptable to the Russians. Trying to suture three vastly different political and economic ideologies into a single pact didn't seem possible.

There had to be a common bond, but so far no one on the team had a clue as to what that might be.

Finally, at 2000, David called a halt saying "ok, folks, let's call it a day. Go home, think about our objective and what we have done so far, which was to eliminate every option we could think of, and get some sleep. Hopefully, one of us will come up with something that will save our careers. Be back here at 0800." He didn't need to say 0800 sharp. Everyone in the room knew his obsession with punctuality.

Being a non-exempt civil service employee, Tammy had left hours ago. David could have approved overtime but knew that, like most working moms, she had kids to pick up, dinner to cook, and if working late, a babysitter to schedule. Besides, he thought, it was only their first day on this project. They weren't in an emergency, jump out your ass, mode just yet. As they were leaving David noted, "don't worry about breakfast tomorrow, I will call Tammy and ask her to pick up some bagels or something on her way in."

David lived near Germantown, Maryland, about forty miles from his office in D.C. He had purchased an older, modest, farmhouse and ten acres of land, a year after moving to Washington. Restoring the house and maintaining the property was both his therapy and escape from the pressures of his job. However, he also rented a small apartment just a few blocks from the Truman Building. He stayed there when working late thru the week and didn't feel like dealing with the soul-crushing traffic on I-270 and everything inside D.C.'s beltway.

David shared the apartment with Kelly Meadows who, like David, lived elsewhere but sometimes needed a workweek retreat. Kelly was a Research Analyst with the General Services Administration, GSA. They had met while taking a postgraduate evening class at The George Washington University and had become good friends. Neither David nor Kelly were romantically involved with anyone, and they considered their relationship to be, more or less, platonic. In reality, they defined themselves to be, what is often referred to as, "friends with benefits." They enjoyed each other's company, shared amazingly similar social and recreational interests, and frequently vacationed or spent long weekends together. Somewhere along the line, they discovered that they were also physically compatible. Yet they staunchly considered themselves to be friends, not lovers.

They had long ago agreed that neither would bring a date to their apartment. It was important to each of them that this was to be neutral territory and a place of rest and, except when their work schedules intersected, solitude. The apartment was David's destination tonight, and he secretly hoped that Kelly wasn't there. He had way too much to think about. Kelly would understand, but David didn't want to waste a second doing anything but concentrating on the task at hand. This ability to single-mindedly focus, to mentally obliterate distractions, was sometimes a blessing and sometimes a curse. It was also something he did without knowing he was doing it.

But right now, David was starving. He made a slight detour and stopped at one of his favorite downtown restaurants, the Jade Palace. The Palace was a Chinese mom and pop, rather mama-san and papa-san, joint that had been around forever. It stayed in business by selling delicious food at, for D.C., reasonable prices. David found a parking space just a short distance down the street and went inside. He made a show of studying the menu although, for the most part, he knew it by heart. It didn't matter; he almost always ordered the same thing, pork lo mein, two spring rolls, and an order of steamed dumplings. His order was assembled, boxed up, and ready to go in less than ten minutes. Faster than McDonald's and twice as good. David gave his Visa to the elderly lady behind the counter. She entered the amount into a credit card reader and then, holding the card by its upper edge with both hands, handed it back. David never failed to be amused by the formality the older generation Asians used when exchanging business cards. They did the same thing when returning a credit card. Hold it with both hands at the top then respectively, and with an almost imperceptible bow, return it to the customer. It was a refreshing change to be treated with a little respect and civility now and then. David accepted the card, put it in his wallet, and thanked the mama-san as he took his order and turned to leave.

Then it hit him. The credit card thing had been the trigger. He had the "how do you appease the Russians and Chinese after we destroy one of their allies" answer. For just a split second, David stopped dead in his tracks. Then he felt a surge of adrenalin and double-timed back to his car.

After arriving at the apartment, David opened his laptop and sat down at the small kitchen table. Using a State Department approved, encrypted, version of Microsoft Word, he pecked out his original idea and then started adding notes, questions, and any other thoughts that popped into his head. He wolfed down the lo mein without really tasting it. His mind was racing as he laid out his theory and began to rationally explore arguments that he might, undoubtedly would, encounter when presenting it to his team. He worked furiously until midnight. Then, realizing he was exhausted, starting to get a little loopy, and had to get up at the crack of dawn, he stopped. David saved what he had written, turned off his laptop, and cleaned up what remained of his dinner. He showered and climbed into bed, physically drained but mentally wide awake. Light but refreshing sleep finally overtook him around 0200.

David had never needed an alarm clock. By merely concentrating on a specific hour, something deep inside his hypothalamus set some internal trigger, and he would wake up at the appropriate time. His brain alarm went off at 0600, and he crawled out of bed. David dropped a Dunkin Donuts pod into his Keurig and did a set of twisting and stretching exercises while the coffee brewed. He then went to the bathroom, brushed his teeth, and started to get dressed. By 0630 he had completed his morning routine and was heading to his car. It was a little after 0700 when he parked his car, negotiated the Truman Building maze, and arrived back at the Pit.

David wasn't surprised that he was the first to arrive. He had a hard-charging, highly motivated, group of professionals. But there were limits, especially in the morning. That was ok. Being there first gave him time to fire up his laptop and to get ready to jump start this morning's discussion. He went back over the notes he had written the night before, edited a few, and added some additional thoughts that had occurred to him during the drive to the Truman building. Knowing that Tammy had copied what was on it, David wiped off the whiteboard as he prepared to open the meeting.

By now his team members were starting to arrive. Although not the least bit scientific, David knew the order of arrival would reflect their devotion to duty and overall professional drive and commitment. The first, Ellen, walked in around 0720, sat down near the end of the table where David was standing, and started reviewing her notes. Tammy came in next carrying a sack filled with bagels, cream cheese, and daily pastry specials from Casey's Coffee on 23rd Street. By 0750 everyone had arrived and were starting to munch on the carbohydrate-laden breakfast and steaming coffee.

David stood up and began the meeting by asking the group if anyone had any ideas that hadn't been discussed, and subsequently eliminated, the day before. There were a few light-hearted comments about meeting induced brain death, but no one had any new, groundbreaking, suggestions. Then, picking up a dry erase marker, David said, "well, I had a revelation.

As we have discussed, ad nauseam, neither the Chinese or the Russians are going to let us, or our buddies in Seoul, establish a footprint anywhere near what is now their border with North Korea. That's a given. It ain't gonna happen.

Conversely, we can't allow them to benefit from our action and to continue to loom over South Korea. I kept telling myself, from a political and social perspective, we are light years apart. But there must be a single thread, some unique bond, that our people, and our governments, share with one another.

Then last night I found the answer staring me straight in the face. A little old Chinese lady. She had probably already been working ten hours straight and would keep at it for another four or five. The answer to this seemingly unsolvable riddle is business. We can't just make a few patches and slap a new coat of paint on some treaty we, or any other country, have used in the past. In today's world, we need a radically original approach. The Chinese are working their one billion asses off in a collective effort to become the number one economy on the planet. They are getting close. The Russians are beginning to turn the corner on economic recovery since the USSR started unraveling in 1990. And despite the financial doom and gloom you hear on CNN, the U.S. economy is still running on turbo with no real slow down on the horizon. Nobody wants another long, drawn out, tax consuming job babysitting its misbehaving neighbor. The superpowers want to get back to the business of business. We don't need to develop another treaty to govern North Korea. We need to, jointly, create an international corporation to take its place."

The room was, for just a few seconds, silent as a tomb. Then light bulbs started coming on. Ellen spoke up first. "Sure wish you would elaborate boss. Unless I dozed off, it sounded like you were suggesting we replace the DPRK government with a company; like, oh I don't know, Kimchee, Incorporated."

Sporting a huge smile David pointed at Ellen with a dry eraser and said, "you got it!" He moved to the whiteboard, wrote Kimchee, Inc., turned and said, "we're going to have to work on the name, but you nailed the concept." Beginning what would turn into a sermonette, he continued, "Rather than a post-war treaty, we replace the existing, soon to be former government with an international corporation. For the sake of discussion, and because Kimchee, Inc., reeks, let's call it the Asian Independent Free Trade Union, AIFTU, or phonetically, Ah If To.

Don't worry; this will also change once our beltway bandit marketing consultants get hold of it. AIFTU would be overseen and directed by a seven-person Board of Directors. The Board is to be composed of appointed representatives from China, Russia, the U.S., and Korea. There would also be an elected representative from the EU and two members at large who would be selected by the other five Board members. The Board is not to be self-perpetuating. Rather membership, representing the countries and groups I just named, is to be spelled out in the corporate charter and with defined term limits. In a nutshell that is my recommendation to replace the DPRK.

I will pause now and give you an opportunity to tell me why this, never been considered in the history of the world idea, will not work. Unless I hear something that would make this plan completely unworkable, or unless someone has a more palatable suggestion, I will continue and add a few more, almost as radical, ideas."

All eyes focused on David, and for a short while, other than a few, undirected expletives, no one made a complete sentence. Robert, the oldest, and least open-minded, member of the team spoke up saying "well we are in this deep, I say let's forge ahead. There has to be a cliff out there somewhere." David thought to himself, ah yes, Robert, just as I expected, the last to drag himself thru the door this morning. David said, "thank you, Robert, let's proceed."

Picking up from where he had figuratively, pressed the pause button David continued. "If this concept is accepted within the INR, I propose that we, and our legal staff, of course, flesh out our proposal and get it in front of the Secretary and POTUS, as soon as humanly possible. It is critical that it be presented to the Russians and Chinese before we launch a strike.

Like the treaty itself, I will use that term just for the sake of discussion; a post-war agreement has never been presented to opposing forces before the shooting starts. In effect, we are telling the Russians and Chinese that we are tired of the DPRK's shit, we are going to clean their clock, and when it's over, we want you to join us in running the place. Hopefully, if we present our plan correctly, a preemptive discussion will prevent retaliatory strikes by the other two superpowers. If not, we can pretty much kiss civilization as we know it goodbye. Maybe the cockroaches will do a better job of living in harmony with the planet than we have. But let's hope the Secretary can sell it. Whether you like his politics or not, he is a master of diplomacy. With all this in mind, it's time to start defining some of the details we want in the treaty document. More will come as it is developed, but several crucial points need to be included from the get-go.

David and his team worked feverishly for the next ten days. They began adding substance to the basic concept of an international corporation as the replacement for a former government. The team clung to David's "there is no such thing as good writing, just good re-writing" advice. As soon as an acceptable idea emerged, the team pounced on it. They collectively converted the concept into treaty lingo then edited the wording until it was concise, unambiguous, and seemed politically acceptable to all future government signatories.

As soon as the wording for each requirement was drafted, Tammy would incorporate it into the evolving document, smoothing out the grammatical rough edges as she went. As such, by the end of each day, they had a readable, unmarked, version which they could take home, review, and wordsmith, even more, the following day. By the time the INR Director's deadline was at hand, the team had a document which, although politically unorthodox, they all felt would meet with the Secretary's approval. Russians, Chinese, and POTUS acceptance would be another matter altogether.

The treaty, or more accurately the corporate charter, would be simultaneously presented to Russian and Chinese Secretary of State equivalents immediately following POTUS approval. From this point forward, it would be referred to as simply the AIFTU Charter. This approach would help avoid what would inevitably become a constitutional sticking point if it appeared the POTUS was making unilateral treaties.

At the end of the month Jim Phillips, the INR Director, called an early morning group meeting of all three teams. Each leader was instructed to bring their entire squad and sixteen copies of a doubled spaced brief of their proposal. They gathered in a conference room down the hall from Jim's office with each group seated around three, previously staged conference tables facing a podium at the front of the room. David was cautiously optimistic about the reception their AIFTU Charter would receive. However, he was also well aware of the current administration's reputation as being rabidly conservative and their proposal was, at best, at the opposite end of the governmentally traditional spectrum.

At precisely 0900 Jim and his Administrative Assistant entered the room and called the meeting to order. Standing next to, but not behind the podium he opened the meeting saying, "good morning folks. For the past twelve days you have, I hope, been working on what could well be one of the most important documents that will be produced in this century. This morning I will ask each team leader to present an overview of the brief of his or her team's proposal to the group as a whole and me. As I noted when I originally scheduled this meeting, you will have thirty minutes to present your proposal. At the end of your overview, you can add as many details as you can squeeze into your block of time. Please hold your questions until three plans have been presented. At that time, you can attack each other's work to your heart's content during our scheduled question and answer session.

Following this morning's meeting, I will give myself forty-eight hours to review and consider each of the documents and decide which I will present to the Secretary. I know you all are chomping at the bit, so who wants to go first?" Before the other two team leaders could respond, David raised his hand and said "Jim, our plan is pretty radical. For that reason, I would suggest that we present last so as not to distract from what the other groups have done." Pointing at the team leader on his left Phillips said "that's fine with me. Steve, why don't you get us started."

For the next hour, the two other teams reviewed their proposals for a post-war treaty with the DPRK. Each plan was structured largely around a blending of the existing armistice with North Korea and the Paris Peace Accord agreement with Vietnam. These plans were designed to appease the Chinese and allow the U.S. to disengage from a conventional, ground-based, conflict. They were also intended for post-war negotiation with both the Russians and Chinese. This assumed the other two superpowers would not jump into the fray once the shooting started. That wasn't going to happen; at least in David's mind.

PowerPoint images summarizing salient points from each treaty document were displayed on the screen at the front of the room. David focused on Jim's facial expression and body language as each slide was presented. Subtle changes in expression, a lifted eyebrow or a furrowed brow, suggested Jim was not pleased with what he was hearing.

In the back of his mind, David felt the other treaties would have worked fifty years ago. They would not work in an age when the U.S., China, and Russia were military and economic contemporaries. The team leader presenting the second treaty started to go over her thirty-minute limit, and Jim called "time." "David, you're up. Let's hear your definition of "radical.""

David walked to the front of the room and clicked the laptop's remote-control mouse, starting his team's PowerPoint presentation. The night before he had prepared slides which would allow him to summarize the central AIFTU Charter concept in ten minutes. He would provide critically important, supporting, details, in bullet list format, during the last twenty minutes of his time allocation.

As he presented the summary on the first slide, David continued to watch Jim's posture and facial expressions. When he stated the proposal to replace the DPRK government with a superpower controlled, for profit corporation he saw Jim sit up straight and, leaning slightly forward, focus on the slide. Without pausing, David, sensing Jim's undivided attention, launched into key elements of the AIFTU Charter.

"As I said, the concept is way out of the box. We think it will be acceptable to both the Russians and the Chinese. However, it must be presented, preferably jointly, to their representatives before we initiate hostilities. To avoid even limited nuclear retaliation, it is imperative that we get their buy-in to this concept before we launch our first cruise missile.

We suggest that the POTUS direct the Secretary of State to arrange a Top-Secret meeting at an undisclosed neutral location with his Russian and Chinese counterparts. We are aware that you are far more adept at orchestrating such a meeting, but I would be remiss if I didn't clearly state the need for total, internal and external, secrecy. We don't want any cameras flashing, or social media scoops, alerting the DPRK, or the general public, to our intentions.

During the meeting, after he has discussed the basic corporation concept, the Secretary must lay out a plan for what happens immediately after the surrender. That would be the formal formation of the AIFTU Board. At this point, there will be plenty of room for "next step" negotiations.

The first thing the AIFTU Board must do is disband the DPRK military. North Korea currently has the fourth largest army in the world, over 1,200,000 active duty soldiers. Their current economy couldn't absorb such a massive increase in unemployment. Initially we, well the Board, would give former military personnel the opportunity to work in civil service type jobs. For example, all weapons and firearms must be collected, disassembled, and scrapped for use in what will become AIFTU manufacturing subsidiaries. Just imagine the mountains of tires, petroleum, and OD green paint for that matter that can now be used for peaceful, profitable, purposes.

I will use this military personnel repatriation task to transition or segue if you are musically inclined, to another critical AIFTU element. Everyone living in the former DPRK will be free to stay or emigrate to any country that will accept them. For the first time in their lives, they will be free. The entire concept of citizenship will have to be redefined. The AIFTU is not a country; it's a corporation. Perhaps those adults living there should be some level of employee or be given similar corporate membership. We felt it best to let the legal beagles work out this, and the hundreds of other details when they develop the official AIFTU charter. The takeaway here is, disband the military, eliminate and repurpose all weapons and weapon production facilities, and provide individual freedom.

Under the direction of the Board, the AIFTU should be given a specified length of time to show a profit. We propose ten years. They will be charged with transitioning from a dictatorial, hermit kingdom to an industrialized free trade zone. This will take some time and concessions by the nations represented on the Board and the AIFTU stockholders. These concessions will take the form of investments and assistance in recruiting manufacturing and other industries.

The wall clock tells me that I have roughly two minutes remaining in my presentation. Although there are scores of other details that will eventually be part of the AIFTU charter, I will close with one globally significant, positive, point. In addition to being an international free trade zone, the AIFTU should set a corporate goal of having a zero carbon footprint in ten years. This will set an example for the rest of the planet while simultaneously making peaceful use of the nuclear materials in the weapons they currently love to parade around.

Jim, that at least summarizes my team's recommendations. We know it's something that has never been done before or, as far as we know, even considered. But we don't think there is any other way to neutralize the DPRK and at the same time appease three global superpowers who deeply distrust one another. The Russians and Chinese have a mad dog in their front yard. But from their perspective, it's keeping the U.S. and South Koreans at bay. This eliminates both threats and gives each of our economies a profitable shot in the arm." With that, David closed his PowerPoint presentation and sat down in his chair.

Jim stood up, walked to the front of the room, and addressed the entire group. "I want to thank each of you for the extraordinarily hard work you have done. Each of your products is individualy brilliant.

When we started this morning, I said that I would give myself forty-eight hours to review the details of each and then select one that I would present to the Secretary. However, I have changed my mind. I am convinced that replacing the DPRK with an international, superpower managed and controlled corporation, will not only work, but it's also most likely the only way to prevent starting world war three.

That is the concept we will present to the Secretary. If anyone can sell it to the POTUS, he can. I will get David and me on his calendar immediately." Looking directly at David, Jim said "between now and then I would like for you and your team to focus solely on the AIFTU charter. Continue to polish it up, hammer in any additional details and have it ready for prime time by the end of the week. Effective now, the charter, this briefing, and everything relevant to this plan is classified Top Secret Sensitive Compartmented Information, TS-SCI."

CHAPTER 8

At the harbor, just north of the DPRK city of Munchon, workers methodically loaded shipping containers on the Nan Feng. The Nan Feng was a medium-sized Chinese container boat making its last stop before sailing to San Juan del Sur on the Pacific coast of Nicaragua and then on to Los Angeles.

The transfer truck-sized containers were loaded with cheap men's and women's clothing, one of the DPRK's most significant exports. Packed near the rear of container number 40760, behind cardboard boxes of women's pants, were ten wooden crates. The sides of each, sequentially numbered, crate was stenciled, in English, with "Sewing Machine Parts." Neither the dock foreman or the Nan Feng's Captain was aware of the crates or their contents. The ship's manifest simply listed "clothing."

As part of the purchasing process, Khalid had intentionally specified that the goods be shipped by boat with Chinese registration. Although sometimes contentious in many areas, trade relations between the U.S. and China were better than they had ever been.

The Chinese were also teasing the Nicaraguan government with plans to build a one-hundred-and-seventy-mile long canal across their country. Although "on again and off again," they continued to conduct feasibility studies and construction plans. These efforts poured millions of dollars into the economy of the poorest nation in Central America. This combination all but insured that the Nan Feng would not undergo an "open container" inspection during stops at either port. All containers unloading at Los Angeles would be automatically scanned for radioactivity, and most were externally sniffed for drugs, as they were placed on receiving vehicles. However, the Nan Feng's cargo, would wiz, untouched, thru customs, most of it on the way to Walmart and Costco distribution centers.

CHAPTER 9

Khalid landed at McCarran International Airport in Las Vegas, Nevada on Monday at 1300. Once the plane stopped, he retrieved his carry-on bag from the overhead compartment, deplaned, and started following the signs toward ground transportation. His bag contained a change of clothes, a toiletries case, and $20,000. The cash, in used $100 bills, was in neatly bound stacks of $1000. In the bottom of his bag, he also had a license plate and a small, sealed, bag of uncut cocaine. He had stolen the plate from a truck in the parking lot of a hotel in San Antonio, Texas. Using a computer in the lobby of the hotel in San Antonio, Khalid had found a three-year-old Ford Econoline van at one of the numerous used car lots on Tropicana Avenue just east of the Vegas strip. He called the dealer, discussed the van, and negotiated a five percent reduction in the list price. Khalid didn't care about the price at all. He just wanted to minimize any suspicions the dealer may have when he made the purchase.

Khalid hailed a cab and gave the driver the address of the car lot. Once they arrived, he paid the driver and gave him a five-dollar tip. Enough to please but not enough to bring unwanted attention to the dark passenger. He immediately saw the van he had selected. It had been pulled in front of the office and washed in anticipation of his arrival.

Khalid hadn't been on the lot more than two minutes before a grinning salesman popped out of the office and headed his way. Khalid explained that he had previously spoken with the sales manager, arranged to purchase the van, and was just there to pay and be on his way. The salesman's face showed more than a little disappointment at losing the prospect of a new sale, but he walked Khalid into the office and introduced him to the manager. Khalid and the sales manager shook hands and then walked back outside and physically looked over the van, inside and out. The manager said, "she's clean as a whistle, fueled up, and ready to roll." They walked back inside and completed the purchase and registration paperwork. Khalid counted out the agreed upon price, and the sales manager gave him his temporary registration and two sets of keys. They shook hands again. As they walked out the door, the manager said, "that registration is good for thirty days. I hope you enjoy her; she's a real workhorse." It was obvious that cash was king with that guy.

Khalid turned west on Tropicana and headed toward its junction with Interstate 15. Along the way, he pulled into the parking lot of a strip shopping center and went inside Dick's, a medium-sized sporting goods store. There he purchased a Gerber utility tool which, among its fourteen distinct functions, included a Phillips and a flathead screwdriver and a three-inch knife blade. He also bought a pair of leather gloves and a hooded, plastic coated, rain jacket.

Next, he stopped at Boots and Saddles, a small western wear shop, and bought a pair of Lucchese pointed toe calf hides, shelling out $425.00. He told the clerk to dispose of the box the boots were shipped in; he would wear them and carry the loafers he had worn when he came into the store. Once outside, he slipped on his New York Yankees baseball cap. For the casual observer, and as long as he didn't open his mouth, he passed for a typical, conservatively dressed, Mexican.

Finally, Khalid walked to a Kroger's. He was starving. Grabbing a shopping basket, he ambled around the store picking up a six-pack of Mountain Dew, a bag of barbecue potato chips, and three Gala apples. He then found his way to the deli and ordered a large roast beef sub. After going thru the self-checkout, he went back to the van and placed his food items in the passenger seat where he could easily reach them as he drove. He then rummaged thru his carry-on bag and fished out the stolen license plate. He had been careful to position the van so that the rear was not visible by any of the security cameras spread over the parking lot. He got out, and using the Gerber's flathead screwdriver, removed the temporary, cardboard, license plate and replaced it with the one he had stolen in San Antonio. He folded the temporary plate with the intention of dropping it in the first trash receptacle he passed when he left. He didn't want to take even the slightest chance of anyone connecting any dots linking him and the Econoline; at least not at this stage of the game.

While at the hotel in San Antonio, Khalid had used Google maps, and its satellite view, to locate a Love's truck stop near the junction of highway 91 and I-710. After finding the truck stop, using a combination of Google and the online Long Beach phone directory, he had found and contacted, one of the scores of independent container delivery truckers. For the most part, these were legal, Mexican immigrants who were paid on a "per unit" basis to move shipping containers from one of the Los Angles ports to "big box" distribution centers. They frequently worked sixteen to twenty hours a day stopping only to refuel, defecate, or grab a catnap between loads. They ate pre-made sandwiches or food truck burritos while driving. Almost all of them carried, and used, some form of urinal. All of this was to pay off barely legal loans on their trucks. This was about as close to indentured servitude as you could find in the U.S.

Their plight, and mistreatment by local trucking companies had been well documented and was even featured on a *Twenty – Twenty* segment. Regardless, it persisted without getting any better.

Khalid had offered the trucker, Hector Rodriquez, $3000 to pick up a container from the Maersk pier on Terminal Island, deliver it to the Love's, and help him load his portion of the shipment into his van. He would send the paperwork needed to authorize picking up the container, and $1000 in advance and would pay the balance upon delivery. Hector jumped at the chance. Although slightly concerned about the legality of the container's contents, this was more profit than he would make in a month hauling his regular loads. And, unless there were a major traffic jam, this job would take less than six hours. Shit, as far as he was concerned, the container could be stuffed with dead babies, three grand was three grand.

While still in the shopping center parking lot, Khalid programmed his cell phone's GPS to take him from Las Vegas, via I-15, to a Holiday Inn Express on the outskirts of Los Angles. According to the GPS, the trip would take a little over four hours, not including a restroom break. Khalid waited until he was on I-15 before he started eating his sandwich. The roads leading out of Las Vegas weren't all that complicated, and they weren't choked with traffic, but he didn't want any distractions that may cause him to have an accident. A stolen license plate, a fake driver's permit, and a forged passport would guarantee him a trip to jail followed by deportation. More importantly, it would entirely derail the mission. Knowing this, he had to ensure that he made the person on his driver's license look like he was competing for some Citizen of The Year award.

The I-15 route passed directly thru the Mojave Desert. The harshest, most desolate, landscape in the U.S. Most Americans would consider this part of the country as being God-forsaken at best. However, Khalid felt right at home. The Mojave was almost lush compared to Saudi Arabia.

The drive and the solitude gave him an opportunity to mentally review and refine his plans for the next several days. Khalid ate slowly, savoring every bite of his roast beef sandwich and munching thru half of the potato chips. After finishing his meal, he meticulously folded up the wrapper, and the single napkin he had been using and placed them back into the carryout bag from Subway. He couldn't understand why Americans generated so much trash. They used scores of plastic bags every time they shopped in their overstuffed grocery stores. The rest of the civilized world charged for every bag a shopper used. This single practice went a long way toward keeping trash off city streets, at least in Western Europe and the Middle East. He supposed it would take a cataclysmic event before the Americans would ever learn. He smiled, thinking that he was going to help make that happen.

Knowing he may temporarily soon lose cell phone coverage, Khalid called Saad and Abdulla and gave them an update on his progress. Like Khalid, they had been in the U.S. for months. Each was living with a Middle Eastern "host." These were an immigrant family or single males who had been living in the U.S. for at least ten years. Saad was in Chicago, Abdulla was in Alexandria Virginia, and Khalid lived with an Iraqi couple in Chicago.

The hosts had not been recruited from the ranks of immigrants. Instead, like hundreds of others throughout the country, they had, following meticulous screening and background checks before being sent to the U.S. by the MA. Their roles were to find employment, assimilate into American communities, and to wait. The waiting was almost over. The hosts were told that their guests were there to check on the status of other sleeper cells and to recruit new members for the MA. They had no idea they were about to play a part in the largest, most well-coordinated, terrorist attack in history.

For the past several months, Khalid, Saad, and Abdulla had been working on their team's attack plans. The MA had provided them with the names and contact information of men near each target city who had been selected for this mission. Since their targets were geographically dispersed, Khalid and Saad spent the first several weeks flying from city to city making face-to-face contact with each of the martyrs who were selected for this mission.

Since his target would be concentrated in the front of the U.S. Capitol building, Abdulla was spared this exhausting travel and the ever-present threat of being identified and detained by airport security. This was mainly a perceived threat. At least as far as they knew they were not associated with any organization, much less an organization that was considered hostile or listed on a Homeland Security watch list.

Nevertheless, they took every precaution to blend in with the business commuter crowd. Although growing a beard is a *Wajib*, mandatory, for all Muslim males capable of doing so, Khalid and Saad were always clean shaven when traveling. They considered themselves to be exempt from any rules which may raise a flag and thus endanger the mission. They wore conservative business attire and carried an expensive briefcase and laptop computer. There was nothing on the computer, including email trails, which could link them to one another or the MA. They could, and routinely did, pass the most rigorous scrutiny that the local TSA could muster.

After making contact Abdulla, Saad, and Khalid began the process of briefing their associates in each of the target cities. They went over, in painstaking detail, Abdulla's visions, the strategy that would bring about a glorious new age for Islam, and their individual, crucial, role in achieving this goal. In each city, Khalid and his martyr studied Google Earth maps of their target airports. They identified primary, and alternate, runways, and directions planes would use during takeoff. They also selected locations as close as possible to each runway where a pickup truck could be parked for a brief period.

Using this knowledge, they drove around each airport to physically see the sites they had selected. Once they agreed on a spot where a truck could be parked, they returned to the location at precisely 1100 to observe the way planes taxied down the runways and the points from which they would typically lift off the ground. In almost every instance in every city this "eyes on" inspection resulted in at least minor changes in their launch site selection. They were also careful to observe vehicle and pedestrian traffic patterns near each launch site.

Each warrior would have his SA-20, armed and ready, in the back of his pickup before arriving at the position. However, they would still need a short span of time to park the truck, get in the back, and wait for a plane to line up and begin its approach for takeoff. The operator would switch on the SA-20's target acquisition control system and focus on the aircraft using the aiming device located on the side of the launch tube. After the operator presses the target mode switch, the SA-20's navigation software finds and locks on to, the heat signature generated by the plane's engines. Once the missile is "locked on" it produces an audible tone letting the operator know it has found its mark and is ready to launch. With the heat generated from a jet engine, the missile guidance system can lock on an aircraft in less than three seconds. After hearing the target acquisition tone, the operator keeps the plane in the aiming device sights until he is ready to launch the missile. He would do so the instant the plane's wing wheels lift off the ground.

Khalid had spent over two months traveling to each city, finding launch sites, and physically rehearsing every detail of the attack process. He had also arranged the purchase of pickup trucks in each town. These were always a late model, seemingly dependable vehicles purchased from used car lots using cash supplied by the MA. He and his team were ready.

At the same time, Saad and Abdulla were working to prepare their respective teams. Like Khalid, Saad, at least initially, had to spend considerable time traveling from one target city to another. The churches in each location had previously been selected by Abdulla. From a park bench, or sitting in their car, he and his respective accomplice observed the congregation entering Sunday morning worship services. They also recorded, and then watched, services broadcast by the local television station. This allowed them to see the way parishioners dressed as well as the physical layout of each church.

Saad helped his martyrs find an upscale apartment near their target churches which they started attending as soon as they unpacked. Although Saad never attended services, he would watch them on TV each Sunday. His men tried to sit in the same location where they would be visible when the camera panned the congregation. Saad was usually able to watch them in real-time, and was pleased with the way they seemed to be interacting with their "fellow Christians."

He had established a circuit, flying from one of his cities to the next on Sunday afternoon as soon as his man returned home from church. By the end of June, all his men were well established in their new communities and being warmly accepted in their church homes. This church community acceptance allowed Saad time to focus on his other, equally critical task, hacking into the DPRK's government and military computer networks.

Abdulla's preparation did not require near as much travel as did Khalid and Saad. His team consisted of two men that he, with assistance from the MA, had arranged to immigrate to the U.S. as war refugees. Both were from Syria, and both had extensive military experience. They also shared a bitter, but well disguised, hatred for the U.S. The American public believed that immigration policies, and the vetting process, were much more stringent than in years past. However, based on their supposed status as refugees, his men were granted Humanitarian visas and welcomed with open arms.

Abdulla was living in a one-bedroom apartment on the outskirts of Alexandria, VA. He had arranged for housing for his men in a similar complex south of the beltway. Although modest by U.S. standards they were the most luxurious accommodations his men had ever seen, much less lived.

Abdulla found a small building whose owners had recently gone out of business. Most American cities had numerous business zoned areas that, once prosperous, were now in economic decline and littered with abandoned buildings. Abdulla paid a handyman he found on Craigslist to do some cosmetic restoration, exterior painting, and a sign saying, "Carson Delivery Services." He also had him mark two parking spaces immediately in front of the building with "No Parking, Business Loading Zone, Violators Will Be Towed at Owners Expense."

Once these preparations were completed, even though his mission was over three months away, Abdulla began looking for a vehicle. He needed a truck whose flatbed sides were paneled and at least two meters high. They had to be tall enough to shield his team and their 81mm mortar, from anyone passing by. Obviously, the top had to be open. After several days of internet searches, he found a 2016 Chevrolet Silverado 3500 for sale. It was outfitted for a landscaping company that was going out of business. The truck was located near Charles Town West Virginia, about seventy miles northwest of his team's "office."

Abdulla and both of his men made what turned out to be a two-hour drive to Charles Town, paid the asking price, and drove the truck back to the Carson Delivery Services parking lot. It was perfect. It was beat up just enough to look like a work truck but not so much that it seemed unprofessional. It also had high, corrugated aluminum, sides and a sheet metal floor. The original plan, as briefed to the MA, had been to bolt the mortar's base plate to a truck floor. However, one of his men had suggested that they line the floor with bags of potting mix. This, he said, would provide a stable platform and would lessen tube movement when a round was fired.

CHAPTER 10

Khalid arrived at the hotel at 1920. After registering at the front desk, he called Hector. He told him he was in town and wanted to meet at the Love's truck stop as soon as possible the next day. Hector promised that he would schedule Khalid's shipment for the following day. He said that, depending on I-110 traffic, he should be able to arrive at the Love's by 1000. Khalid had Hector give him a description of the truck he would be driving and directed him to park as far back in the truck lot as possible. Khalid told him that he would be waiting and would call no later than 1030 if he had not spotted his truck.

Khalid estimated that it should not take over twenty minutes to load his shipment if, as he had requested of the shipper, the crates weren't buried too far back in the container. After making the pick-up arrangements with Hector, Khalid called Saad and brought him up to speed on his progress. As they had previously discussed, Saad would now make reservations at a motel on the west side of Dallas. He would also inform Abdulla, and the next day the two of them would start driving toward Texas. Khalid had estimated that, once he had the shipment loaded in his van, it would take him twenty hours to drive to Dallas. He said he would make the drive in two days and instructed Saad to plan accordingly.

In keeping with their increasingly heightened vigilance, Saad would not reveal the exact location of the motel until Abdulla and Khalid were, respectively, three hours away from Dallas.

The next morning Khalid woke up at 0600, said his morning prayers, and went downstairs for what the Holiday Inn Express passed off as breakfast. Despite its lack of appeal, Khalid polished off two boiled eggs, a pancake, orange juice, and what appeared to be a cheese Danish. He then grabbed two bananas and a cup of coffee to go. Back in his room, Khalid showered, brushed his teeth, and packed his bag. He threaded his belt thru the multi-tool carrying case and slipped the gloves he had purchased into a side pocket on his new rain jacket. He also tucked the bag of cocaine into the right front pocket of his jeans. At 0830 he loaded his bag into the passenger seat of his van, turned on his GPS, and started driving toward the Love's.

The traffic on highway 91 was, for Los Angeles, moderate and Khalid arrived at the truck stop shortly after 0900. He drove around the truck parking lot looking for a vehicle which matched the description that Hector had given him of his semi. Satisfied that Hector had not yet arrived, he found a parking space where he could observe the road leading into the service area.

Shortly before 1000 a late model, red, Kenworth sporting flame decals, towering twin exhaust pipes and hauling a standard shipping container pulled off the road and headed toward the "trucker lot." Khalid waited while the driver backed into a parking space on the far side of the lot and turned off his engine. Khalid then drove to where the truck was parked, pulled behind it, and backed up until the rear of the van was about ten feet from the doors on the container. He got out, put on his rain jacket, and walked around to the driver side door of the truck.

A middle-aged Mexican was climbing out of the cab, and Khalid said, "Hector Rodriquez?" The man replied, "*si, hola senior* Khalid." They shook hands and then walked to the rear of the container. Hector gave Khalid the stamped loading and customs documents he had received at the terminal and the keys to the padlock on the container. The padlock was laced with a thin strip of metal bearing a serial number which matched the number on the loading document. This indicated that the container had not been opened since it was loaded on the container ship. Using the snip on his new multi-tool, Khalid broke the metal seal and then unlocked the container. As he was putting on his gloves, he turned toward Hector and said, "ok amigo, let's get her unloaded, and you can be on your way."

As Khalid had known would be the case, the rear of the container was stacked, floor to ceiling with cardboard boxes strapped to wooden shipping pallets. Fortunately, the strapping material was made of strips of plastic which, again using his multi-tool, Khalid was able to cut easily. Once he cut the straps on the first pallet, Khalid removed one of the boxes and handed it to Hector who placed it on the ground underneath the rear of the truck trailer. They continued in this manner until they had removed the entire rear layer of boxes.

To his relief, Khalid's cargo, ten long wooden crates, were stacked neatly in the center of the container. Khalid drug the first one he could reach from the stack until the end of the box could be tilted down onto the floor. As he suspected, the crates were heavy but not so much that one person couldn't maneuver each. After getting three crates on the floor, Khalid jumped down from the back of the container, and together he and Hector loaded them into the van.

They continued this process until all ten crates were loaded. Khalid closed the rear doors of the van and then instructed Hector to get into the shipping container so that they could reload the boxes. Hector climbed into the back of the container, and Khalid handed him a box until, one by one, they had reloaded what they had removed to get access to Khalid's cargo. Khalid then climbed into the container and told Hector that they needed to make sure everything was secure enough to be transported to its final, true, destination.

They shifted boxes around until they appeared to be appropriately organized and then, pointing to one of the severed plastic shipping straps laying on the floor, Khalid said "Hector, would you hand me that piece of plastic." As Hector turned and bent down to retrieve the plastic, Khalid stepped slightly forward and thrust the knife blade on his multi-tool into the right side of Hector's neck, about three inches from the bottom of his chin. Using a technique he had been forced to learn when he was only sixteen he pushed hard and forced the blade forward and slightly to his left severing Hector's carotid artery and slicing thru his larynx.

Hector's hands flew up to his neck, and he clawed furiously, but uselessly, in a reflexive response to the pain. Blood spurted like water from a fire hose spraying all over the boxes in front of him. Using his left hand, Khalid kept Hector, and his gushing blood fountain, facing forward as his knees started to buckle and he sank, spasmodically, to the floor. It was over in a matter of seconds.

Khalid had managed to keep most of the blood off himself. However, his gloved right hand and sleeve of the rain jacket were splattered and dripping red. He unzipped his coat and, using his left hand, pulled it off inside out trapping the blood on his right sleeve. He pulled off his gloves and neatly folded them inside the bloodied jacket.

Khalid then removed the packet of cocaine from his pocket, tore the top back halfway, and sprinkled the contents inconspicuously on some of the boxes and around the floor of the container. He knew that with Hector's erratic work schedule it would be days, if not a week before his family reported him missing. When they finally did find him and his truck, nestled among scores of others in the Love's lot, an investigating team's K-9 squad would lead them to believe this was a soured drug deal.

Khalid climbed out of the container, wiping anything he touched as he left and taking his folded rain jacket, then closed and locked its doors. He drove his van around to the pump stations in front of the Love's and topped off his tank. After pumping his gas, he walked inside, stuffing his jacket and gloves into the trash can outside the front door as he went inside. He knew they would be shredded by the recycling company that serviced the counties surrounding Los Angles long before Hector and his truck were discovered.

Khalid went inside the first empty stall inside the Love's men's room. As he relieved himself, he checked his shoes and clothes for blood. He saw stains on the leather soles of his right shoe. When he returned to his van he would put on his boots and discard the shoes at the first rest stop he came to on I-10. After flushing the toilet, Khalid thoroughly washed his face and hands and went outside and climbed into his van. He pulled away from the pump, drove to the end of the lot and stopped his engine. Turning on his laptop, Kahlid retrieved an emailed document he had received from his supplier in the DPRK. It listed, in coded Arabic, the contents of each of the cases he had removed from the shipping container.

He crawled into the back of the van and found the one he needed. Using the snips on his multitool, he cut the two hard plastic shipping straps wrapped around the case. He then removed the screws which secured the top of the case to its sides. There was a total of twelve screws which, using the multitool, took both time and effort to remove. He was glad that he had instructed Abdulla and Saad to bring a battery powered drill and Phillips bits, for use when they would meet in Dallas. After he had removed all the screws, he slid the top back. Packed inside were several stacks, he didn't take time to count them, of two-kilo blocks of Semtex, boxes of detonators, and preconfigured lengths of detonation cord and blasting caps.

He removed one block of Semtex, a push button detonator, and a blasting cap. Khalid knew that Semtex and blasting caps would normally never be shipped in the same container. That was a recipe for disaster. However, this was exactly the configuration he had requested. Had there been an accident while on the ship, or during transport, the resulting explosion would have made it extremely difficult for authorities to identify the contents of the cases; or anything or anyone within fifty meters. Khalid put the top back on the case, screwed it down again, and took his block of explosive back to the front of the van. He connected the detonator to the blasting cap and pushed the cap into the block of Semtex. If the police stopped him, he would slip the safety cap off the detonator, push the button, and meet Allah.

Once he had finished rigging the explosive, Khalid entered Dallas, TX into his GPS and started the twenty plus hour drive east. It was almost 1130, and he estimated that he could make it to El Paso before his adrenaline wore off and he had to stop for the night.

CHAPTER 11

Jim Phillips and David Stakley were sitting in the waiting room outside the office of the Secretary of State of the United States, Robert, "Bulldog," Pitts. It was 0920, and they were there for a 0930 appointment; you weren't late for a meeting with the Bulldog.

Robert Pitts didn't look, act, or think like a typical Washington D.C. politician. He was seventy-three years old, five feet, seven inches, tall and barely tipped the scales past one hundred and sixty pounds. He sported severely close-cropped, gray hair. A style he had adopted fifty plus years ago after joining the Marines.

It was during Marine Boot Camp that he had earned his nickname. Some long since forgotten Drill Instructor had tagged him with that moniker after he had been knocked down three times during pugil stick training. He got up each time and kept fighting until he finally pummeled his exhausted, bigger, opponent to the ground; who didn't, or couldn't, get back up. The name stuck and everyone who knew or met him quickly understood why.

Bulldog held the unprecedented distinction of being the only Secretary to hold that office back to back; from one president to another and Democrat to Republican at that. He was that good; quite simply the best international delegate in the country's history. He exuded warmness and had a genuine Will Rogers, "never met a man I didn't like," presence that made everyone that met him feel like a lifelong friend. However, he had zero tolerance for incompetence, tardiness, or bullshit. He called a spade a spade; sometimes he called it a "fucking shovel."

At precisely 0930 the Secretary of State's office door opened, and Robert Pitts came out. Most elected officials, and senior level civil service staffers, would have buzzed their Administrative Assistants and told them to "show their visitors in." Not the Bulldog. Walking across the outer office reception area Pitts, wearing a congenial but serious face, enthusiastically shook each man's hand.

"Jim, David, you don't know what a relief it is to see you this morning. The POTUS has been on my ass all week. The DPRK is pushing us into a corner, and the big guy is ready to come out swinging. As he ushered the two men toward his office he told, Trish, his Assistant, "hold my calls unless it's the POTUS. Tell anyone else I will return their call just as soon as I finish saving the planet." The Bulldog's droll sense of humor often had a disarming effect on even dire situations.

Walking toward to a round mahogany table near his office window, the Secretary said "sit down gentlemen but don't get too comfortable. Now is not the time to relax. Ok Jim, give me a thirty-thousand-foot view of your treaty proposal. We will dive deeper into any points that I don't understand or don't, at first blush, agree with."

Jim Phillips immediately launched into a high-level explanation of the AIFTU plan David's team had developed, asking David to interrupt any time he felt additional clarification was necessary. The Secretary allowed Jim and David to lay out the basic concept and salient points of the AIFTU charter without interruption. When they had completed their overview, the Secretary sat back in his chair and, lacing the fingers of each hand together forming his familiar "I'm thinking about it" pose.

No one spoke for several seconds until the Secretary said "boys, that's about the most outrageous scheme I have ever heard. I like it. No, I love it! I don't think I could have come up with anything like this, at least not in the timeframe you guys had to do it in." David smiled and said, "you just need to eat more Chinese takeout, Mr. Secretary." The Bulldog gave David a quizzical look and replied "I don't know what the fuck that means but when the smoke clears you can elaborate over a bottle of single malt Scotch; that is if the boss buys in on your proposal. And, if we can sell it to the chinks and Russkis." The Bulldog's "calls a spade a spade" reputation was not without merit.

Raising his hand and extended index finger, indicating a pause in the conversation, he pressed a number on the telephone sitting on his desk. Immediately a female voice said, "yes Mr. Secretary." "Trish, please call the Chief of Staff and tell him I need an urgent audience with the POTUS, subject, code name Top Knot. No other attendees. He will not know the code name. The POTUS will tell him what he needs to know. Then, clear my calendar for the rest of the day and all day tomorrow." "Yes sir, Trish replied."

Returning his attention to Jim and David, the Secretary picked up where he had interrupted himself. "All right let's talk about how we are going to present this to the Chinese and Russians, assuming we get a green light from the President." The Secretary's use of "President" rather than "POTUS" signaled a subconscious shift in his perception of the gravity of the situation. This almost imperceptible change wasn't lost on David.

"The instant the President blesses the plan I will call the Chinese Foreign Minister, Wang Yi, and Sergey Lavrov, the Minister of Foreign Affairs of Russian Federation, or as they are better known, the Russian MFA. They are aware of how precarious things

THE ENEMY OF MY ENEMY

have become with the DPRK, and I think will be more than willing to hear what we have to say.

Jim, I hear what you are saying about the need for an ultra-covert meeting and agree in concept. My only departure from your recommendations is the setting and security. Rather than a neutral country, I think we need to be more conciliatory toward the Chinese. They are closer geographically, and as trade partners to the DPRK than the Russians or anyone else for that matter. And besides ourselves, they would have the most to lose if we go to war with the fat guy. Let's give em a bone right out of the chute and suggest we meet on their turf. Somewhere way off the international beaten path but still on Chinese controlled soil. Let's shoot for Hainan. It's an island province of China off the southern coast of the mainland. Since the Chinese control the island's airspace, we can scoot in, meet with our, hopefully, soon to be business partners, and fly out again without ever popping up on Fox News.

Also, I appreciate your suggestion of using a Secret Service - CIA team for transportation and security. However, we both know there is a mole in Langley. The agency has been watching her and her handler for months but aren't ready to take them down just yet. They think by keeping her on the line a bit longer they can work their way up the spook food chain and land some bigger espionage, and maybe political, fish. We sure as hell don't want to run the risk of leaking this operation. Instead, let's engage our friends at Blackwater. I mean Academi, I keep forgetting they renamed themselves after that little incident in Baghdad. We don't need a huge entourage.

I will take point, and do the back-slapping because that's what I get paid for. David can go since he knows the AIFTU Charter inside and out. That's all it will take for the initial meeting. Academi can whisk us over there on their new Gulfstream 550. That thing cruises at over 600 miles per hour. Of course, in addition to the flight crew, they will want to send a four or five-man security team. There is no need for them, but that's how they earn their money, so we will play along and let them pad their expense line.

If I know Yi, he will want to wine and dine us before getting down to business. We will go along so that he can show off for Lavrov. But when I call I will try and instill a sense of urgency. So, David, if you have a date this week tell her that duty calls. Pack a bag for no more than a one-night stay, and put yourself on one hour, wheels up, standby.

Jim, David, any questions, comments, or concerns?" Getting no response, he continued, "if not let's get ready to get this show on the road. Excellent job gentleman, please tell the rest of your team that I truly appreciate the work they have done. They don't know it yet, but so does the rest of the country." The three men stood up, and the Secretary walked around the table and shook their hands. As he walked them to his office door, he noted "I know you understand this meeting, and this entire effort, is top secret sensitive compartmented information. However, I wouldn't be doing my due diligence if I didn't remind you. Not a word to anyone without my personal, face to face, permission." "Clear sir," Jim said as he and David walked out the door.

A little after 1600, as he sat at his desk reading the details of the AIFTU document, Robert's personal, encrypted, cell phone range. The phone's display showed only **********, and he knew who it was. He answered, "Robert Pitts." "Bulldog, can you be in my office at six p.m.?" a familiar voice barked. Pitts knew that wasn't a question. "Yes Mr. President," Robert replied. "Good, come in thru the bathroom window."

Robert knew that meant for him to use the semisecret entrance from a closed off alley on H street. It passed thru a winding, underground, tunnel exiting into the White House basement. The President, and select, carefully screened, visitors sometimes used this entrance when they didn't want their comings and goings seen by the public. "I got an urgent message from the Chief of Staff that you were ready to brief me on the Department's progress on Top Knot. I'm ready to make something happen on the peninsula. We've had about all of that fat guy's shit that we're going to take. See you at six." Robert smiled at the President's use of twelve, rather than twenty-four, hour time, and distances were, by God, measured in miles, not kilometers. In most areas, the guy was a one hundred percent, USDA grade A, certified, anachronism. A throwback.

On the other hand, he was, is a political genius. Picking up his office phone, Robert pressed his Assistant's intercom number. She answered on the second ring. "Geez Trish, what took you so long? Are you napping on government time?" Long accustomed to the Bulldog's wit, she replied, "forgive me, Mr. Secretary, it will not happen again." "Well see that it doesn't. Now call my driver and tell him he's up for some overtime. I need to be at the House no later than 1745. Tell him to do whatever it takes to be here in time to make that happen. Then call my wife and tell her I will not be home for dinner. I am not sure when I will get there. I will call her when I leave the House unless I get other marching orders." "I'm on it sir, and unless you need something else, I will be leaving after I speak with Mrs. Pitts." "Thanks, Trish, I will see you sometime tomorrow."

Robert hung up the phone and, picking up where he had left off, returned to reading the AIFTU charter. Barring any other interruptions, he thought, I have just enough time to get thru this thing before the driver shows up.

CHAPTER 12

Saad was in his element. For the past several weeks he, like Khalid, had been traveling from one target city to the next, working to get his martyr teams settled into their new, albeit temporary, homes and communities. He felt good, and took a great deal of satisfaction, about his preparations to destroy the infidel places of worship. His teams were in place and were, from all observations, being assimilated into their respective communities and congregations. However, his real passion lay with his task of hacking into DPRK computer networks and subsequently using them as decoys to fool the Americans and their South Korean lackeys. This was proving to be a far more significant challenge than he had anticipated.

While traveling, Saad always made sure that the hotel he was staying in provided internet access to their guests. However, he never used their free wi-fi. His laptop was equipped with an ethernet card and cable which he plugged into the hardwire connection in his hotel room. Every Holiday Inn and virtually all other hotels had provided this service for years. They were a long way from secure, but his encryption software and the firewall on his laptop would keep all but the most technically adroit snoops from breaking into his system. This plus the fact that he seldom stayed at any one hotel for more than a few days made for an acceptable level of, at least computer, security. Saad had contacted an old friend, and fellow computer guru the very next day after Abdulla had made him responsible for transmitting fake communications from the DPRK to the Americans.

Mustafa Azizi had been born in Basrah, in 1985, on the Iraqi side of the Euphrates river. His father and two uncles had been killed during the bloody and eventually pointless, eight-year war with Iran. Due to the loss of his father, and male relatives, Mustafa's mother, along with him and his five-year-old sister, had been forced to flee from Iraq shortly before his third birthday. They found refuge with his mother's sister, and her family, in Al Jahar, Kuwait shortly before Iraq – Iran hostilities ended in 1988.

Although they had a roof over their heads, and enough food to eat, Mustafa and his mother and sister were little more than servants to their adopting family. Mustafa grew up dreaming of the day when he would finish school and go out on his own. He also grew up with a white-hot, burning, hatred for Iran and the Iranian government.

Mustafa was barely five years old when Saddam Hussein's Republican Guard burst into Kuwait. Within two days the Kuwait military had been overran or driven into neighboring Saudi Arabia and Bahrain. For the next seven months, Iraqi forces occupied the entire country, raping and looting as they pleased. In late January 1991, after failed negotiations, and repeated warnings to withdraw its troops, the United States, and its allies, launched a massive attack on the Iraqi military in Kuwait. The intensity, and ferociousness, of the assault, was unlike anything ever seen before, or since.

In February Iraqi forces, with their tails tucked between their legs, began withdrawing, actually a blindly panicked flight, north up highway 80 toward the border town of Safwan. As they fled, the humiliated Republican Guard took their wrath out on anything, and anyone, along their escape route. Unfortunately, Mustafa, and what was left of his family found themselves in the center of this exodus. Up until now, Mustafa's aunt's family, and the neighborhood where they lived had not suffered any damage by the occupying Iraqi forces. This took a horrible change for the worse on a cold February morning.

Mustafa was getting out of bed, and his mother and her sister were preparing breakfast when they heard shots fired and the rumble of diesel engines. When they looked outside, they saw two army trucks, with a dozen or so soldiers in each, slowly driving up their street. They stopped two doors down. Soldiers climbed out and started going from house to house on each side of the road. Mustafa's step-uncle, Hassan, came out of his bedroom and joined the women looking out the living room window. They watched as soldiers entered the house across the street. More shots were fired, and minutes later two men came out, one carrying a green canvas bag and one carrying what looked like a laptop computer and a heavy coat.

As they watched the soldiers move to the next house, someone pounded on their front door. Hassan walked to open the door but was not fast enough. Before he could get there, a huge Iraqi soldier rammed his shoulder into the door splintering the wood around the latch and ripping the bolt out of the wall. Four men, each carrying a rifle, barreled into the room. Holding one another, Mustafa's mother and her sister, screamed and moved to a corner of the room.

Taking a step back, Hassan cried "please don't hurt us. We are Iraqi, just like you." "Shut up pig," the big man snapped. "Bring me all the money you have in the house. Dinar, dollars, euros, everything you have. And any gold or silver. Now!" As Hassan scurried away toward his bedroom two of the men started ransacking the kitchen, eating the bread and fish the women had prepared and looking inside the refrigerator and cupboards. The other two men moved to where the women were huddled, clutching one another and crying. The big Iraqi grabbed Mustafa's mother's wrist and bellowed, "shut up you sluts!" As he was pulling her away from her sister's grasp, Hassan came back into the room holding out a shoebox-sized metal case and pleading again "please don't hurt us, we are Iraqi." The second man grabbed the case and opened it as the big Iraqi pawed at Mustafa's mother. "That's all," the soldier screamed at Hassan. "A big fine house like this and this is all the money you have." Pointing at a chain around Hassan's neck he said "I said everything! Give me that gold, and your rings." As Hassan removed his gold necklace and his wedding ring the soldier turned to the women saying, "you too, give me all of your jewelry."

Mustafa and his sister watched in sheer terror, huddled together, still standing next to the window where they were when the soldiers burst into the house. They were both wailing, scared beyond anything they had ever felt. Mustafa's mother and her sister hurriedly removed their rings and placed them in the soldier's outstretched hand. Leering at Mustafa's mother, and roughly caressing her face with the back of his hand, the big Iraqi suddenly ripped off the hijab from her head. "You leave her alone" Mustafa screamed.

Holding the gold necklace, rings, and the case Hassan had given him, the smaller soldier said "is this everything? No more money? No silver coins or gold?" Holding his hands in front of him as if in prayer Hassan moaned, "that's all we have. Now please leave." The soldier replied, "no, we have unfinished business," and fired a three-round burst from his rifle into Hassan's chest.

Mustafa's aunt screamed, and her knees buckled. As she dropped to the floor Mustafa's mother, also screaming, tried to steady her but the big Iraqi grabbed her hair and jerked her toward him. "You're coming with me bitch," he growled pulling her toward one of the bedrooms. The two soldiers who were in the kitchen slung their rifles over their shoulders and, looking toward Mustafa's aunt and grinning, entered the room. The soldier with the money case sat it down, and the three of them rushed over to where she was standing, kicking and pushing chairs out of their way as they went. One of the soldiers grabbed his aunt, and the other one yanked his sister away from Mustafa's arms.

With tears streaming down his grimacing face, Mustafa balled up his tiny fist and started pounding the laughing soldier's arm screaming "no! leave her alone!" The soldier who had been carrying the money case spun around, and with his left hand holding his rifle's barrel and his right hand on the stock, butt stroked Mustafa hard to the side of his head. Mustafa fell to the floor, unconscious, with blood streaming down his face. As much as it would hurt later, the blow was a blessing. He didn't hear the screams that went on, and on. Or, the rifle shots.

Much later, when Mustafa woke up, the house was cold and silent. The front door was wide open, and furniture was strewn all over the living room. Hassan's lifeless body lay where he had fallen. What seemed like liters of blood covered the living room floor and soaked its ornate Persian rugs. Cans of food and utensils had been raked from the kitchen shelves and lay scattered over the floor and countertops. Mustafa was bitterly cold, and he wandered, still somewhat dazed across the living room toward the nearest bedroom. He entered the room, looked at the bed and started screaming.

Stumbling as he went, Mustafa ran blindly from the room and out the front door of his dead aunt's house. His left eye was swollen almost shut and oozing blood from the gash caused by the rifle butt. The entire side of his face was grotesquely bruised and a searing pain shot thru his head and neck with every, staggering, step he took. Still, he ran, wailing at the top of his voice, tears streaming down his cheeks.

A small crowd was gathered around the front of the house across the street. The house belonged to a Kuwaiti family who was close friends with Hassan, his wife, and Mustafa's mother. Two uniformed members of the Kuwaiti National Guard, carrying a body on a stretcher, were emerging from the house as several weeping neighbors looked on. A wailing Mustafa, running full speed across the yard and into the street, was oblivious to the commotion. One of the women, another neighbor's wife, standing near the rear of an ambulance in the driveway, saw Mustafa as he ran out the door, across the front yard, and into the street. Clutching her black over-garment, her *abaya*, to keep from tripping, she scurried out into the street and scooped Mustafa into her arms. "Mustafa, child" she cried, "what's wrong little man?" Mustafa could only sob hysterically. The woman starting walking toward Hassan's house saying, "let me get you back to your mother." Frantically squirming in her arms, Mustafa howled "nooo, not go in house!"

Breaking away from the group of men watching the Kuwaiti soldiers carrying the stretcher, the woman's husband ran over to where she and Mustafa were standing. "Omar, go over to Hassan's house and tell Mustafa's mother that he is terrified and that he does not have a coat and is freezing cold." The man ran across the yard and entered the front door of the house. A few, long, seconds later he slowly shuffled out the front door. His wife, Farah, still holding Mustafa, was walking across the yard and had almost reached the front of the house. Raising his arms, the man said, "Farah, stop, for Muhammad's sake, do not go in there. Take him to our house. I will tell the soldiers they need to come over here right away. Go, I will explain later. The boy can't go in there." Farah knew something must be terribly wrong and holding Mustafa even tighter, walked, hurriedly, toward her own home."

All of this had occurred Friday. That night Mustafa, although apparently in shock, stayed with Omar and Farah just down the street from Hassan's house. He stopped crying shortly after sundown but would not let go of Farah, even as she attempted to prepare their evening meal. Although he hadn't eaten all day, Mustafa only picked at his food. Finally, around 2200, he fell asleep in Farah's arms, and she gently tucked him into her and Omar's bed and returned to the living room.

Sitting on their sofa, close together, Omar said "our office will most likely be closed all next week as we try to clean up the mess the Republican Guard left when they were running out of town. However, the International Red Cross has set up a temporary screening center at the Italian embassy in Kuwait City. As soon as traffic is allowed back on highway 5, I will drive over there and discuss Mustafa and his situation." Taking Omar's hand, Farah said "perhaps we should consider letting him live with us. Maybe even adopting him. It has been Allah's will that we not have children of our own. This may be his way of sending us a son." Omar gazed at his wife's face for several seconds and the said "perhaps."

On Wednesday Omar received word that the highway leading to Kuwait City was open for civilian traffic. In less than an hour after leaving his house, he was in the Italian embassy and talking to a British Red Cross worker. It was surprisingly easy to get permission for Mustafa to live with him and his wife until the Kuwaiti government returned to normal and resumed business as usual. The worker explained that official adoption was another matter altogether. This would have to be discussed with the Ministry of Health and Human Services. The worker explained that it would take some time, but given the circumstances, and the sudden and dire need for orphan placement, she felt very optimistic. She collected Omar and Farah's personal and financial history, and contact information, and promised to pass this along to the proper official as soon as she could determine just who that may be. A smiling Omar thanked the worker and left, driving back to Al Jahra and giving the news to Farah.

The Emir of Kuwait, Sheik Jaber al-Ahmed al-Sabah, ending over seven months of exile, returned to the capital sixteen days after Iraqi occupying forces fled. Much of Kuwait City had been damaged, dwellings and businesses ransacked. Thick, black, suffocating, smoke filled the air from oil wells the retreating Iraqis had set on fire. Still, his homecoming marked the beginning of a return to normal for the people, and government, of Kuwait. Three months later, Omar received a call from an official at the Ministry of Health and Human Services telling him that he and Farah could begin the adoption process.

Omar and the company he worked for did very well over the next several years. Just before Mustafa's fourteenth birthday, Omar was offered a position with Al Ahli Bank in the heart of Kuwait City. Along with his new job came an increase in both salary and prestige. The family moved to a newly developed, more exclusive, neighborhood on the outskirts of Kuwait City and Mustafa began attending Hamad Al-Rujaib High School, only a few blocks from his father's office.

It was here that Mustafa developed a passion for computers and programming. He also developed a knack for hacking into networks, and databases, that was strictly off limits. By the time he graduated from high school, Mustafa had earned a reputation. Among the loosely organized group of international, activist hackers, known as Anonymous, he was regarded as someone who could hack his way into any system at any time. In reality, it was his alter ego, who went by the pseudonym Simcard, who rightfully earned that status. Although he experienced a couple of "near misses"

with the Kuwaiti internet police, and their technically inadequate,
national firewalls, he had managed to work "under their radar" and
to maintain Simcard's anonymity. His brush with the authorities
didn't deter Mustafa. Instead, he learned from his mistakes and
never repeated his technical errors. Even at seventeen, he was really,
really, good, and was getting better.

After graduating from high school, Mustafa, at Omar's urging,
and financial support, enrolled in Al Faisal University's College of
Science and General Studies at the Riyad, Kingdom of Saudi Arabia,
campus. He majored in computer science with minors in English
and mathematics. Although something of a loner, Mustafa did very
well in college. He graduated in the top ten percent of his class and,
following a government-sponsored job fair, found himself on the
receiving end of three job offers. It was by pure coincidence that one
of the soliciting firms was owned, and managed, by Saad's family.

CHAPTER 13

The black Gulfstream 550 received its final approach clearance and landed at Andrews Air Force Base at 2000. Except for the runway landing lights, it was pitch dark when David and Robert Pitts arrived twenty minutes later. This was as planned. The Secretary had decided that it would be best if his driver took them to Andrews. Traveling in a State Department Suburban wasn't exactly inconspicuous, but it would be less so than nighttime helicopter transport. The Bulldog knew that there was always a cadre of camera-toting reporters stationed around key points in D.C. It was an insignificant price to pay for living in one of the most open governments on the planet. At this time of night, even D.C. traffic was light, and they could leave the State Department Building without peaking anyone's interest.

At the base's gated entrance, everyone's identification was checked and electronically verified. Once they cleared the entrance gate, the driver proceeded west on Perimeter Road, turned left on Menoher Drive and drove to another, guarded gate adjacent to the main runway. Just past the mechanical gate arm six steel bollards, mounted in the pavement, blocked vehicle entrance. One of four, armed, uniformed guards checked their credentials again, even more thoroughly than at the main gate. At the same time, K-9 escorted Military Police looked underneath the Suburban using mirrors and lights mounted on long poles. After the security team determined they were who they were supposed to be, the gate arm was raised, and the bollards were mechanically lowered into the pavement.

Once inside, the driver proceeded toward the runway and pulled parallel to another government vehicle; a white Ford Taurus parked next to the waiting Gulfstream. After they came to a stop, David and the Secretary grabbed their bags and got out of the Suburban. At the same time a slender, pantsuited female got out of the Taurus. Speaking to the Bulldog, and handing him a clipboard, she said, "Mr. Secretary, I have the information you requested. If you would be so kind as to sign for it." The Bulldog scrawled his name and passed the clipboard back to the lady. She compared the signature to another document she was carrying and then, apparently satisfied they matched, handed the Secretary two brown accordion folders. "Thank you," the Bulldog said, "I'm sorry you had to come out here so late at night." The lady replied, "I am honored to be able to do so Mr. Secretary. Have a safe journey."

David and the Secretary walked to the steps at the front of the plane. There they were greeted by two men, one Oriental and one Caucasian, both in their late thirties, and with what appeared to be zero body fat. Except for somewhat shaggy hair and a short, cropped, beard on the white guy, they could have passed for active duty military. Each was dressed in black cargo slacks, a black long sleeve, black crew neck shirt, and black boots. There appeared to be a theme here. The man on the left thrust out his hand and said "gentlemen, I am Douglas Cho, your security team leader and this is Captain Lawrence, our pilot. On behalf of Academi, and our entire team, welcome aboard. We have a fourteen-hour flight, and a refueling stop in front of us so if you are ready, hop on."

Once in the plane, David and the Secretary stowed their bags in overhead compartments. As they were doing so, Cho introduced them to the co-pilot and the other members of their six-member security team. As the plane started to taxi down the runway he reviewed their flight plan, "this particular aircraft has a range of six thousand seven hundred miles. The distance to Hainan is a hair over eight thousand four hundred miles. We plan to refuel in Athens, Greece on the way over and on the way back. We do this so that we don't have to gas up while we are in, what Academi considers hostile territory. We don't want a Chinese ground crew to come within a fifty-meter radius of our ride while it's on the ground.

Captain Lawrence, the co-pilot, and three members of our security team will stay with the plane the entire time. Two of my thugs will stay outside, on the tarmac while the third rests. They will rotate continuously until we are back in the air. The plane is also equipped with ground sensing radar which will alert the crew if anyone, or anything, comes within that fifty-meter zone I mentioned. The remainder of our team will be at your side everywhere you go. And yes, that includes the men's room.

Just a note about our team. Every member, to include the pilots, are former military. The security team was all either Army Rangers, Special Forces, Marine Raiders, or Navy Seals. We are all airborne qualified and are conversant in at least one foreign language. Each man, we refer to ourselves as Operators, can lead a mission such as this one on their own. We tend to rotate leadership based on geographic location and specialized skill sets which may be required. At all times, during our time on the ground, each operator will be armed. Except for the DPRK, we have agreements to that effect with just about every government on the planet. I suspect you knew this already, but I would not be doing my due diligence as an Academi Team Leader if I didn't remind you.

Gentlemen, unless you have any questions, I will get out of your hair. I suspect you have preparations you need to attend to. If you have any questions or need anything at all, let me or any member of my team know. Oh, one other thing. Since this is a stealth mission, I suggest you remove the SIM card from your cell phones. As long as they are in there, the NSA can locate them. And if the NSA can do it you can be damned sure every other jack-leg intel agency on this rock can do it. If you need to make a call, myself and each of your assigned operators, will have a secure satellite phone. They can call other secure links, land lines, or your run of the mill Obama phones as long as you have a number. They can't be traced and will show up as unknown number on all caller id's." With that, Cho turned and walked to the rear of the Gulfstream joining the rest of his team.

The Bulldog swiveled his leather-clad seat around and faced David, "you have to admit, the seats on Academi's plane beat the hell out of Delta." He handed David the two portfolios the courier had given him on the tarmac before they boarded. "These are CIA dossiers on Wang Yi and Sergey Lavrov. I want you to read over them and then give me any insights you might glean if any. The reports are somewhat cut and dry, but the analysts generally try and summarize their reports with their impressions of what makes someone tick. They are classified TS-SCI, not necessarily based on the content but related to the intelligence sources they reveal. Of course, you would know that, being a former INSCOM Analyst yourself."

With a grin creeping across his face the Secretary continued, "your dossier was amusing in its own right. Outside of a couple of instances when you were in college, you were a pretty straight-laced lad. After we finish discussing Yi and Lavrov, we will shred the reports. Our plane is equipped with an NSA certified shredder. We don't want anyone, not even our escorts to know what we know."

For the next hour, David poured over the two dossiers. There was official, government released, photos of each man, and a few that were anything but official. The documents described their family, education, political and professional experience, and a wealth of personal and financial history. The Russian seemed to be fond of vodka, that was no surprise, and French pastry. He was also reputed to have been a chess master before rising to his current position. Yi's file was not as extensive, most likely due to the difficulty in getting reliable human intelligence, or what intelligence agencies referred to as HUMINT, out of China.

Nonetheless, it did describe a highly intelligent, very well educated professional politician who had clawed his way from village manager to an important position in the Politburo. Both men were devoted party members, happily married, and spoke fluent English. Each man was also independently wealthy; extremely wealthy.

After he had completed his analysis of the dossiers, David turned to the Bulldog and said, "looks like these guys are cut from the same bolt of cloth boss. No dirt or even anything shady for that matter. Just two, ambitious, hardworking guys who apparently love what they do and are good at doing it. There was one thing that jumped out. Both are deeply invested in the stock market. Heavy on mutual funds but also major holdings in individual stocks, most of which are U.S based but with production facilities in China, Vietnam, and South Korea. I would say this would be their mutual Achilles heel. Both would be seriously hurt, financially, if the market bottomed out. Yi more so than Lavrov, but still, both would be in a world of hurt."

"My thoughts exactly," noted the Secretary. "And if all three of us start lobbing nuclear firecrackers at each other there will be no market. We all lose and lose big. That's our hook, David. We must convince them that the earth has a malignant tumor, the DPRK, and we are going to remove it surgically. Sure, there will be financial and political shockwaves. But if China and Russia stay on the sidelines, and don't get militarily involved, things will recover. And when the smoke clears, metaphorically speaking, we will all be better off, even, no especially, your average Nork."

David smiled at the Bulldog's use of the slang term for a North Korean. He had heard it thousands of times during his time in Seoul. He knew it wasn't used in a derogatory manner, no more than Brit or Yank. Chuckling to himself he thought unless of course, you were talking to an Aussie; nork was their term for tits.

David closed the tops on the two portfolios just as Cho and another operator walked up the aisle. When he got within earshot said "gentlemen, unless you had dinner before we left, you should be getting hungry by now. The galley is stocked with gourmet, microwaveable meals, fruits, and beverages, including the Secretary's favorite fifteen-year-old Scotch. If you like I will show you where everything is and give you a hand warming things up. We have found that it generally works to everyone's benefit if we stay out of the way and let our clients get whatever they need."

David said, "that sounds great, but before I start rummaging thru the fridge, could you show me your shredder. I have some things I need to make disappear." "Sure," Cho said, "it's right inside this drawer" as he pulled a rectangular contraption from a sliding cabinet. "This one is a bit different from the one in your normal office.

As you can see, it's quite portable. You set it over the commode in the head and feed your documents thru it in smaller batches. They are simultaneously cut in two directions. Vertical and horizontal. The result is a fine powder-like substance, about the consistency of grits, and impossible to reassemble. But we take it a step further. As each batch is shredded, it falls into the toilet, and you flush it away. It takes a little longer, but the end result is totally unrecoverable. Unless you want to make Paper Mache."

David laughed, took the shredder from Cho, and proceeded to the head. As was department protocol for TS-SCI material, the Bulldog joined David to witness the document destruction. When they had finished destroying the dossiers, David and the Secretary fixed themselves dinner. As the plates were heating in the microwave, the Bulldog poured each of them a double Scotch on the rocks.

Although painstakingly long, the remainder of the flight was uneventful. The Gulfstream was incredibly comfortable. Its fully reclining, leather upholstered, swivel seats were more luxurious than anything David had ever experienced. You could rest, not just suffer thru the flight as with commercial airlines. David's circadian rhythm told him it was well past his regular bedtime. He took one of the blankets from his overhead storage and stretched out for a catnap. He slept all the way to Athens and thru the refueling stop.

CHAPTER 14

Khalid started nodding off around the time he reached the outskirts of El Paso. His GPS indicated the Days Inn El Paso West was only a couple of exits away. He eased off I-10 onto the South Desert Blvd exit, drove about a quarter mile, and turned into the Days Inn parking lot. Khalid registered at the front desk and asked to stay on the ground floor. He would move his van later if he couldn't see it from the room's window. The alarm was on, and Khalid knew he could make it out his door and into the parking lot in seconds if it went off. He would sleep with his pants and boots on just in case.

Once in his room, Khalid called Abdulla and Saad and let them know he was at the halfway point. He told Saad that he would call when he reached Abilene, Texas which he calculated to be right at three hours from Dallas. As they had discussed previously, that would be when Saad would give him the location of the hotel where they would rendezvous, stay the night, and distribute the materials in the crates.

After ending his call with Saad, Khalid opened his laptop and logged into his account on Dmail. He composed an email to each of his five soldiers. Even though each man had a personal email username, Khalid used the blind copy, or bcc, function on Dmail to further protect their identities. In the message, he told them he would be ready to meet them at a location of his choosing in two days. He informed them that the designated city would be at least one day's drive from their current location. They must be on standby and ready to leave at a moment's notice. As with the Dallas rendezvous with Saad and Abdulla, the exact location would be withheld until the last minute. He directed them to purchase a tarp large enough to cover a crate and the bed of their pickup along with bungee cords to strap it down. Also, he asked them to visit local Goodwill and Salvation Army stores or neighborhood yard sales, and purchase used lawn and gardening tools to put in the back of their vehicle. This would lead the casual observer to think they were simply one of the thousands of day workers in every state. The boxes they were soon to receive would simply blend in with the other equipment.

Later, he would suggest that Saad take the same precautions with his team. After completing his communication tasks, Khalid showered and drove to the nearest Tex-Mex restaurant; there was one on every corner in El Paso. He wasn't in the mood for fast food and thought he would try the local cuisine. He also wanted to be able to sit down, be served, and eat off a real plate with real, metal utensils for a change. He wasn't disappointed. The service was fast and courteous, and the more than ample portions of food, whatever it was, was delicious. No wonder so many Mexican women were fat. After dinner, Khalid went back to the Days Inn, read the free copy of USA Today, and went to bed. He had another ten-hour drive in front of him tomorrow.

The next morning Khalid woke up at 0600 and, as was his custom said his morning prayers. He washed his face, packed up his laptop, and left the hotel. He stopped at a nearby Waffle House for breakfast and then got back on I-10 heading east, for the next leg of his journey.

Khalid drove from El Paso, well past Van Horn, Texas. There he got on eastbound I-20. This would take him all the way to Dallas.

Four hours later he passed thru Abilene where, as planned, he called Saad, got the name and address of the hotel where they would meet, and entered them into his GPS.

The hotel Saad had found, another Days Inn, was off I-20, just south of Dallas. He had reserved a two-bedroom suite using the name on his forged driver's license. He had already checked in and Abdulla, traveling west from Washington, D.C., was only a couple of hours away. Following the directions on his GPS Khalid pulled in to the parking lot just minutes before 1700. Traffic had been light and driving well within the speed limit; he had made excellent time.

He noted two other vans parked next to one another, and correctly assumed they belonged to Abdulla and Saad. After seeing the number of cars, and general activity in the parking lot Khalid determined they would need to drive to another location to offload and distribute the cargo he was carrying. He had passed a Home Depot after getting off I-20 and onto the Lyndon B. Johnson Freeway on his way to the Days Inn. It would work. An enormous, mostly unmonitored parking area filled with apathetic shoppers trying to get as close to the store's front door as possible. They would pay scant attention to three men in three unremarkable vans moving boxes from one vehicle to another. "That's about as good as it's going to get," he thought.

Khalid got out of his van, locked the doors, set the alarm, and made sure nothing suspicious or worth stealing was visible thru the windows. He found his way to the room number Saad had given him on the phone and knocked on the door. Seconds later a beaming Abdulla opened the door and, placing his arm over Khalid's shoulder ushered him into the suite's living room saying, "come in my brother. It seems like forever since we last saw one another." At the same time Saad entered from one of the adjoining bedrooms, thrust out his hand and said "welcome Khalid, I trust you had a pleasant, albeit long journey. Let's have tea and talk for a while. We have a lot of catching up to do." "And plans to review," added Abdulla. Khalid and Abdulla sat down at the small table in the suite's kitchenette as Saad heated water for their tea.

After everyone was seated, Abdulla noted "based on your ongoing emails; it appears that our preparations are starting to come together. Since our first strike is only a few weeks away, let's take this opportunity to bring one another up to date and to discuss any problems we may dealing with or foresee in the near future.

Khalid, I think the first order of business is the status of our shipment. I, for one, have had very little sleep since you left for Los Angeles. I know this cell phone silence is a necessary evil and is in the best interest of our mission security, but I am dying of curiosity. Has everything been accounted for?"

"I am sorry Abdulla," Khalid replied, "I have not taken the time, nor the risk of opening each crate. I have reviewed the list of parcels, and their contents that our supplier sent me. Based on that, it appears that he shipped exactly what we ordered, but we will not know for sure until tomorrow when we open each crate. I did open one of the Semtex shipments and configured a suicide device I could have used in the event the police stopped me. Everything in that crate exactly matched what the supplier had written on the invoice he sent. I don't want to sound flippant, but it looks like one more night of fitful sleep is in order."

"You're right, as usual, Khalid," Abdulla replied. "I didn't intend to sound pushy. As it relates to weapons procurement and other nefarious skills, you are by far the most experienced person I have ever met, much less the three of us. Please indulge me if I seem a bit apprehensive, I'm only looking out for one point six billion fucking Muslims."

Abdulla's exaggerated facial expression and waving hand motions, told Khalid and Saad that he was being humorously sarcastic. But they both knew that his sarcasm was a subconscious manifestation of a deep-seated fear of failing at what he considered to be the most significant undertaking in the entire history of Islam. They also knew it was their duty to support and encourage Abdulla, and his vision, regardless of the circumstances. They would not fail in their roles.

Without missing a beat, and resuming a more serious demeanor, Abdulla turned to face Saad. "We are fast approaching the time when we need to send out our first set of fake messages from the DPRK to the Americans and their Asian allies. In your last update, you indicated that you, and your team of computer gurus, were having problems hacking into DPRK networks. Update us on where you are in this effort and whether or not we need be concerned at this point."

Looking more confident than he felt, Saad replied, "progress has indeed been slower than I like. For you to better understand what we have, and have not, accomplished I need to give you a little background. I will need to get a bit technical, so if you don't understand, or have any questions whatsoever, please interrupt me.

Several years ago, one of my family's companies in Riyadh recruited, and hired, a young Iraqi man, Mustafa Azizi, who had just graduated from the Al Faisal University's College of Science and General Studies. Mustafa was an orphan who had been adopted by an upper-middle-class, childless, Kuwaiti couple. His birth father had been killed during the Iraqi – Iranian war, and he and his mother and sister had moved to Kuwait to live with her sister and her husband.

His mother, aunt, and sister were raped and brutally murdered by Iraqi Republican Guard soldiers who were fleeing Kuwait

City after coalition forces destroyed most of their invasion forces. As I understand it, the Kuwaiti family found Mustafa wandering the streets in shock. He had witnessed his aunt's husband's murder, was beaten unconscious, and then discovered the savagely ravaged women when he awoke. He was just a child at the time and, as you can well imagine, severely traumatized.

The Kuwait couple adopted him, raised him like he was their own son, and sent him to school. He turned out to be something of a momma's boy and a total, complete, nerd. However, he's also a workaholic and a computer genius." With a devilish smile, Saad added, "just the kind of employee our business prefers; no social life, works all the time, and never complains. Well, to make a long, complicated, story short, he worked for us a couple of years and then, based on my recommendation the MA recruited him to work for one of their shell companies.

At the time the Iranians were going full speed ahead on their efforts, like the DPRK, to join the nuclear weapons club. The MA leadership were convinced that with India, Pakistan, and Israel having the bomb there were already plenty of opportunities for disaster in the Middle East. The world for that matter, but they were primarily concerned with our front yard. So, our friends the MA Sovereign Council decided to surreptitiously, do something about it. Based on someone's brilliant idea, they engaged a small team of computer experts to do something akin to what we are attempting to do with the DPRK. That is, create mischief with the Iranian nuclear weapon laboratory computer network. Mustafa was on that team, and they succeeded beyond the MA's wildest expectations. Khalid, you have a lot more history with the MA than I do, but even you may not know what I am going to share.

Mustafa and his team worked night and day for over a year. One small group was charged with finding their way into various government and academic network servers and workstations. At the same time another group started developing code for the infections, Trojan horses, viruses, etc., they planned to insert once they got past network firewalls.

Finally, sometime around 2007 they got past the security systems and began what they referred to as "time released infections." The malicious code they had developed was designed to sit idle for months but to spread across network nodes, without doing any harm while it did so. Then at a predetermined date, it would start taking control and wreaking havoc. This particular virus strain targeted what is referred to as programmable logic controllers, or PLC's. Computer geeks never use comprehensible words when an acronym will do," Saad quipped.

"PLC's are used to automate electromechanical processes that control machinery, medical devices, or in this case, the centrifuges that are used to separate nuclear materials. You probably read about the cyber attack when it was finally discovered in 2010. The combined virus, Trojan Horse infestation was given the name Stuxnet by a Russian antivirus software provider that isolated it in another network. By then it was too late, tremendous damage had already been done.

It has been estimated that almost twenty percent of the centrifuges used in their nuclear program had been damaged or destroyed. And somewhere in the neighborhood of one hundred thousand computers infected, and thousands of automated machines crippled. Stuxnet literally brought the Iranian nuclear program to its knees. But here is the brilliant part. Everyone, the Iranians, the Russians, and the global press said the attack was the result of an American – Israeli cyberweapon. Our guys and the MA were never even suspected."

After Saad had finished, Abdulla spoke up. "That is all well and good Saad, I appreciate the level of technical competence you have injected into our cause. But when can we actually break into the DPRK network and start sending bogus messages? The fuse is burning, and this is one task that doesn't have a plan B."

With his face and tone, expressing a combination of frustration and guilt, Saad noted "trust me, Abdulla, I share your concerns. You, of all people, should know the complexities of establishing a timeline when dealing with computer software. It's virtually impossible to establish an accurate target date for completing even the simplest of programs. It's not like building a road. You seldom know how far you must go, what obstacles will encounter, or how much work can be accomplished by you or members of your construction crew.

My team's task is further complicated by the fact that the overwhelming majority of DPRK citizens if you can call them that, have no access to computers and the internet, and very little cell phone coverage. This makes standard phishing, and similar tactics, just a point shy of impossible to use. Regardless, I will Dmail Mustafa tonight and tell him the future Caliph of all of Islam wants a status report."

Abdulla could tell Saad was a tiny bit irritated. He punched Saad playfully on the arm, laughed, and said "dial it back a click *"namur."* In your email, tell him your old, totally Type A friend would like for him to update the three of us, via speakerphone, tomorrow morning at 0700 our time. That will be 1600 in Riyadh which will let him get a good night's sleep and ample time to prepare whatever he intends to tell us. Now, let's the three of us have dinner. We need to be rested tomorrow so we can go distribute the goodies Khalid has brought us."

Minutes later, as the three men were getting ready to leave, Saad's disposable cell phone rang. Answering it, and turning on the speaker, Saad said: "you will not believe this, it's Mustafa!"

CHAPTER 15

The United States presidential election campaign, as had become the norm, informally kicked off the year before the actual election. However, this was proving to be anything but a typical election. The sitting president, a marginally competent, short-sighted, playground bully had surfed into power on a small wave of anti-liberalism and overall voter apathy. He maintained a core group of loyal followers, comprised mainly of blue-collar workers with two-digit IQ's, greedy business owners, and far right wing, ultra-conservative, closet racists.

Even these were starting to slip into an increasingly silent, politically ignorant, minority. Since coming into power, the POTUS had proven himself incapable of fostering even the most basic bipartisan agreements and had singlehandedly wrecked, or severely weakened, relationships with even long-standing allies. His approval ratings were the lowest since Gallup began conducting its polls in 1945. Even so, he had convinced himself that he could win a second term. He was dead wrong.

There were some potential, and generally viable, contenders, for the Democratic presidential candidacy. There was also a plethora of political pariahs, card-carrying communists, and those just on the fringe of sanity who seriously thought they had a shot at the presidency. The Democratic Party primaries had whittled these numbers down to a handful of well-known politicians, media celebrities, and business leaders. A series of nationally broadcast debates resulted in reducing the field even further. There was no small degree of concern expressed that corporate controlled media had an undue influence on who would, and would not, be selected to run. Prospective candidates were invited to participate in the debates based, to a substantial degree, on the whims, and political affiliation, of network owners.

The Democratic National Convention was held in the Kansas City Convention Center, also known as Bartle Hall. It came without the disruptive protests that had become the hallmark of national conventions, of both parties. And, thanks to a well-organized combination of Kansas City law enforcement and the National Guard, there was no public violence. Any pockets of rioting, or attempts at looting, were quickly squashed and never made their way to major news channels.

There were endless, vile and bitter, rants against the sitting POTUS woven throughout each speech given by every presenter. These attacks began with the opening speaker, a popular, and generally well-respected senator from North Carolina, and didn't end until the microphones were turned off on Thursday night.

After the final convention ballons and confetti dropped, the two-time governor of Wyoming, as was long anticipated, easily walked away with the nomination. His pick for Vice President was a Hispanic female and former Secretary of Labor under the previous administration. Both candidates appeared insanely popular in every national opinion poll.

Nashville's government officials formally submitted their application and began lobbying, to host the Republican Convention two years earlier. For years, city planners had been working to change Nashville's reputation from just a country music Mecca to a more rounded, virtually crime free center for business, education, and commerce. With the Republican National Convention, RNC, they got more than they had bargained for.

Where the DNC had been comparatively free of organized protests and generated no widespread riots, violence, or looting, its Republican counterpart was a barely contained eruption.

At his request, the President was the opening speaker, and from the time he took the stage until he angrily stalked off, he was heckled and booed. Outside the Nashville Convention Center, four massive Jumbotron's displayed his image and boomed his speech to a seething horde of onlookers. The fact that the convention was held in July, the hottest month of the year, and its effect on the crowd's mood, was akin to pouring gasoline on a smoldering ember. Fights and attacks broke out among sign swinging factions each time the President made even the least controversial point in his speech. And he had a lot of points. Gunshots rang out, and dark spots appeared on one of the Jumbotron screens exactly where the President's head had been just seconds before.

On Tuesday, the second day of the convention, the state by state roll call vote resulted in the nomination of the Republican Senator from Texas as the party candidate for President of the United States. Not since 1856 when the 14th president, Franklin Pierce, was passed over in favor of James Buchanan, had a sitting president not been nominated by his party for a second term.

The newly appointed presidential candidate, a combat veteran and trauma surgeon by training, was highly regarded on both aisles of the Senate. He was a keenly insightful, tactician, who could see all sides of most issues and arrive, objectively, at whatever his stance may be. He was impervious to lobbying efforts, and his background and political dealings were squeaky clean. He chose, as his running mate, the CEO of one of the most successful online merchandising companies in the country. Together they represented a sensibly conservative force that, given the opportunity, may reunify the Republican party while simultaneously presenting a challenge to the equally legitimate Democratic ticket. Unfortunately, the current state of the party was anything but unified, and time was not on their side.

As in the past, the convention ended Thursday night with the newly nominated candidate making his acceptance speech. The protests, outside the convention hall, had died down considerably. Inside, the raucous crowd's anger, for the most part, had been replaced by optimism.

On the other hand, the POTUS was seething. His political days, and power were numbered. At best he would have to ride out the five-month remainder of his term as a lame duck. He would have to watch the campaign, and the November election, like every other citizen. He would be forced to stand by impotently for almost three months until the newly elected president, most likely that "damn Democrat," was sworn into office, his office, in January.

Despite the popularity of the recently nominated Republican candidate, the party would be fragmented, sufficiently split to tip the scales in favor of the Democrats. His first thought was to run as an independent. Thanks to over twelve months of pre-convention fundraising and big-ticket, favor-seeking, contributors to his war chest were more than adequate. He still commanded a small, but fiercely loyal following who would support him until the second coming. Most of his top officers, and cabinet, chosen based on political favors or campaign contributions, would stick by him even after he was kicked out of office. Especially, the Secretary of Defense and Attorney General, and the Chairman of the Joint Chiefs of Staff. But the more he thought of an independent campaign, the more it soured on his palate, the madder he got and the more he thougth, "Fuck em, fuck em all."

On Friday morning, as workers shoveled confetti off the convention hall floor, the United States woke up to find itself with two exceptionally strong, more than capable presidential candidates. Unfortunately, for the next six months, it would have an increasingly bitter, famously vindictive, Commander in Chief who would become progressively unstable.

CHAPTER 16

David woke up two hours after the refueling stop in Athens. In the chair across the aisle, the Secretary was still sleeping off a Douglas Cho administered dose of zolpidem, aka Ambien. Zolpidem was a department of defense, DoD, approved medication sometimes used by military pilots and Special Forces, to sleep when it is necessary outside their normal circadian rhythm. Its use gained notoriety when taken, with near disastrous effect by Seal Team 6 before attacking Osama Bin Laden's compound in Abbottabad, Pakistan. To counter Ambien's well-deserved reputation for post-use grogginess, Cho would give the Secretary a stimulant, Dexedrine, once he woke up and again right before their meeting with Yi and Lavrov. The Bulldog needed to be at the top of his game when serious discussions began.

After leaving Athens, they flew over the Mediterranean then across Sadia Arabia, Oman, and the Arabian Sea. David reread the AIFTU Charter or at least the salient sections that they wanted to drive home with the Russians and Chinese. As he read, he massaged his notes. This was to refine further the points which he and the Secretary hoped would convince the two diplomats that this approach was in the best interest of their respective countries, and themselves.

As the Gulfstream approached the southern tip of India, the Bulldog snorted loudly and awoke. "Where are we David," he asked as he adjusted his seat and sat up. Looking at the GPS monitor in the front of their cabin David replied "we are just west of Mumbai, then on to the Bay of Bengal. We should be about three hours away from Hainan. Plenty of time to have some breakfast and discuss sticking points that might have come to you while you were sleeping. I'm telling you, Mr. Secretary, I've got to have one of these chairs in my living room."

As they were talking, Douglas Cho magically appeared carrying a plastic glass of water and two pills. "Here is your Dexedrine whenever you are ready Mr. Secretary. *One pill makes you larger, and one pill makes you small* he sang." The Secretary took the pills from Cho's hand and, taking a sip of the water told him, "geeze Cho, you are way too young to remember Grace Slick and the Jefferson Airplane. For that matter, I barely remember them; the sixties were pretty rough on some of us." Cho chuckled saying "I don't want to add insult in injury Mr. Secretary, but my dad used to play those old songs when I was growing up."

David got out of his chair and went forward to the head to relieve himself and to splash his face with cold water. After he finished, he opened the door of one of the refrigerators and began rummaging around. Dragging out two trays he turned to the Secretary and asked, "how about a ham and cheese omelet and, according to the label, hash browns boss?" "That sounds perfect, I'm famished," replied the Secretary. After David heated the trays in a microwave, he made coffee, pulled two orange juice containers out of the fridge and brought everything back to the small table in front of their seats.

As they ate, the Bulldog looked across the table at David and, leaning slightly forward said "David, there is one thing that I need to share with you. There is a chance that what you and I are about to do could be in vain regardless of how successful we are during our meeting. What I am about to share with you is way beyond classified. It is also mainly based on personal, empirical, evidence. It is not the result of any official feedback or investigation. Just my gut. David, I think the POTUS is going insane. Hell, he may have already passed insane, waved at it, and is on his way to flat out crazy. Yes, I am well aware of the mummers, and whispered comments, among the White House staff. There has long been conspiracy speculation spewing out of the talking heads, and some, no most, of his comments seem to come out of nowhere. But, he and I go back a long way, and I see more than that. The other day when I was briefing him on this operation I noticed, and not for the first time, a strange, distant, look in his eyes. Something I haven't seen since the war, and then only a couple of times. It was like his eyes were focused in my direction, but he wasn't looking at me. They weren't the blank look of someone in shock, and I could tell he was hearing and processing everything I was telling him, but something just wasn't right. I may be reading him totally wrong, or a little paranoid and overreactive myself. But I'm not. Something's not right, and I'm flat out worried. David, I'm not sure what I expect you to do with this information, or if I should have even shared it with you. But, it's something we need to keep in the back of our minds as we negotiate this deal. The consequences of failure could be far greater than we can imagine and buddy, I've got a vivid imagination."

David sat in stunned silence, trying to read any subliminal signals on the Secretary's face. He wasn't necessarily surprised at the information the Bulldog had shared with him, but he was surprised that he shared it. He and an overwhelming number of Americans had their concerns, as did much of the planet. But he had never expected such a blunt confession from the United States Secretary of State. This indeed was a cause for concern.

Just then the pilot opened the cockpit door, leaned out, and said "sorry to interrupt, but we are about one hundred miles west of the city of Sanya on the island of Hainan. We have started our final approach. I thought you would like to know that we have an escort, two to be exact. If you look outside either the port or starboard windows, you will see a brand-new Chinese J-20 fighter, one just off our wing tips on each side of the plane. The J-20 is what they would throw up against our F-22 or F-35. Apparently, it's as stealthy as they claim or at least we didn't see them on our radar. We wouldn't have seen them at all if they hadn't of pulled up right next to us. The pilot on our port side even gave me a "hookem horns" sign. Or at least that's what it means in Texas, who knows what it means in China.

David looked out the window next to his seat. There, about twenty meters off, and slightly ahead, of the starboard wing tip was a sleek, dark gray jet with a bright red star on its vertical stabilizer. Oddly, David felt comforted by the sight of the fighter.

Douglas Cho walked up from the rear of the plane and joined David and the Secretary as they observed the Chinese fighters. "Looks pretty damn impressive," mused Cho, "I've read that they still have a lot of technical problems, but even so, they are still only the second military to operate a 5th generation stealth fighter. After us of course.

Guys, we have had radio contact with the Chinese officials on Hainan. Our accommodations tonight, and your meeting tomorrow will be at the Pullman Oceanview Sanya Bay Resort and Spa, or as we say in Chinese, Sānyà wān bó ěr màn dùjià jī⊠diàn jí shu⊠liáo zhōngxīn," Cho said smiling. "That's easy for you to say," joked the Bulldog, grinning ear to ear.

Assuming a more serious expression, Cho continued, "I suspect one of the reasons they are putting us up in the Pullman has to do with its proximity to a small military airport right next door. Less than a click away. Foreign Minister Yi and his vehicle drivers will pick us up on the tarmac, at the door of the plane, as soon as we taxi to a stop. He took your request for secrecy to heart. As much as they like to prance around, no other dignitaries will be there. From there we will go directly to the hotel. Your suites are ready and waiting. Karwoski and I will shadow the Secretary. Phillips and Henderson will do the same with Mr. Stakley. Remember, except when you are in a classified, closed-door conference, we will be within twenty feet of you at all times. I have explained this to my Chinese counterpart who said he would expect nothing less.

As usual, we don't expect any trouble, but we will be armed and ready just in case. Of course, since there are a billion of them and eleven of us, the odds aren't really good if the shit truly does hit the fan." "That's the spirit Douglas," chimed the Bulldog. "Just remember, there's an ironclad "no live Secretary of State, no payment" clause in our contract. Then again there has never been a government contract that a beltway lawyer couldn't breach." Just then the fasten seat belt light came on, and Cho went back to his seat in the rear of the plane.

They came in across the bay, from the southwest end of the runway. The Gulfstream virtually floated down to the airstrip without the jarring impact David had grown accustomed to on most commercial flights. No doubt about it, these guys were pros. The plane braked and then made a hard-right turn into one of three parking areas. There were what appeared to be military planes, twin-engine props, lined up in two of the parking lots. The lot they stopped in was deserted except for three limousines. Black-clad drivers stood at parade rest next to the rear passenger doors of each vehicle and two men, wearing suit and tie, stood a few feet apart, waiting for the plane to come to a stop.

As soon as they stopped, Cho got out of his seat and came forward saying "gentlemen, welcome to China, and even though I have never been here, my ancestral home." He went forward, opened the plane's door, and lowered its gangway steps. David and the Secretary got their bags from the overhead storage compartments and started walking forward. One of the operators, Karwoski, said "Sir, if you don't mind, we will take your bags for you. Chinese officials, especially at this level, put a lot of weight on status and appearance. You too Mr. Stakley, if it's ok. Besides, it gives our guys something to do and lets the Foreign Minister, and his staff, know we are your security detail and are here to serve you." "Thanks, son," the Bulldog replied, "that reminds me of when Jimmy Carter was President. He always made a big deal of carrying his suit bag. But the Secret Service knew that was only for show; it was always empty." Everyone laughed for just a second, then the Secretary, putting on a completely somber face started down the steps.

When the Secretary reached the bottom step a slim, late 50's looking man, with smartly combed, jet black, hair stepped forward, bowed, and thrust out his hand. Speaking perfect English, he said, "Mr. Secretary, welcome to Hainan, it is so good to see you again. You look remarkably well, especially considering you just survived a fourteen-hour flight." "Thank you, Minister Yi, I appreciate the compliment. However, if I look anything like I feel, I question its sincerity." Both men smiled, then the Bulldog said, Minister Yi, please let me introduce my very able associate, David Stakely." Knowing well the custom, David bowed to Yi and said, "Minister, it is an honor. I want to thank you in advance for your hospitality, and for the escort. They were very impressive."

Returning David's bow then shaking his hand Minister Yi replied, "the honor is mine Mr. Stakely. I understand that you work in the INR Division of the State Department and that it was you who orchestrated much of what we will be discussing tomorrow."

David was more than a little surprised by the last comment and, looking at the Bulldog, perceived that he was as well. Before David could reply, Minister Yi said, "but we can talk at length about that later. For now, let us take you to the hotel, and you can freshen up. Mr. Lavrov, the Russian MFA and his associate, arrived earlier this afternoon. If I know him, he is soaking in the hotel spa, or roasting in the sauna, as we speak. We have drinks, and an intimate dinner planned for 1900. We will send an escort to your room to show you the way.

David, the Secretary, and the Chinese Minister got into the lead limousine and Cho, Karwoski, Phillips, and Henderson, along with a Chinese escort loaded into the second vehicle. The small procession drove from their location on the tarmac to Sanyawan Road, proceeded for less than a quarter mile, and then turned right into the Pullman Sanya Bay Resort complex.

Cho hadn't been kidding when he said the resort was next door to the airport. As they drove, Cho noticed the complete absence of traffic along their route. When he pointed this out to their escort, he informed them that traffic had been detoured to allow repairs to be made on the street. He then smiled and told the group "well that, plus we didn't want any tourists snapping photos of the Minister and the Secretary. Also, we will arrive at the rear entrance of the resort and enter without drawing any attention to ourselves. Your suites, a special dining area, and conference room are on the fourth floor of a wing that has been closed off to the public. It's too bad you will not be able to take advantage of the amenities the resort has to offer, or the pristine beach, but I get the impression our respective bosses aren't here for the scenery." As they were talking, the vehicles came to a stop and parked next to a non-distinct door on the rear of what appeared to be a large hotel.

After stopping, and turning off the limousine engines, the drivers, and each escort, came around and opened the passenger side doors. Following Minister Yi, David, the Secretary, and the rest of the entourage entered the building. Once inside, Minister Yi led them down a brightly lit, deserted, hall to what appeared to be a service entrance elevator lobby. There they were met by a well-dressed man who Minister Yi introduced as Mr. Wong, his head of Security. He bowed, shook their hands, and said: "on behalf of myself, and the staff at Sanya Bay Resort, welcome."

Handing first the Secretary, and then David, a zippered leather portfolio" he continued, "please accept this humble welcome packet. Inside are the keys to your respective suites. One key for yourself and one that you can give, if you so desire, to each of your security staff. We have also included three, individually numbered, cell phones along with business cards for my team and me. These phones can be used anywhere on the island, or China for that matter. Of course, they don't meet your government security requirements, and you may be concerned that they could be used as bugs to monitor your conversations. They aren't, but their use is totally up to your discretion. Myself, or either of the escorts you have already met, will be your primary point of contact should you need anything at all. One of us will be available twenty-four hours a day.

You will notice the absence of hotel staff. During your stay, this section of the resort, for reasons of security and anonymity, is off limits to all hotel employees. And so, gentlemen, whenever you are ready your escorts will show you to your suites." At that point, Minister Yi chimed in, "thank you, Mr. Wong.

Mr. Secretary, David, as I mentioned earlier, we have dinner scheduled for 1900. You should have ample time to settle in and freshen up between now and then. We will have breakfast and begin our meeting at 0730 tomorrow morning. Your escort will knock on your door at 0715. Unless you have any questions, I will see you shortly."

CHAPTER 17

Motioning for Abdulla and Khalid to sit back down, and turning on his cell phone's speaker, Saad said "Mustafa, your timing is perfect. We were just now talking about you. By "we," I mean another MA associate and the future Caliph of all of Islam. I am placing you on speaker so that you can brief the three of us at the same time. I pray you are calling with good news." From the cell phone speaker Mustafa's, disembodied, electronically amplified voice rang out, noticeably tinged with excitement.

"Saad, and my brothers, the short answer is yes, I am calling with good news. We have had success beyond my wildest dreams, and I am ready to give you spectacular proof of what we have accomplished.

As you know, since the beginning of our mission, and up until just a couple of weeks ago, we have been stymied. We couldn't find a way to break into the DPRK network. Shit, we couldn't find a network for that matter. The North Korean civilian population lives in an information technology stone age. Individual cell phones and personal computers are practically non-existent. And internet access is either severally restricted or outright illegal."

Slipping into the short cell phone pause, Saad interrupted. "Mustafa, based on the excitement I perceive in your voice, I can only surmise that you are getting ready to launch into one of your technical dissertations on how to build a watch. But first, I only want to know what time it is. You grabbed our attention when you teased us about "spectacular proof." Could you elaborate a bit more? And then you can share the details in as much computer speak as you wish."

Without skipping a beat, Mustafa continued. "Please forgive my exuberance, my brothers. I will try to restrain myself. We have indeed cracked into several DPRK government networks and have been doing a little snooping. I am now prepared to predict with a high degree of confidence that the North Koreans will test another Hwasong-16 within a week."

Mustafa paused, and Saad jumped back into the conversation. "Mustafa, is that it? Is that the proof you want to share with us? I've done no network snooping but could still guess, with about an eighty percent degree of confidence that those lunatics would be testing their newest space toy during the next few days. If nothing else, to piss off the Americans."

Then Mustafa sprang the trap he had set. "Ah Saad, now it's you that is jumping the gun. You interrupted before I could elaborate. Let me start all over. I predict that weather permitting, the Norks will conduct a test launch of their ICBM next Thursday at 2300 local time. It will fly east by northeast for, let's say, thirty seconds before it takes a nosedive toward the Sea of Japan and self-destructs forty seconds after liftoff. That's unless you want to change the amount of time it is in flight. How is that for precise confidence?

Now, may I proceed with my explanation of how we were able to open their kimono, or hanbok, or whatever Norks wear?" This time it was Abdulla who responded. "Mustafa, this is Abdulla. We are totally, and completely, impressed. If, as you imply, you can make this happen as proof of your and your team's, success there will surely be a reward for all of you when, as they say, "the dust settles." Please proceed, I promise there will be no further interruptions." Mustafa continued.

"For weeks on end, we struggled. We kept running into technical dead ends. As I described, the DPRK has virtually no computer infrastructure to break into, outside of their highly restricted government networks. Compound this with our need to use language translation software to switch between Arabic, Korean, Chinese, and English. Even the characters on our keyboards often required two or three conversions.

After the first week, we abandoned Arabic altogether. As it turned out, we made ninety percent of our progress using English. Finally, one of my associates tried an approach we hadn't previously considered. He switched his target. Instead of Nork networks, he went after the Chinese. We all knew that China was the DPRK's largest trade partner, and besides the Russians, one of only a few that provided them with any scientific or technical assistance. I should note that, ironically, the Americans have unknowingly made tremendous contributions to the DPRK. All the software on their desktop and mainframe, computers, as well as network firewalls and virus detection software originated in the United States.

As it turned out, once we got inside their networks, this gave us the keys to the kingdom, metaphorically speaking. Anyway, using a keyword search algorithm on a communication data stream, my team member came across some emails from a Chinese advisor and his DPRK counterpart. This eventually gave us a universal resource locator, aka URL, on the North Korean side of the exchange. Although I am greatly oversimplifying things, that was all we needed. Once we had that URL, which by the way belonged to their rocket propulsion laboratory, we started peeling the onion. One URL leads to another, then two more, until we were able to go just about anywhere we wanted to inside their network. Once inside, we knew exactly where we wanted to go.

As with the Iranians, well the entire planet for that matter, the DPRK relies heavily on something called SCADA. This is an American acronym for Supervisory Control and Data Acquisition. SCADA is a set of computer software that monitors and controls various electrical or mechanical processes. The average person never sees or thinks about what they do. But they are everywhere and embedded in just about everything. For example, right here in Sadia Arabia, a SCADA system controls our power grid and even our traffic lights. The North Koreans, just like every other government, rely on some flavor of SCADA to control their hydroelectric dams, railroads and guess what, their rocket engine thrusters. The good news is they work surprisingly well and are extremely reliable. The bad news is they are ridiculously easy to hack. Insanely insecure. I guess that's good news for us hackers.

So, my brothers, we are inside their military and government networks. We can do just about anything even their most skillful programmers can do. As we speak, my team is implanting Trojan horses and diverse types of viruses that will allow us to gain even more control. If we so desire, we can crash programs or bring down entire sub-nets. We are also, sweeping the trail, or covering our tracks as they say in the movies. Just like in Iran, they will never know who got past their firewalls and penetrated their networks.

Saad, whenever you are ready, we can begin transmitting messages to the Americans, South Koreans, Japanese, or anyone else for that matter. I can show you how it's done. Or, you can Dmail me the verbiage you wish to send, the individual or group you want to receive it, and the date it should be transmitted, and I will take care of it."

Relieved, and deeply satisfied with his team's accomplishments, Saad looked at a beaming Abdulla who said, "the American presidential election is the first Tuesday of November. The archangel has directed that our first strike be less than three weeks later, the day before the American Thanksgiving holiday. We will send three messages in November. The first will be the Thursday following the election. Let the Americans revel, or wail depending on which party wins, about their new president. Then we jerk them back to reality with a venomous warning from their nemesis, North Korea.

The second, even more, threatening message will come the Monday before our attack. They will, of course, ignore both. Then on Wednesday, as their little darlings start to head home from college, to be with mommy and daddy on turkey day, ka-boom! There's not a dry eye in the entire U.S. Our third November, "we warned you," message will be transmitted on Thanksgiving Day.

Mustafa, I will compose each message personally and Dmail them to you. As is our practice, I will copy Saad and our other associate here, to keep them in the loop. Please proceed with whatever preparations, and DPRK network meddling, you need to make. Thank you again for your, and your team's, contributions to our cause. A reward beyond anything you can imagine awaits you once we are victorious and I sit on the throne of the world Caliphate.

Keep a close eye on your Dmail inbox and call Saad immediately should you have any problems, any whatsoever. We will be anxiously awaiting the news of a failed North Korean ICBM launch." Abdulla ended the call and motioned for Saad and Khalid to get up. "Indeed, that was wonderful news, Saad. Excellent work. Now, let's have dinner and celebrate our success. We have a big day tomorrow. In the morning we will split up the weapons and explosives that Khalid has lugged halfway across the country. Then we begin the most dangerous leg of our mission."

CHAPTER 18

Despite his exhaustion from spending almost sixteen hours in a steel tube, hurtling along at six hundred miles per hour, forty thousand feet in the air, David had slept fitfully. He had opted not to take the Ambien Cho had offered to help him sleep. He tended to steer away from putting anything, whose components he couldn't pronounce, in his body. Hell, he didn't even take an Ibuprofen unless he thought his head would explode. Last night's dinner, preceded, during, and followed by copious amounts of vodka, Scotch, and some God-awful Chinese liquor was an exception to his rule. David hadn't been drunk, but he was thankful that all he had to do was walk back to his room. He couldn't have driven anywhere. He was amazed at how much vodka Lavrov had been able to put away, without any noticeable effect.

Dinner had been an absolute delight. Minister Yi was a gracious host and the meal, some of the dishes David had never seen before, were indescribly delicious. Even though David was a raving fan of Chinese food, he had never had Peking Duck authentically prepared and presented, as it had been served last night. The entire meal had been fantastic, more importantly, he had been able to get to know Yi and Lavrov, and even the Secretary, on a more personal level.

While David was at dinner, one of his security operatives, Henderson or Phillips, had set the clock next to his bed to alarm at 0600. Although he was wide awake, and surprisingly refreshed considering his disrupted sleep pattern, and last night's alcohol consumption, he welcomed the alarm. He crawled out of bed and was heading to the shower when he detected the smell of coffee. After slipping on a hotel robe, David opened his bedroom door and went into the suite's living room. Henderson was standing next to a hotel room service cart which was loaded with pastries, Chinese dumplings, and what was obviously a large pot of coffee.

"Good morning boss, I trust you rested well. They just brought us a small feast. There's also juice, tea, and coffee." Taking a cup and filling it with steaming coffee David replied, "this is exactly what I needed. They are also going to serve us a working breakfast at our session this morning. You and Phillips should dig into this while I shower and get dressed." "We sure will," Henderson replied. "Phillips should be back shortly. He and Karwoski are just checking out the room where you and the Secretary will be meeting with Minister Yi and Lavrov. Nothing to fret about, it's part of our standard operating procedure, SOP."

Smiling, and nodding in agreement, David responded, "yep, one thing the Army, and my time with the State Department, taught me was that SOPs were there for a reason. Regardless of how goofy they might seem." Both men chuckled as David returned to his bedroom.

David and the Secretary followed their Chinese escort down a hall, back to the area where dinner had been served the night before. The guard had knocked on David's door precisely at 0715. If nothing else, these guys were punctual. Along the way, they were met by Sergey Lavrov, his associate, and their escort. When the group arrived at the conference room where they were to have breakfast and their meeting, they were greeted by Minister Yi.

The room had been rearranged to accommodate a round table and six chairs. Nameplates were on the table thus signaling their seating arrangement. David and the Secretary would sit across from Yi and Lavrov who would be next to one another. David realized this was a not so subtle signal that they considered themselves to be allies. At least for this meeting. After the obligatory greetings, the men exchanged barbs about the previous night's dinner and the amount of alcohol they had consumed. Once they finished breakfast the table was cleared, and the resort wait staff vanished, closing the conference room doors behind them.

As was customary, the host, Minister Yi, started the meeting saying "Robert, you have come a long way to meet with Sergey and me. What pray tell brings about this sense of urgency and the need for such a clandestine gathering? I trust that our presence here is indicative of our respect for your wishes. But, quite frankly, we are more than a little curious about your objectives."

Placing his hands flat on the table, and with a somber expression on his face, the Bulldog looked first at Yi then at Lavrov. "Gentlemen, the situation on the Korean peninsula is fast coming to a boil. Your DPRK ally has an arsenal of nuclear weapons and now has the means, via their new and improved Hwasong-16 ICBM, to deliver them. We, the United States, our allies, the rest of the planet for that matter, can't let that happen."

As soon as the Secretary paused, Lavrov interjected, "Mr. Secretary, Robert, I think I speak for both Minister Yi and myself. We wholeheartedly agree and, at least my country, plan to strictly enforce the economic sanctions we have agreed upon. Yes, I know we may have let them slide a bit in the past. But we too understand the gravity of the situation. We know, especially considering their recent ICBM advancements, it's getting worse every day. We are standing on the brink of what could be a world-wide disaster."

Nodding his head, Minister Yi added, "we concur with Sergey, China is also prepared to enforce the agreed-upon sanctions and even stronger ones if necessary. However, Robert, I don't sense that you came all this way, in what amounts to a diplomatic panic, just to get our concurrence on ratcheting down economically on the DPRK. We could have discussed that with a conference call. What's the real purpose of this visit?"

Raising his eyebrows ever so slightly, and slowly nodding his head, the Bulldog responded. "You're correct Wang. We didn't come all this way to eat Peking Duck, although in retrospect, based on last night's dinner, it would have been worth the trip. We are here for two, critically important, purposes. First, I need to inform you of what we intend to do. Not talk about, do! Second, and by far the most important, is to respectfully request your concurrence with, and participation in, what could well be the most significant international treaty ever proposed.

Sergey, Wang, you, and the people you represent, know that we are at, no, we have passed, a crisis point on the Korean peninsula. Way back in the sixties, in one of his more notable speeches, President John Kennedy stated, incorrectly I might add, that the Chinese combine two characters when they write the Mandarin word for crisis. One represents danger, and one represents opportunity. Yes, Wang, before you correct me, I know, linguistically speaking, this isn't accurate. But it's a wonderful metaphor. Self-help books and management consultants have been using it for years, and it makes an incredibly valid point. Keep this analogy in mind when David expands upon the treaty I just mentioned. But before we get to treaty discussions, I need to share with you our intentions for the near term. I am going to cut to the chase. The next time that lunatic dictator threatens the United States, one of our allies, or displays his progress, or even intentions toward expanding the DPRK's nuclear weapons program," here the Bulldog, looking intensely, first at Yi then Lavrov, paused for just a second, "we're going to annihilate his ass, and his military."

Despite their years of political training and experience, David detected a shudder of surprise and fear, in both Lavrov and Yi. Before they could respond, the Bulldog continued. "The time for diplomacy has passed. For the first eighteen years of my life, I lived on a ranch in Central Texas. My father was a loving, compassionate, man. But when he saw a rattlesnake, he killed it. He didn't walk around it or let it have its own space, and wait for it to bite one of us kids, or Lord knows, one of his dogs. No, he killed it then and there. Gentlemen, we have been tiptoeing around this way too long. Like we say in Texas, it's snake killing time."

David felt a tingle run up his spine. The silence in the room was palpable. The Secretary let his words sink in. Looking first at Lavrov, then turning his focus back to the Bulldog, Minister Yi spoke up. "Robert, those are very serious words. The scenario you are painting would start another Korean war that could drag on for years and this time cost the lives of millions. Worse still, it could start a worldwide nuclear war and bring about the end of civilization as we know it. We have feared this for over half a century. Mr. Secretary, how can the United States entertain such a notion?"

Pushing his chair back from the table, more for effect than anything else, the Bulldog fired back. "That's precisely why we are here Wang. We don't want to get bogged down in another regional conflict any more than China or Russia does. And we damn sure don't want to start world war three. Now, take a deep breath, and let me explain our plan.

Although North Korea only has a population of twenty-five million and change, its active duty military is over nine hundred thousand. A piss ant country, whose citizens are starving, one third the population of France, yet with an army over five times the size. It has the fourth largest active military in the world, and they have another five million, trained, reservists. The DPRK has as many tanks and submarines as the United States.

Let that sink in for a minute. I don't know where the hell the park them all. Well actually, thanks to our satellites we know exactly where they are. But I'm digressing. Equally troubling is their current military doctrine. The Norks have no intention of fighting a limited, conventional, war as they did in the fifties. Or, as in Vietnam and Afghanistan, replicating the mistakes the United States continues to make. When the time comes, North Korea plans a massive, all out, assault across, and under, the DMZ. That's right, under the DMZ.

At last count, they had over twenty, hardened tunnels that could transport upwards of fifteen thousand troops and vehicles per hour behind South Korean lines. They just blow out the last few meters of rock and dirt and *voila*, a military superhighway. And, using what amounts to slave labor, they are continually expanding and improving these things. Who knows what they have today?

At the same time, using aging but plentiful transport aircraft, and ships, they will insert their special forces troops directly into South Korea and possibly Guam. They have the largest special forces in the world, twenty-five brigades or over one hundred and twenty thousand, highly trained, battle ready, troops. And I haven't mentioned their chemical and biological weapons. Or their eighteen thousand heavy guns and multiple-tube rocket launchers. These things are capable of raining over three hundred thousand conventional or biochemical shells per hour on South Korean and American forces.

I could go on and on, painting an even more alarming picture of their military capabilities. Suffice it to say that a conventional war against North Korea, on Korean soil, isn't winnable. They know it, you know it, and we know it. The North Koreans don't plan a limited engagement, and we don't plan on a conventional, non-nuclear, fight. That brings me back to the point you were making Wang. The sole purpose of our trip was to prevent, as you noted, a worldwide nuclear war. Everything else we are going to propose amount to nothing but details toward that end."

David felt a sense of relief come over everyone in the room. The Secretary settled back into his chair subtlety conveying a return to normalcy. With a serious expression, but looking a bit more relieved, Lavrov commented, "I concur, Robert, from an American and South Korean perspective, the future looks nothing but bleak if hostilities do break out. And it's not too rosy for Russia or China either. This is especially true given our physical proximity, and relationship with the north. So, as you say, cut to the chase and tell us what role you see for our countries should, or as you imply, when this evolves into open conflict."

"Thank you for that segue Sergey," the Bulldog replied, "the first part is simple. We suspect that in the very near future the DPRK will commit, what the civilized world considers to be, another egregious act of war or illegal weapons test. When that happens, we are going to strike. There will be no warning, there will be no limitations, and there will be no mercy. The first part of our mission here is to inform you of our intentions and to ask that your countries take no actions when this occurs. We do suggest that you find a reason to recall your ambassadors, diplomats, and anyone else you aren't willing to sacrifice. Especially from Pyongyang, any military sites, and biochemical or nuclear weapon production plants. As you might suspect, they will be the first to go.

I will personally try and give each of you at least twenty-four hours' notice before we pull the trigger. However, I can't guarantee that will be possible. It would be prudent to begin to quietly remove your key staff as soon as possible after our presidential election, if not sooner. I don't see our sitting POTUS coming out ahead and who knows what his frame of mind will be if he does lose. As I see it, the world should be on high alert from the day after the election until January 20.

In summary my old friends, I have shared our intentions to put an end to the madness that has festered in North Korea for over seventy years. And I have pleaded with you to stay tolerantly on the sidelines once we begin this task. This brings us to the other reason we requested this face to face summit. What happens afterward? What role should our respective nations play in a postwar Korea?

My associate, Mr. Stakely, David, has been instrumental in the development of our suggestion for this eventuality. He has been beyond instrumental; it was his brainchild. For that reason, I will ask him to give you an overview, a summary, of what we refer to as a charter rather than a treaty. This approach will facilitate a peaceful transition from the harshest dictatorship on the face of the planet to a free, and productive, member of the United Nations."

Taking his cue from the Bulldog, David pulled four neatly bound and indexed, copies of the AIFTU charter from his attaché case. Getting out of his chair, he walked around the table and ceremoniously presented the document to Yi, Lavrov, and then the Secretary. The formality of this gesture would not go unnoticed, especially by Yi.

"Gentlemen, this document summarizes a radically new concept in international relations. For want of a better term, we call it the Asian Independent Free Trade Union or AIFTU. Its development was completely serendipitous. We were trying to come up with a treaty that would appease the three superpowers, China, Russia, and the United States from a military as well as a governance perspective. Simultaneously, it would eliminate the need for costly treaty oversight, provide a path for economic and social recovery, and provide a degree of freedom and prosperity the indigenous people haven't experienced in over half a century. Not to mention eliminating the tension in South Korea and Japan.

What evolved was the document you have in front of you. It's far better than what we set out to develop." For the next two hours, David walked Lavrov and Yi thru each section of the charter. Both he and the Secretary fielded questions and addressed every concern raised by the other two diplomats. David could see the men's demeanor move from skepticism, thru guarded acceptance, and finally to unexpressed, but obvious endorsement.

When David had completed his review, the Secretary tagged in, without waiting for a response or further questions, to close the deal. "Wang, Sergey, I suspect neither of you is empowered to accept our proposal formally. Or to even acknowledge your approval for that matter. However, I beseech your positive consideration and ask that, when you return, you present it in that light to your respective Politburos. And I implore you to do so as quickly as possible. I don't want to seem overly dramatic but boys we could well have the fate of humanity in our hands."

For just a few seconds, the room was quiet. No one spoke. Then, without consulting Lavrov, Yi, turning his gaze squarely toward David, took command of the meeting. "Mr. Stakely, you have developed, at worst, an intriguing concept. I am not sure how to categorize what you refer to as a charter. It is an odd mixture of capitalism and what could pass for a form of national socialism. Without a doubt, it is the most unique, and I dare say most promising, approach toward national reconciliation that I can imagine."

Turning his attention toward the Bulldog, and without missing a beat, Yi continued. "Secretary Pitts, you are correct in assuming that I cannot unilaterally approve China's acceptance of this proposal. In fact, I am probably going out on a limb by expressing my personal satisfaction. However, I will pledge my support. I will attempt to meet with the General Secretary immediately upon my return to the mainland. Naturally, I cannot guarantee his, or the Central Committee's approval. But, I will do my best to convince my countries' leadership that this may be our only option for a peaceful, and profitable, conclusion to what is obviously imminent hostilities."

Turning toward Lavrov, Yi said "Sergey, I am sorry I did not give you an opportunity to speak. That was not very diplomatic. However, I could not contain the need to express my opinion. Please, forgive my blunder and share your feelings with us."

Lavrov released a bit of nervous energy by collecting and carefully stacking, his copy of the AIFTU charter. "No offense at all Wang. In fact, you gave me the opportunity to collect my thoughts relative to the situation on the Korean Peninsula and on what we have heard this morning.

My feelings are very similar to your's Wang. The DPRK is like a tick that has latched on to Russia. Although not as closely allied to them as China, it's sucking the blood out of our fragile, but improving, economy. We know we need to pull it off and squash it but getting it to release its hold on us has proven to be extremely difficult. Like yourself, I cannot officially agree to anything. Fortunately, or unfortunately, depending on how the wind blows, I do not have to get our Central Committee's approval. I only need to convince our President that this approach will be in the best interest of Russia and the Federation.

Mr. Stakely, you have done a commendable job in presenting what I consider to be a brilliant concept. I'm sure Secretary Pitts will find a way to reward your skills and creativity. Perhaps a more relaxed, and extended, return to this beautiful resort. Or if he's truly grateful, an all-expense paid vacation on the shores of our Volga. During the summer of course. However, as with my Chinese colleague, my immediate task will be to get on our President's calendar and to try and get his approval. As you know, he tends to make his own decisions. But he does listen to recommendations from his staff, and his actions are generally thoughtful and well planned. Never rash. Minister Yi, Mister Secretary, I will do my best to get back with each of you by the end of the week."

CHAPTER 19

Saad and Khalid climbed into Abdulla's van. With Abdulla at the wheel, the three proceeded to an Applebee's less than a mile down the access road from their hotel. After dinner, Abdulla drove back to the Day's Inn and parked next to Saad and Khalid's vehicles which were at one end of the hotel, away from the front entrance. By now it was getting dark. The lights in the parking lot barely illuminated the sidewalk and the first row of cars. Everything else was shrouded in shadows.

This was just fine with Abdulla. After they stopped, Saad got out and walked to his van. Opening one of the rear doors, he retrieved six rubberized magnetic signs and gave Abdulla and Khalid two each. Saad held one of the signs he had kept, near the rear of the driver's side of his van and, walking forward, started to unroll it. The white sign, which was six feet long and three feet wide, stuck securely to the side of the van. Large, black, block, letters spelled out "Steller Carpet Cleaning" on the first line. Smaller font on the second line read "214-590-9279."

In less than a minute, the van transformed into what appeared to be a commercial vehicle. The signs Saad gave to Abdulla and Khalid said the same thing, giving the appearance of small business fleet vehicles. When they completed putting signs on each side, of each van, the three men returned to their suite.

The men talked until shortly after 2200 when Saad, stifling a yawn, said he was tired and needed to go to bed. Abdulla set the alarm on the clock in the Day's Inn suite to go off at 0600. Saad and Khalid were in the bedroom of the suite, but Abdulla had volunteered to sleep on the fold out couch bed in the living room. He relished this bit of privacy, especially when he knew the dreams would come later in the night as they almost always did. He was not disappointed.

Despite the excitement, and anticipation of the events expected the following day, Abdulla immediately fell into deep, REM, sleep. It was shortly after midnight when the first, misty, images started flowing.

He was moving, gliding, just slightly above a street, heading toward an enormous stone and steel structure. A stadium of some sort. Along each side of the street, crowds sank to the ground on their knees and bowed, arms outstretched toward him as he passed. They were cheering, no chanting, Abdulla the prophet of Allah, ruler of Islam, a descendant of Muhammad, death, and destruction to all infidels. As he entered, the stadium morphed into a colossal mosque with four massive, redwood tree sized, columns reaching up to the sky. A gold dome capped the center of the magnificent structure. The crowd followed closely behind him as he moved but stopped as he entered the mosque thru gigantic, wooden doors that slowly, and silently opened. As he glided toward the center, a long, ornate, silk rug rolled out along his path. On either side of the carpet, throngs of ghostly images sank to their knees and soundlessly mouthed his name. Then with a blinding flash of light, the angel appeared in front of him, flaming sword in its right hand and holding a crystal goblet in its left.

Abdulla stopped a few feet from the angel, opened his arms and attempted to speak. But his words wouldn't form. Then he felt, more than heard the voice. "Do not speak! Only listen!" The voice went on and on, louder and louder until at last the angel raised the sword, pointing it toward the center of the dome. A blue streak of energy arched downward enveloping the angel, and with deafening, unending thunder he was gone. Covering his ears to shut out the sound, Abdulla burst out of sleep and sat straight up on the couch-bed. Now fully awake, he reached over and turned off the screeching alarm clock.

"*Sabah alkhyr* Abdulla," Khalid said as he walked, fully dressed, into the living room. "I trust you had a good night's sleep." "Yes, *sabah alkhyr* to you as well" Abdulla replied, trying to shake out the sleep, and images from his dream and to regain consciousness.

Abdulla rolled out of bed and began getting dressed as Khalid heated water, for tea, in the suite's microwave. Seconds later, Saad walked into the living room dressed but carrying his shoes. As tea bags steeped in the heated water, the three men kneeled together and said their morning prayers. When they had finished praying, they sat around the small kitchen table and had a meager breakfast of the tea Khalid had brewed along with bread, cheese, and fruit they had purchased the night before. They thought it best not to have their morning meal in the tiny Days Inn dining room. Especially beginning today, the fewer hotel staff and guests that saw them together, the better. No use in taking any chances.

As they ate, Khalid reviewed their plans for the morning. "We will leave separately, with myself going first. Travel east on the inter-state for exactly one and one-half miles then take exit 217b. You will see a Home Depot just off to your right on the access road. I will find adjoining parking spaces near the access road side of the lot and wait for you there. As soon as you arrive, we will take the tops off of the crates, starting with Saad's shipment, verify the contents, and then transfer them to your van. By the time we have finished, you will appreciate bringing those battery powered drills. The tops of each crate are held in place by at least ten, long, wood screws. They are relatively easy to remove using the Phillips bit on an electric drill, but a pain in the ass if we had to do it with a screwdriver manually.

We will work together until each of our shipments are loaded into our respective vans. Then we will depart, again individually, Saad and I for our separate rendezvous points with our teams, and Abdulla for his trip back to Washington. If there are no questions or comments, I will be on my way. Give me a five-minute head start then Saad and then Abdulla." Khalid took a final sip of tea, picked up his bag, and left the room.

The drive to the Home Depot took less time than he had expected. During breakfast, it had occurred to Abdulla to tell Saad and Khalid that the voice was no longer confined to his dreams. He heard it almost constantly now. Usually just a murmur in the background, like overhearing indistinct conversations in a crowd. But sometimes it was loud, occasionally unbearably loud. However, he hadn't said anything. Maybe it was best they didn't know. Or at least any more than they already knew.

Abdulla turned off on exit 217b and onto the access road heading east. The Home Depot was on his right, about one hundred meters down the road. He spotted the two vans as soon as he pulled into the parking lot. They were parked so that the rear of one vehicle faced the rear of the other, about six feet apart. Kahlid's rear doors were open, and the two men were inside, apparently already at work on the crates. Abdulla parked next to Khalid, grabbed his tool bag, got out and walked to the rear of the van.

The lid to one of the wooden crates had already been removed. Saad and Khalid were gleefully digging into its contents like children during *Eid Al-Fitr*. Packed inside the container was five, neatly stitched, canvas vests. Each vest had two rows of pockets which held what appeared to be blocks of Semtex, eight blocks in each row. Each block was linked to its neighbor by a short length of detonation cord connected to a blasting cap which was embedded in the center of the Semtex. As they quickly inspected the vests, Khalid commented, "apparently our North Korean suppliers do not adhere to the same safety standards as the rest of the world.

Shipping these suicide vests pre-configured with blasting caps could have been disastrous. Semtex itself is exceptionally stable and safe in its own right. Like its American counterpart, C-4, it can even be burned without causing an explosion. During Vietnam, GI's routinely dismantled Claymore mines removed the C-4 and used small balls of it to heat their rations. It normally requires some type of detonator, like a blasting cap, to cause it to explode. Regardless, the vests seem to be configured properly and will no doubt do the job they are intended for when the firing mechanism is pressed and released."

Khalid then reattached the top of the crate and Abdulla, and Saad picked it up and slid it into the back of Saad's van. The three men continued their task, opening each box, verifying the contents, and then loading it into the applicable van.

Because of its combined weight, Abdulla's shipment was packed into four separate crates. One contained the long mortar tube and its attached bipod leg assembly. Another held the mortar's base plate, and one, the heaviest, included five, high explosive, shells. The last, and smallest of all the crates contained the mortar's GPS tracking system computer.

A smaller, square case, was packed with ten *Baek-Du San*, nine millimeter, pistols and boxes of ammunition. Abdulla took two, one for himself and one for his mortar team. One other crate contained individual blocks of Semtex, rolls of detonation cord, blasting caps, and a dozen press and release triggers. The remaining five crates were identical. Each was about six feet long, eighteen inches in height, and eighteen inches wide. Khalid removed the top from one of them.

Inside, surrounded by styrofoam packing pellets, was a long, OD green, fiberglass tube with two pistol grips. It was the latest DPRK shoulder-fired, surface to air missile, an SA-20.

Thanks to the battery powered drills and adrenaline-fueled motivation; the three men completed their task in less than twenty minutes. The shipment of explosives and weapons were distributed to Abdulla, Khalid, and Saad, and packed into their vans, according to their assigned attack plans. They were now ready to travel to their rendezvous points. But before they did, Abdulla called a huddle.

"Saad, Khalid, the beginning of the end of the infidel's supremacy is in sight. We know well the legend of the mighty Phoenix. It lived for five hundred years and then it would burst into flames and be consumed by fire. But from the ashes, a young, new Phoenix would arise. This is an apt analogy. Except it will be the infidel who is consumed by fire and it will be the new Islamic caliphate, a new world order, that arises from the ashes. And we my brothers, will be the instruments of this transformation.

As we slept last night, I was once again visited by the archangel. All of heaven is pleased with the mission on which we are embarking. Allah will guide and protect us. The time is almost upon us. The men we have trained will soon join the other martyred souls in heaven. A magnificent reward awaits them. And you too will be rewarded, both here and when your soul leaves your physical body. Before we go our separate ways, I want to say thank you from the very bottom of my heart. Thank you for your faith, thank you for your devotion to Islam, thank you for your courage. But most of all, thank you for being my friend and confidant.

THE ENEMY OF MY ENEMY

Khalid, your mission is just a few weeks away. Once the Americans have their senseless presidential election they, or at least half of them, will be in a state of euphoria. Three weeks later your team will slam them into the dirt." Khalid smiled at a mental image of a jet, and its passengers, smashing into the end of an airport runway. "You must purchase your ticket for a return flight to Riyadh right away. Plan to drive to Montreal and leave from there. There is little doubt that the FAA will shut down American civilian airspace, at least temporarily, as soon as they learn that five planes have been blown up during takeoff. Of course, our spoofed messages, before and after, will direct the blame toward North Korea. But we should count on airport security being even tighter than it was following nine eleven.

Saad, the same thing goes for you. Plan your return flight for Christmas morning. The Americans will be in a complete state of shock after five of their churches are blown apart. It will be all over the news, and they will be pointing fingers, trying to lay blame, one faction against the other. The police will be running around like roaches, at least in your target cities. But airport security will not be greatly increased if at all. Regardless, get out of here. Go back home and wait for my signal. Once my task is complete, I too will return, and we will begin the second and last, phase of our mission.

CHAPTER 20

The *Musudan-ri* missile launch site is in the remote northeast corner of Hamgyong Province. During the Japanese occupation, the area was known as *Taep'o-dong* from which the North Korean Taepodong rockets take their name. Even by North Korean standards, the area was at best austere and forbidding. The weather was brisk with highs in the mid-forties. The bone-chilling winter was over a month away. The missile test compound was built in the center of a large forest surrounded by small vegetable farms and terraced rice paddies. It was visible only to the prying eyes of the low-earth orbit (LEO) spy satellites circling one hundred and twenty miles above. The latest American KH-14 series satellite has a resolution powerful enough to determine the brand of cigarettes a soldier is smoking when he is walking guard at Musudan-ri; a practice which would garner him six months forced labor. Although the orbital paths of these satellites are highly classified, the DPRK military is keenly aware of their capabilities.

For this reason, they take extraordinary measures to conceal activities at the launch compound. Much of the complex is hidden underground in an elaborate system of caves and interconnecting tunnels. Massive concrete colored camouflage nets are mounted on towers encircling the main and alternate launch pads.

These nets disguise the missiles as they are being assembled before being launched.

Today was an exception to the normal level of concealment and security. Camouflage nets had been removed, and a Hwasong-16, the pinnacle of North Korea's ICBM technology, mounted on its sixteen wheel transport vehicle stood in the center of the main launch pad. Unlike its predecessor, the Hwasong-16 was a solid-fueled weapon capable of being launched within minutes rather than the hours required of its liquid-fueled cousin. Aside from its propellant system, it was physically identical to the Hwasong-15. This allowed it to be mounted, with very few modifications, on the same, highly mobile, launch vehicle. It was also capable of producing nearly one hundred tons of thrust giving it the ability to deliver a fifteen hundred kilo payload to any point on the globe.

There was a single gravel-topped road leading from a larger, but virtually deserted paved road to the launch compound. Typically there were only a few military trucks or OD green sedans moving to and from the heavily guarded front, and only, gate of the launch site. Never any civilian vehicles of any kind. However, for the past several hours there appeared to be a constant stream of vans and even a large bus moving down the road and thru the gate. The Norks were getting ready to put on a show.

Except for regularly scheduled and highly choreographed parades and annual displays of live artillery fire, the general public or foreign press was never allowed to witness military exercises. Today was to be an exception to this rule.

Bleachers had been erected a mere two kilometers away from the ominous looking missile. DPRK television crews had been stationed inside three shielded, concrete bunkers less than two hundred meters away. The bleachers were packed with military brass and high-level government civilian employees. In an unprecedented gesture, the two representatives of the Neutral Nations Supervisory Commission, NNSC, a Swiss and a Swedish General Officer, were invited to attend. These two men and their staff of four men each are stationed on the South Korean side of the DMZ living in cabins less than three meters from the North Korean border.

The NNSC was established in 1953 and charged with monitoring the Korean conflict cease-fire agreement. The NNSC had initially included representatives from Czechoslovakia and Poland, who were to live on the DPRK side of the DMZ. However, after the collapse of communism in Eastern Europe the DPRK government expelled these representatives leaving the task of monitoring the cease-fire agreement to the Swiss and Swedish representatives. However, they aren't allowed access to North Korean ports or facilities and thus have a mission which is impossible to achieve despite being contractually obligated to do so. Just one more, small, example of the absurdity of trying to deal with the hermit kingdom.

Two officers from the Syrian Arab Air Force were in attendance. The logic behind there invitation was twofold. First and foremost, it was to show off North Korean military prowess to what most of the world considered an equally distasteful dictatorship. The second reason was that over the last four years Syria had purchased tons of materials for the production of chemical weapons. This was one of the few sources of trade income from one of the few countries that bought anything from North Korea. The chemical weapons business promised, at least somewhat, the possibility of opening a pipeline for the "under sanctions" sale of other, even more, nefarious weapons and black market goods. DPRK officials had also invited a small delegation from China and Russia to attend today's launch. Without providing an explanation, both countries had declined the offer. This did not arouse any concern or suspicion from the North Koreans who considered a lack of diplomacy and goodwill to be normal behaviors.

In the U.S. and throughout the region, Intelligence Analysts observed the activities and launch preparations using streaming images from spy satellites. They concluded this was another test of the Hwasong-16's range and targeting capabilities. They were wrong.

This version of the DPRK's ICBM arsenal was already capable of hitting a target anywhere on earth. Since the Hwasong-16 was mounted and fired from a wheeled vehicle, it could be transported to and launched from virtually anywhere in North Korea. And its solid fuel propulsion system would allow it to do so in a matter of minutes.

No one in the bleachers or viewing the preparations knew it but today's launch was designed to test the miniaturization and reentry capability its warhead. For the last several years the North Korean's had mainly focused on the development of missiles, their guidance systems, and the mechanics of building nuclear weapons. Up until recently, they had placed scant little effort into solving the problems caused by reentry heat. When a warhead re-enters the earth's atmosphere at nearly thirty thousand kilometers per hour, its exterior could potentially reach a temperature of eleven thousand degrees centigrade. This would essentially evaporate the warhead long before it reached its target. For the past two years, DPRK scientists had been working frantically to address the problems caused by this phenomenon. Previous warhead designs had proven partially successful. There was widely positive anticipation that the design of the dummy warhead sitting on top of the Hwasong-16 would resolve this final, nagging, problem. This would make the DPRK a nuclear force to be reckoned with on a global scale, not just a regional bully. For this reason, today's test was a matter of national pride. Everyone who was even remotely involved knew that it had better go off without a hitch.

The Hwasong-16 was scheduled for liftoff at 2300 hours local time. For some long-forgotten reason, large-scale missile tests were always planned for the late evening. Some said this was for security reasons although daylight or darkness made little difference to the ever-present spy satellites. Others implied but never, ever, said it was merely because the Supreme Leader enjoyed seeing the spectacle created by a night launch. Regardless, this was when they were staged.

The Supreme Leader arrived by helicopter at 2145 hours. Two sedans were there to meet him and the two Army generals who were his constant companions when making appearances such as this. There was also another television news crew who would follow the Supreme Leader and his entourage, filming every fake smile and every wave of the hand to unseen and nonexistent, onlookers. Careful observers would note that the Supreme Leader never smiled unless he was looking directly at the camera or knew he was being videoed. If a camera crew mistakenly captured his normal stone-faced expression, that section of the video was quickly, and permanently, edited out upon their return to the studio. Typically, sounds of cheering and music would be dubbed over the video footage before it was shown to the public. Today's news footage would never be broadcast.

The Supreme Leader was driven to the bleachers which were now packed shoulder to shoulder with Korean military and civilian dignitaries and the few foreign guests. At a signal from a female Army officer, inconspicuously tucked out of the TV camera's line of sight, the crowd stood up, cheering and clapping as the Supreme Leader exited the sedan. Another officer discreetly guided him to a podium sat up in front of the bleachers. As he stepped behind the podium, the audience sat back down in perfect unison. It was 2200 hours.

The Supreme Leader began what would become a fifty-five-minute speech. Starting first with extravagant praise for DPRK scientists and military leadership. He quickly transitioned into a diatribe against the Americans, Japan, and the puppet South Korean government. He went on to say that today's test of the Hwasong-16 would put the entire world on notice. The DPRK was now, or soon would be a full-fledged nuclear power. It was no longer relegated to just homeland defense or enemies in or around the Pacific. Its nuclear arsenal now included multi-megaton fusion weapons. And the Hwasong-16 would allow them to deliver one or more of these so-called hydrogen bombs to any city in the United States.

The North Korean members of the audience sat ramrod straight, never taking their eyes off the Supreme Leader, paying rapt attention to his every word, and speaking not a word to one another during his oration. Most of the audience had heard stories of the Army officer who, years ago, had dozed off while the dictator was speaking. The officer had been executed by a firing squad using anti-aircraft machine guns. And his family sentenced to twenty years of forced labor at one of the scores of prison camps located throughout the country. North Korea had a "three generation punishment rule." If someone is convicted of a crime and executed or sent to prison, the entire immediate family and two following generations would be imprisoned as well. From that perspective, the officer's family got off relatively light. For whatever reason, whenever the Supreme Leader was speaking, or even within sight, the audience appeared to be more like robots than human. Finally, the Supreme Leader concluded his speech with a promise to destroy the Americans in nuclear fire and biological pestilence if sanctions against the DPRK weren't lifted.

When he was finished speaking, the Supreme Leader turned and began walking off the stage. The audience immediately stood and, except the Swedish and Swiss representatives, started clapping and cheering. Not with the joy and exuberance any other group of people in any other country might display for even a mildly motivating speaker, or grammar school play for that matter. But with a spirit inspired by fear and total ignorance of the world outside their highly guarded borders.

As he left the stage, the Supreme Leader was guided toward a large metal table, and five leather office chairs a few meters in front of the bleachers. He, his two Army General companions, and the senior scientists in charge of the ICBM and nuclear warhead programs respectively sat down to observe the launch. As soon as they were seated the general sitting to the right of the Supreme Leader gave a hand signal and the countdown began.

A large digital clock mounted on poles off to the right of the bleachers showed the time remaining. Large similarly mounted speakers also began booming the countdown when the clock indicated thirty seconds remained. At ten seconds, the Supreme Leader picked up the enormous pair of binoculars lying directly in front of him and started looking at the missile. Three, two, one; with a blinding eruption of light, fire exploded from the bottom of the Hwasong-16. The sound was deafening and continuous as the missile vaulted from its launch platform. The Supreme Leader jumped out of his seat and started clapping with the wild, unrestrained enthusiasm of a kid at a magic show. The Korean spectators immediately did the same. The two NNSC officers stood up as well, albeit slowly and they did not clap or cheer. They knew this was far from a joyous event.

Ten seconds after liftoff the fifty-ton missile was eight thousand feet in the air traveling at the Mach 1, the speed of sound. It was a perfect launch. Twenty seconds later it had climbed to thirty-eight thousand feet and was moving three times the speed of sound. Then things went wrong, terribly wrong.

Inside the missile's first stage, a newly designed, steerable exhaust nozzle started moving to one side. The nozzle was developed to allow the missile to make computer initiated directional changes in mid-flight. It was doing just that. Only these changes weren't in the instructions the DPRK scientists had programmed into the computer. The Hwasong-16 started turning to the northeast, directly toward Sapporo, Japan.

There was sheer panic inside the mission control bunker. Looking back and forth at an array of television screens then to computer monitors, the launch commander started screaming questions, then orders to bewildered technicians. Thirty-five seconds after liftoff the missile was flying at full speed, not straight up as intended but parallel to the sea below. Knowing the test was doomed the launch commander ordered a technician to destruct the Hwasong-16. The technician removed the safety cover from a control panel, then flipped the self-destruct switch. Nothing happened. He flipped it off, then on again. Still nothing. Then the missile started diving straight for the ocean at full speed. At one kilometer above the water, traveling more than four times the speed of sound, the missile exploded.

Neither the spectators in the bleachers nor the Supreme Leader witnessed the destruction of the Hwasong-16. It was out of their line of sight when it exploded. For several minutes the Supreme Leader was jubilant, smiling, clapping his chubby hands, and raising his arms upward victoriously. The crowd, still on their feet, were also clapping and cheering wildly. Then a landline telephone used to communicate with the control bunker before the launch, rang. One of the scientists answered it before the second ring. Those looking at the man's face saw his expression change in an instant from joy to terror. For several seconds he spoke with the person on the other end of the line then laid the phone on the table and tapped the General sitting next to him on the shoulder. The General turned curtly toward the scientist, clearly annoyed at the interruption, and the two had a brief, hushed, discussion. The General picked up the phone, spoke and then listened for a few seconds before thrusting it back to the scientist.

By now the Supreme Leader noticed the commotion out of the corner of his eye and turned toward the two men. The General bowed slightly and then coming as close as he dared whispered something to the Supreme Leader and the second general. The three men stopped their celebration, the General said something to one of the female officers and followed the Supreme Leader, whose smile had vanished, walking toward their sedan. The officer, displaying the composure of one who did not fully understand what was happening, announced to the spectators that today's demonstration was over. Everyone must follow their guides and load back onto the buses. There would be a price to pay for the missile's failure.

CHAPTER 21

November would prove to be one of the most infamously momentous months in the history of the United States. The year's hurricane season should have been drawing to a close. Instead, hurricane Valerie, after devastating the Cayman Islands, had slammed across Cuba and the Florida Keys. It was regaining strength as it hovered over the warm waters of the Gulf on a path that would take it directly across St. Petersburg. It had gone from a category four to a three after passing over Cuba. But it was predicted to regain its strength to category four again when it reached the west coast of Florida. Valerie was the fifth hurricane of the season and the third category four. In addition to marking the end of hurricane season, November was also presidential election month. Metaphorically speaking, there was also a political storm raging across the country.

The presidential candidates themselves had, at least initially, conducted themselves in a respectively civil manner. Especially when compared to the previous campaign which ushered in the, soon to be former, sitting POTUS. However, things erupted when the Republican candidate, by far the more conservative of the two, against his campaign advisors' recommendations, dropped a political bombshell in October. For the last two decades, the country had wrestled with three politically and emotionally polarizing issues. Eking into first place was the questions surrounding the second amendment. The overwhelming majority of conservatives maintained it was their constitutional, if not God-given, right to purchase and carry virtually any type of firearm. This included what was generally referred to as assault rifles and even the mechanisms which could convert them into automatic weapons. The infamous "bump stock." They also demanded the absolute minimum in government restrictions and registration requirements. Most liberals were lumped squarely on the other end of the continuum. They vocally maintained that it was never the founding father's intention to do more than to provide for a "well-regulated militia." They were firm in their belief that no one had a right, or need, to possess a weapon who sole purpose was to kill other homo sapiens. This continually simmering issue was brought to a boil with each mass murder which seemed to be increasing in ferocity and frequency.

The second most divisive issue du jour hovered around immigration and welfare. Conservatives could not separate the two. They screamed for strictly enforced, quota-based, legal immigration policies and iron-fisted control of U.S. borders. Or at least it's southern border. A multi-billion dollar barrier had served as a campaign platform for years. However, funding never materialized, and the U.S. Mexican border remained as porous as ever. Liberals argued that immigration, even when illegal, was, in fact, healthy and in the best interest of the U.S., Mexico, and other Central American countries. Nearly one hundred billion dollars are sent back to the relatives of Central American immigrants each year with over forty percent going to Mexico alone. It is a fact that Mexico is America's third largest trading partner. And the belief that immigrants perform jobs that U.S. workers do not want, or will not do is the backbone of pro-immigration arguments. Conservatives see an inextricable link between immigration and welfare abuse. Although, they are quick to point out that there is more than enough to go around in homegrown third and fourth generation food stamp, public housing, "baby momma" communities. They don't say it out loud, but they mean black.

Finally, in the Bronze position of political contentions is healthcare. It has long been a liberal position that all healthcare is a fundamental human right and that it should be managed, controlled, and paid for by the federal government. Since the majority of Democrats were left of center on the political-social continuum, this concept formed the crux of their platform on this issue. The overwhelming majority of conservatives and their Republican party took a polar opposite stance. To them, healthcare was like any other commodity. You worked, you paid for it, and you had total control over your choice of medical provider.

The Republican candidate had a solution that in his mind would address and begin to solve what he saw as causing many of the problems in the United States. It was his position that the principal problem with American society was an apathetic, politically ignorant, citizenry.

He was a physician and followed the same methodology in addressing nonmedical issues that he used in the operating room. He attempted to do a root-cause analysis and then address the core cause of a disease, or problem, rather than treating its symptoms. This worked with cancer, and it would work for society. You might prescribe a Tylenol to relieve a headache temporarily, but you treated the tumor causing the pain. One of his solutions was as radical as battlefield surgery. You did what you had to do to save the patient.

His plan called for an amendment to the United States Constitution itself. He, and subsequently his party, proposed changing the manner by which citizenship is granted. The 14h Amendment to the Constitution bestows citizenship to "all persons born or naturalized in the United States." The Republican candidate firmly believed that this carte blanche bestowing of the rights and privileges of citizenship, but no commensurate obligations or responsibility was the root of all social and political evil in the United States.

The Republican candidate proposed changing the 14th Amendment to read: "All persons born or naturalized in the United States and subject to the jurisdiction thereof, are eligible to apply for United States citizenship and the State wherein they reside upon their seventeenth birthday. To obtain citizenship, applicants must serve a minimum of two years of military, law enforcement, or congressionally approved public service and must take and successfully pass the official United States Citizenship Naturalization Test.

As if the modification to the 14th Amendment wasn't enough, he proposed constitutional changes that would; restrict the purchase, ownership, or possession of firearms to citizens; allow only citizens to vote in state or national elections; establish a national resident and visitor identification system; establish a nationwide electronic medical record.

It was widely accepted, by the mainstream media that when the Republican platform was officially announced there would be an uproar among the nation's Democrats and staunchly conservative supporters of the 2nd Amendment. There was some degree of wailing on both sides that comes with any change. Especially proposed changes in the Constitution, the very law of the land. However, the uproar wasn't nearly as dramatic and pervasive as predicted. The seemingly never-ending gun violence and the unwillingness of congressional leadership to do little more than offer "thoughts and prayers" had the mainstream public demanding action. And when a plan was finally proposed, even one as dramatic as the Republican presidential candidate, it fast gained voter approval. But not sufficient to swing the election.

A record sixty-one percent of registered voters turned out that first Tuesday of November. Overall, the race was amazingly close. Although it would take weeks to finalize the numbers for the popular vote they didn't matter. The Electoral College results gave the Democrats a 283 to 250 victory. Three electors voted for the sitting POTUS, despite his not even being a candidate, one vote went to UGA, the University of Georgia mascot, and, for the second time, one to Faith Spotted Eagle. The popular vote, over sixty-seven million for the Democratic candidate, and sixty-five million for the Republican were one of the closest ever recorded. Shortly after the west coast polls closed on Tuesday night, America had a new President-Elect, a Democrat.

The Republican candidate gave his concession speech shortly before midnight Pacific time. It was widely considered the most gracious and optimistic acknowledgments of defeat ever presented.

Watching alone from his living room in the White House, the sitting POTUS was anything but gracious and optimistic. Boiling, incessant, rage replaced his simmering anger. As he listened to the man he considered nothing more than a loser, and watched the saddened faces of his crowd of supporters; he began forming his own concession. And it wouldn't take the form of a speech.

CHAPTER 22

No one had ever seen the Supreme Leader in such a fit of rage. He started screaming the instant the doors closed on the sedan that drove him from the spectator area back to the waiting helicopter. He demanded the immediate execution of someone, everyone, that could be even remotely responsible for the failure. In an unusual display of bravado, his most trusted General cautioned against a purge that might set back progress on their nuclear armament program. This did not placate the Supreme Leader, but it did cause him to pause his rampage for a few heartbeats.

"You are correct," he said, "but someone has to pay. Arrest the wife and children of everyone who is responsible. Sentence them to hard labor equal to ten times the length of time it will require us to have a successful test of our warhead reentry vehicle. Ensure everyone on the program knows of the punishment. And let them know I was lenient. I will show no mercy the next time I am publicly humiliated." The wild, barely in control, look in the Supreme Leader's eyes, and the spittle at the corners of his mouth sent chills up the General's spine. And he had seen and caused unspeakable horrors.

A small group of Analysts huddled before a bank of monitors in one of the NSA buildings at Ft. Meade, Maryland. For the past ten hours, they had been monitoring activities at the Musudan-ri launch site. The KH-14 spy satellites were maneuvered into position earlier in the day and had been streaming amazingly clear, real-time video to the agency all day. The spooks were extremely interested in watching and recording today's launch of the Hwasong-16. Its solid fuel propulsion system represented an alarming advance in North Korean missile technology. They wanted to observe and catalog the time it took to set up and launch. Far more importantly, they wanted to see the new Hwasong-16 nose cone design.

Their concern increased based on what they saw. It was obvious that the North Koreans had been dramatically successful in their efforts to reduce the size of the nosecone. This was an indicator that they had also been able to reduce the size and weight of the warhead itself. The satellite's telescopic camera had also provided crystal clear images of the refractory material they were using to construct the nosecone's heat shields. This represented another cause for concern. The Hwasong-16's warhead appeared sheathed in an ablative heat shield using some unrecognizable ceramic material. This was an advanced design most likely provided by the Chinese.

The conclusion from their clandestine observations would be a highlighted entry in the President's Daily Briefing (PDB). The PDB is a top-secret document produced by the Director of National Intelligence and provided each morning to the POTUS and a small, highly select group of government officials. Between election day and inauguration it was also offered to the President-Elect. The PDB summarized information about covert CIA, NSA, and foreign intelligence agency activities and foreign and domestic threats. It was considered one of the most closely controlled documents in the world. The PDB was normally presented by a CIA Senior Analyst personally selected and groomed by the Director.

Tomorrow's PDB would state that the North Koreans were now technically capable of exploding a multi-megaton hydrogen bomb over any city in the United States. It had only been a matter of time before this capability became a reality. The combination of the solid fuel propulsion system, warhead miniaturization, and heat resistant nosecone had come together on the Hwasong-16. The North Korean threat was increasing logarithmically. They now had a virtually unstoppable nuclear package. The subsequent step would be mass production. All this information was gathered as the analysts observed the Hwasong-16 as it was transported and set up before its launch. The remainder of the show beamed from the satellite would be just entertainment. Then they saw the missile scream off course and explode in mid-air. Everyone in the room knew this was a game changer.

Just as planned, the first message came on Thursday, the day after the results of the presidential election were officially announced. It was transmitted from one of the two communication satellites the North Koreans had placed in orbit three years earlier.

"The peace-loving citizens of the Democratic People's Republic of Korea have patiently endured the slobbering dog injustices and aggressive abuses from the United States and its bootlicking lackeys far too long. The United States is at this moment given ten days to meet the following demands of the DPRK; 1. Lift all economic sanctions they and their allies have imposed on our country. 2. Immediately repay the DPRK monetary damages these sanctions have inflicted. These are conservatively estimated at twenty billion Euros. 3. Remove all military forces and close all bases everywhere on the Korean Peninsula, Japan, Guam and elsewhere in the Asian Pacific. If these demands are not met by the stated deadline all Americans, regardless of where they may be, will feel the awful wrath of the mighty DPRK. We will attack with every weapon at our disposal to include but not limited to our nuclear arsenal."

The message was transmitted on open channels and received by the U.S. Pacific Command, USPACOM, every intelligence agency monitoring station in the eastern hemisphere, and more than one billion Facebook users worldwide.

Various DPRK agencies which listened to USPACOM saw the message as well. However, their command and control communication were pitifully ineffective. This, combined with a fear of reprisal from speaking out, stymied upward and horizontal information flow. As a result, senior military leaders assumed the message came from the Supreme Leader's staff. Several of the Supreme Leader's closest advisors, whose duties included monitoring social media sources, congratulated him on sending such a bold and forceful demand. And his all-consuming ego and sense of self-importance prevented him from admitting he wasn't the source of the message or its content.

Unlike many of his predecessors, the POTUS received his daily briefing at 0730 every single day he was in Washington. With previous administrations, it was somewhat hit-or-miss, more of a weekly event despite its name and its significance. Not with this guy. As long as he had one finger on the trigger he wanted two other fingers on the pulse of national intelligence. Staff who would receive the PDB was at the president's discretion. This POTUS shared it with his Chief of Staff, the National Security Advisor, Secretary of State, FBI Director, the Secretary of Defense, and the Vice President.

A summary of the new Hwasong-16 warhead test was in the PDB less than eight hours after the missile exploded. Although his eyes were strangely glazed and seemed to be focused somewhere outside the Oval Office, the president's mind was racing. The Analyst went over the paragraph describing the missile's staging, launch, in-flight explosion and the CIA's blunt assessment of North Korea's ability to deliver a nuclear attack.

At the conclusion of the daily briefing, after everyone had grilled the CIA Director and the Analyst presenting the PDB, the

POTUS snapped out of his self-induced hypnotic state and began giving orders. Looking at his Chief of Staff, Abagail McKelvy, he growled "Abbie, set up a meeting in the White House Situation Room for 1300 today. I want everyone currently in this room plus the Chairman and the Joint Chiefs, Secretary of Homeland Security, and the Ambassador to the UN. Tell them to cancel whatever they have planned and to be there on time if not early." Without waiting for a reply or discussion, he turned to the Secretary of Defense. "Dennis, take us to DEFCON 4." More than anything said all morning, or in recent memory for that matter, this statement got everyone's attention.

DEFCON, or defense readiness condition, is a numerically graduated system used by the U.S. government and its armed forces to describe states of wartime preparedness. DEFCON 5 is the lowest or normal state of readiness.

DEFCON 4 calls for a heightened state of alertness and puts the military on notice. When changed to DEFCON 3 the Air Force is ready to mobilize in fifteen minutes. At DEFCON 2 the armed forces are prepared for nuclear war. The entire military is set to deploy and engage with the enemy in less than six hours. The United States has only been placed at this level of readiness once. In 1962, during the Cuban Missile Crisis, the Strategic Air Command, SAC, was ordered to DEFCON 2. All out nuclear war is either occurring or is imminent at DEFCON 1. At or before this stage, select members of congressional leadership are evacuated to secret secure locations.

In 1958 work began on the construction of a 1,100-bed bomb shelter underneath the Greenbriar Hotel Resort in White Sulphur Springs, West Virginia. This was designed to house Congress, the Supreme Court, and the President in the event of a nuclear attack. Its existence was kept secret for thirty years until exposed by a Washington Post article in 1992. After the Greenbriar's secret was revealed, the shelter was abandoned, and construction began on a series of similar sites.

Mount Weather, Virginia and Raven Rock in Pennsylvania are but two of over thirty locations within two hundred miles of Washington, D.C., designed to provide shelter following a nuclear attack. Wartime survival plans call for the President and Vice President to be evacuated to physically separate, secret, locations. All critical government agencies will have representatives moved to the various wartime sites. All sites are connected via redundant classified communication facilities. Plans have been developed which will maintain short-term emergency services until the government, or what is left of it, can be reconstituted. These plans are rehearsed annually using uniquely designated military personnel as stand-ins for various government officials.

The room was silent. Going from one DEFCON to another was serious, serious business. The POTUS had never initiated it. And never unilaterally. Changes in readiness, which were rare indeed, were always made at the direction of the Chairman of the Joint Chiefs of Staff, or the Secretary of Defense, and only after seeking counsel from senior military leadership or cabinet-level intelligence chiefs. Everyone in the room knew this departure from the norm was no reason for celebration. Weekend plans evaporated, and speculations ran wild in anticipation of what the 1300 session would bring.

At a nearly subconscious level, the President's mind was running at full throttle. What had started as a knee-jerk reaction was turning into an embryonic but rapidly forming plan of action. Fueled by personal frustrations and white-hot rage from his humiliation during the Republican National Convention he slid faster and faster down the slope of sanity. Despite his eroding emotional state, the President's mental abilities were strangely sharper and acuter than ever. It was as if one part of his brain had flipped over to an aggressive, primitive, state and other parts were supercharged; running on unspent adrenaline burning energy.

The POTUS didn't become the POTUS because he was weak or indecisive. He had no intention of going "gently into that good night." He was going out with the explosive force of a Krakatoa. His name would go down in history. Not just another president. He would be remembered as the president who changed the world. Like Lincoln, or FDR, or JFK. He wanted his personal eternal flame, and by God, he knew how he was going to get it.

Abdulla was responsible for the actual content of the first message. As he had directed in their Dallas telephone call, he had sent its verbiage to Mustafa via Dmail. Mustafa had subsequently inserted it into a DPRK satellite communication data stream. Abdulla was ecstatic with Mustafa's accomplishments. Not only had Mustafa, and his team been able to spoof North Korean communications, they had destroyed their most advanced ICBM and brought worldwide disgrace to their demigod dictator.

His Allah inspired strategy was coming together piece by piece. In just a few days his warriors would make their first strike against the Great Satan. A few more spoofed messages on the heels of the coming terrorist attacks and the United States would lash out at North Korea. They would probably destroy most of the country and kill millions by doing so. But so what. The godless heathens were like roaches. They needed to be eradicated. Besides, their elimination was part of Allah's plan.

Then the Chinese would attack the Americans and the Russians. They would destroy one another, riding the world of non-believers. Then the army of the Caliphate could easily enslave the Israelis. His initial plans had been to destroy Israel, but with deeper consideration, he had decided it would better serve himself and the caliphate to have a race of slaves. The thought thrilled him to no end. Opening up his laptop, Abdulla began pounding out a Dmail to Mustafa with copies to Saad and Khalid. "Mustafa, you are a true genius. I can't begin to tell you how pleased I am with your performance. Destroying the Hwasong-16 was absolutely amazing, and taping into DPRK communication satellites was an unbelievable accomplishment. But including one billion Facebook users, one-seventh of the earth's population truly exceeded my wildest expectations. Trust me; you will be rewarded when I ascend to the throne of the coming caliphate. But I don't want you to have to wait. I am going to deposit five hundred thousand Euros into your account immediately. Please share it with your team as you deem fit. In the interim, do whatever you need to do to be ready to send another message to the same recipients on the American Thanksgiving holiday. I will compose it and send you the verbiage within the week. Check your Dmail several times each day. Again, thank you. *Allah, Akbar.*"

At precisely 1300 the President, his Chief of Staff, and the Vice President entered the Whitehouse Situation Room. Except for the United States Ambassador to the United Nations, who was on an official visit to France, all those who the POTUS had ordered to attend was in their seats. As the President walked in everyone stood up, the Joint Chief attendees snapping to attention. Taking the chair at the head of the long polished wooden table, with the Vice President sitting to his right and the Chief of Staff to his left, the President gave the customary "please be seated." The monitor mounted in the corner at the end of the room read "Mic OFF" indicating that this session would not be recorded. Before entering, everyone had turned off their cell phones and checked them with the Administrative Assistant at the main entrance of the Situation

Room. Wasting no time on superfluous salutations or preliminary discussions the POTUS began.

"Folks I fear that the day we have all been dreading but that we knew would eventually arrive is here. During this morning's PDB I was reminded that our sanctions are having little to no effect on reducing the nuclear threat posed by the North Koreans. Everyone in this room knows that. Their people are starving, yet their military capabilities are growing. Faster than ours for Christ's sake. But that nagging fact, that thorn in my foot, wasn't what got my attention.

The thing that concerns me the most is the knowledge, the certainty, that if we don't do something now that nothing will be done for months. It is crystal clear that we don't have months. I will be leaving office in less than three months and that *Kumbaya* singing Democrat and his socialist, do-gooder buddies will be making Smores in the Oval Office. All the while the Norks are beefing up their nuclear and biological arsenals and drawing big red targets on their war maps, right on top of Washington, San Francisco, and Tokyo. We can't let that happen. I'm not going to let that happen. We can't continue to "kick the can" to the next Administration. I would normally have said to the next generation, but if we don't do something, and do it now, there won't be a "next generation."

As most of you know, the United States has long adhered to a "qualified no first use" nuclear weapons policy. That means we have pledged not to use nuclear weapons against governments that do not possess a nuclear capability themselves. North Korea no longer falls into that category. They've got the bomb, and now they have the capability of laying it on the White House lawn. Everyone in this room knows that the guy who will be sitting in this chair come January is perfectly willing to roll over and let that happen. Well, not me! I am planning to make a pre-emptive strike before those lunatics get any stronger." The POTUS paused. There wasn't a sound in the room. No one said a word or even breathed. Then he continued.

"Last month I directed Secretary Pitts and his team at the State Department to come up with a proposal, a post-war treaty was my exact words, which we could live with once we bombed those fuckers back to the stone age." The President's formality while referring to the Bulldog subconsciously underscored the seriousness of the meeting. Although, no one in the room felt the least bit otherwise.

"They developed what I consider a brilliant plan. Not exactly a treaty in the literal sense. A far more relevant, workable, and politically acceptable strategy. Then they turned around and sold the concept, covertly of course, to the Chinese and Russians. Robert, to set the stage for the rest of our meeting I would like for you to give the group a thirty thousand foot overview of the AIFTU charter. You can start by telling them what the acronym means. Once you have finished, I will share the next steps in my strategy. I do ask that everyone hold their questions, and undoubtedly you will have a few, until the end. Otherwise, we will be here all night. Robert, you have the floor."

For the next twenty minutes, the Bulldog walked the group thru the AIFTU charter's development and his subsequent meeting with the Chinese and Russian representatives. As the POTUS had directed, no one asked any questions, but they were furiously scribbling notes to themselves.

"Thank you, Mr. Secretary. As you know, last night the DPRK attempted a test of their most advanced nuclear warhead delivery system. The CIA is convinced that the nosecone reentry vehicle will work just fine. It should since it appears to have the same design and incorporate the same heat shield materials as the Chinese warheads. Which of course were copied from ours. Far more worrisome is that its design reflects what appears to be their success in reducing the size and weight of their fusion weapons. That was the last straw. And even though the Hwasong-16 blew up in mid-flight, they turned around and threatened us again. This time with the most aggressive, most belligerent language, they have ever used. But that's not the clincher.

Somehow they were able to post their threat, along with a ridiculous caricature of me cowering before their "Supreme Leader," on every Facebook account on the planet. We've asked Zuckerberg to have it removed immediately, but the damage has been done. So that's it. They've threatened to destroy us.

In 1950 Chief Justice Fred Vinson and the Supreme Court, ruled that the president did not have to wait until an attempt to destroy the government was executed before it interrupts seditious plots. These actions pass the clear and present danger test. These idiots intend to destroy our country and I'm not going to stand for it." The President was on his feet now, pounding his right fist into his left hand, barely under control. "Buckle up folks; we're going to war."

No one spoke. No one moved. Every eye was glued to the POTUS as he paused ever so briefly. His gaze shifted from one person to the next, its intensity ramming his message home. The only sound was the slight hum of the air conditioner.

The President sat back down and, turning to the Secretary of Defense, continued. "Dennis, I want you and the Joint Chiefs, to make whatever modifications are necessary to our Korean Peninsula first strike plans. I know the carrier groups and most subs are on DEFCON 4 standby but start moving any remaining assets into position; lock and load. I want you to brief this group and me as soon as you are ready. That means on or before the first of December. It's imperative that we do this, and everything else the group discusses during this meeting, without alerting our friends in the south. Or Tokoyo, Guam, or anywhere else for that matter. We sure as hell don't need any rumors to get out and be forced to deal with riots or protests in the streets of Seoul.

Now I am going to contradict what I just said." Turning to the Secretary of State the President said 'Bulldog, this would be the appropriate time to suggest that your Chinese and Russian counterparts bring their North Korean Ambassador staff home for a visit. You decide on how to recommend a cover story for doing so. They might want to do it under the guise of the expanded sanctions we are going to slap on them for the latest Hwasong-16 test. This would give them a good excuse, and they should be able to pull it off without unduly raising the Nork's suspicions. Frankly, I don't give a rat's ass how or if they do it. But you made a deal and we damn sure don't want them going back on their agreement not to get involved.

Folks, we have gone over war preparation scenarios in the past. Those were dress rehearsals. This is live on Broadway. There won't be any cuts or retakes and damn few mid-stream corrections. We've got to get it right the first time. I know the Joint Chiefs are itching to tell me that battle plans change the instant the first shot is fired. I'm aware of that, but we are going to make that "shock and awe" from the nineties look like a bedtime story.

Now, two other things before I open the floor for comments, questions, or suggestions. First, we must pull all of this off with the absolute minimum collateral damage. Especially south of the 38th Parallel. Dennis this unenviable task falls squarely in your lap. I know you and the Joint Chiefs have a strategy for doing so. But I want to go on record as saying that minimizing civilian bloodshed is our top priority.

Second, the instant that the manure hits the props I want everyone in this room to report to their assigned shelters. Kissing your loved ones goodbye and heading off to Weather Mountain, or wherever your classified destination may be, is going to be the hardest thing you have ever done. I know that. But when I press that button, the focus of our duty suddenly shifts from family to country. That's all I have for today; we will reconvene as soon as the Joint Chiefs finalize their plan of attack. I will open things up for discussion but keep in mind; our course is set."

CHAPTER 23

Camile Brooks rolled out of her Jackson, Mississippi hotel room bed at 0530 Wednesday morning. She felt great. In fact, she had been on top of the world for the past seven months.

Camile, or Cammy as her husband, mother, and closest friends called her, had graduated from San Jose State University when she was twenty-two. She had earned a BS in Aviation with a minor in Industrial Technology along with her Airline Transport Pilot, ATP, certificate. Cammy had graduated in the top ten percent of her class. She had been interviewed by Delta Airlines during the first semester of her senior year at SJSU and was offered a job immediately after graduation.

Although pleased with herself, she had a nagging feeling that at least one reason she was hired was that she was a she. Like every other large corporation, Delta was under constant pressure to balance the racial, gender, and ethnic composition of their workforce. Especially at senior management and skilled labor levels. Cammy was breaking into an overwhelmingly male-dominated profession. But her sex only got her foot in the door. Her knowledge, flying skills, and leadership took it from there. She also had a healthy dose of ambition and determination. She took every pilot management course Delta had to offer and got in as much simulator time as she could squeeze into her schedule. After working for Delta for only four years, and logging 3,500 hours as a co-pilot, she had been placed into the company's Command Course.

Cammy completed the Command Course, logged another 1,000 hours of flight time, and in April at the age of 28 was promoted to Captain. This was almost unheard of within the industry, and it had never happened before at Delta. She was the youngest Captain in the largest, most well respected, airline in the world. Cammy was almost always chipper and in a good mood. Since her promotion, she had been insufferably cheerful. And her mood was contagious. You just couldn't be sad or down in the dumps when Cammy was around. But her promotion wasn't the source of her joy today.

Yesterday, just when she thought she couldn't be any happier, she had learned that she was pregnant. She and her husband Josh had been trying for nearly a year without even a hint of success. Her period, which normally appeared like clockwork, had been late. During her last layover, she had bought a home pregnancy test at the CVS just down the street from her hotel. These relatively inexpensive kits are designed to tell if urine contains a human chorionic gonadotropin, hCG, hormone. After dipping the indicator stick in a cup of her urine, her $8.99 kit responded with two bright red lines. This was the "you're pregnant" sign she had been praying for. She had followed this up with a visit to her OBGYN who, before she had left for the trip she was on, confirmed the diagnosis. She hadn't told Josh yet. She would surprise him with the news tonight when she got home. Knowing Josh, he would be starting dinner and would offer her a glass of wine as soon as she walked thru the door. She would demurely decline and say, "you know I can't drink when I'm pregnant."

Cammy and Josh had met during her Junior year at SJSU. Josh was a first-year graduate student majoring in physics with his eye on getting his Ph.D., assuming he could wrangle a grant. He didn't want to go any deeper in student loan debt. Josh had grown up in Marin County, just north of San Francisco. Their personalities were nothing alike. Where Cammy was hard-charging and aggressive, Josh was laid back, introspective, and painfully shy.

He was also brilliant, Stephen Hawkins level brilliant. Cammy and Josh had both been members of SJSU's Canoeing and Kayaking club, and it was on a club outing on the Marin section of the Russian River that they got to know each other. Somehow, they had ended up as partners in a two-man canoe. Both were skilled paddlers in their own right, and as it turned out, they worked "hand in glove" as a team. Without thinking about it, Cammy took the rear seat on the canoe, and thus command, and also without thinking about it, Josh was more than happy to oblige her. So, it was from that point forward.

A week after they returned from the canoe trip Cammy called Josh and invited him to a sorority party. She had some apprehensions that Josh may not fit in with some of her loud, obnoxious, sisters. She was pleasantly surprised. Stunned actually. Josh joined in their conversations and held his own even during the most superficial and girlish chatter. However, it was when the music started that she was completely blown away. As it turned out, Josh was an incredibly good dancer.

After the party, they started dating on a regular basis and were married in June, right after her graduation. Delta designated Denver as Cammy's home base, and she moved there in July. Josh took advantage of Delta's family member travel perk and commuted from San Jose to Denver two or three weekends a month for the next year while he finished his Master of Science degree. The day after he received his diploma Josh packed everything he owned into a U-Haul trailer and moved to Denver. In less than three months he received a grant from the University of Denver's Division of

Natural Sciences and Mathematics and began working on his Ph.D. In August they bought their first home, an older, three bedroom stucco with a spectacular view, albeit distant, of the peaks of the Rockies near Golden Gate Canyon State Park. Things were falling into place. He and Cammy were obscenely happy.

After showering, Cammy got dressed in her immaculately pressed black pants, dazzling white shirt, and four stripped Delta Airlines Captain's jacket. Even after seven months, she was still thrilled and proud when she was wearing her uniform and checked herself out in the mirror. She finished packing her suitcase, grabbed her pilot case, and headed down to the lobby to catch the shuttle to Jackson's Medgar Evers Airport. On Tuesday Cammy had flown the Denver, Dallas, Jackson route and as always stayed the night at the Howard Johnson Inn on Airport Road. Not the fanciest digs by a long shot but it was clean, convenient, and apparently Delta's low bidder crew hotel.

You could see the tire marks on one of the two runways from the window in her room. Much to Cammy's chagrin, despite the hotel's attempt at soundproofing, you could also hear jets taking off up until late at night. Today, she would fly the same route in reverse. Assuming no delays in Dalla, she would arrive in Denver in the late afternoon. But today was the day before Thanksgiving. It was the airlines busiest day of the year. Every seat on every flight would be booked. But Cammy loved it. Once the doors closed, she would be the one responsible for getting folks home for the holidays. Despite the routine of having done this for years, it still gave her a warm feeling inside. In the hotel lobby, she hooked up with her First Officer and one of the Attendants that would be on her flight. Together they and two hotel guests boarded the shuttle for the ten-minute ride to the Airport's departure gate lobby.

Akram Al-Sayed was not so good-humored when he got out
of bed. Akram was never in a good mood. Over the years he had
learned to put on a normal albeit never smiling face. Inside he was
filled with hate and loathing toward infidels. Especially American
infidels. Akram was just a baby when his parents immigrated to the
United States from the war-ravaged slums of Yemen.

Although educated and trained as a Pharmacist, his father
and the rest of his family had been forced to live like rats before the
all-out civil war in Yemen. As a clandestine supporter of al-Qa'ida
in the Arabian Peninsula (AQAP) his father had come to the attention of an organization affiliated with the MA. It was through this
connection that the family was able to obtain refugee status and
immigrate to the United States. They had no idea that this immigration support was part of the MA's master plan to implant radical
Islamic sympathizers throughout Europe and North America. The
small Muslim professional community in Jackson, almost all physi-
cians and college professors, had helped Akram's father get a job at
the sprawling University of Mississippi Medical Center (UMMC).

Akram had been homeschooled until he turned thirteen
at which time he entered the ninth grade at Jackson Preparatory
School. Generally speaking, minorities faired quite well at Jackson
Prep. First of all, you had to be smart and extremely well off to ever
set foot in a classroom. Annual tuition, not including books and
incidentals, was well over $20,000. This put everyone on a more or
less equal playing field. Then there was the fact that everyone, staff,
and students, seemed to go out of their way to welcome minorities
and assimilate them into the Jackson Prep culture. This didn't work
with Akram. He was bitter and spiteful from the day he started until
the day he graduated. No one cheered, not even his family when he
walked across the stage to accept his diploma.

Now Akram was a third-year Law student at Mississippi College in Clinton, MS. His disposition had not improved, at all. Four months ago, after arriving home from a late afternoon class, his father had taken him to a park near downtown Jackson. There they met a Saudi who introduced himself simply as Mr. Black.

After this terse introduction, his father said: "Akram, the time has come for you to pledge to Islam and al-Qa'ida." Politely raising the palm of his hand toward Akran's father Mr. Black interrupted saying "Akram, we know you are still in College and that you may feel you are not yet ready to commit to our cause. However, it is not for us to decide when we are ready. It is the cause of Islam that determines when it is ready for us. Akram, that time has come. You are needed. You will be asked not only to serve but to make the ultimate commitment, the ultimate sacrifice for Islam and the glory of Allah. Tell me now! Are you ready? Can you accept the tremendous responsibility of taking the lead in what may well be the most important battle the warriors of Islam have ever been called to fight?"

Akram was overwhelmed physically and emotionally by the force of Mr. Black's impassioned speech. Putting his arm around his father's shoulder and filled with emotions he had never experienced Akram shot back; "I am! Take me, send me, use me in Allah's service." Mr. Black shook Akram's hand, smiled a joyless smile, and said: "your training will begin soon my brother."

Two weeks later, Akram took delivery of a white, late model Ford F150. The truck was one of several loaded on a long-haul, vehicle transport tractor trailer. Akram had received a call arranging the time and place for delivery on a disposable cell phone he had received from Mr. Black. He met the driver in the parking lot of a Walmart near I-20 on the west side of Jackson. The driver asked for Akram's license, verified his name, and then had him inspect the F150 for scratches and damages. Once he had done so, he had

Akram sign an inspection and delivery document, gave him a yellow carbon copy, handed him the keys to the truck, and left without additional discussion.

Following Mr. Black's instructions, Akram unlocked and opened the F150's glovebox. Inside was an envelope which contained $1500 in $10's and $20's and two more disposable cell phones. The following week Akram received a call from Mr. Black directing him to travel to a location in West Central Texas. He wasn't given an address, just longitude and latitude coordinates which he was instructed to plug into the truck's GPS. He was also given a specific day and time he should arrive and instructions to plan on being there for three days.

Akram had been instructed to arrive at the designated coordinates, which ended up being in the scrublands east of Odessa, at 0800 on Wednesday. The drive would take a little over ten hours and, not daring to be late, he left on Monday with plans to stay the night somewhere near his destination. Unfortunately, he could not find a hotel within an hours drive of where he needed to be on Wednesday morning. He had to backtrack all the way to I-20 where he stayed at a Super 8, the first hotel he found.

The next morning he got up at 0500, said his morning prayers, and started following his GPS. After turning off what passed for the main highway, he drove for another twenty minutes until his GPS told him he had arrived at his final destination. It was long dirt, single lane driveway blocked by a locked metal gate with a seemingly endless barbed wire fence on each side. It was 0730, and Akram decided to wait until his exact appointed time before he tried the number Mr. Black had given him to call in the event he was severely delayed or lost. When he checked his cell phone, he decided it really wouldn't matter. It indicated he was in a "no service" area.

He felt the first wave of anxiety, verging on panic. However, at exactly 0800 the gate swung open. Apparently, its electric motor was remote controlled. It was only after driving thru the gate that he noticed two cameras mounted on two inconspicuous poles that he realized he had been monitored the entire time he had been waiting. After driving in a straight line for a little less than two kilometers he came to a single story ranch house surrounded by a large barn, stables, and Quonset Hut structures. He parked in front of the house, got out of his truck, and started walking toward the entrance.

He hadn't taken five steps when a male voice boomed from the front door, "welcome Akram, you are right on time." Two Caucasian men, wearing well used western hats and boots, came out of the house, shook his hand, and using obvious cover names introduced themselves as Mr. Jones and Mr. Smith. The smaller of the two, Mr. Jones, began by saying "come in Akram, have some breakfast and then we will get started. We have a lot of material to learn and practice and you must be proficient when you leave here at 1600 Friday. We also have two very important departure "gifts" for you. These must be guarded with your life. Let's get started."

The men began by giving Akram a high-level overview of his mission. They then drilled down and went over, and over, every minute detail. They reviewed surveillance procedures, target selection, how to exit from the scene discreetly, the planned secondary attack and what to do in case he was stopped by the police before, during, or after his mission.

Using a simulator, they prepared, and dry fired the SA-20 until Akram could do it blindfolded. Then they did it some more. By 1500 Friday Mr. Smith deemed Akram "mission ready." Shortly after 1500, at Mr. Smith's direction, Akram backed his F150 to the front of one of the Quonset Hut's on the west side of the house. Mr. Jones unlocked the double doors of the building and motioned for

THE ENEMY OF MY ENEMY

Akram to back the truck inside. After Akram parked about three meters from the entrance, Mr. Jones pulled a tarp off of a stack of long wooden crates. Even retrospectively, it never occurred to Akram to ask or wonder why there was more than one crate in the stack. Being the only "student" at the ranch, he just assumed that he was the only one who had a mission.

Together Akram and Mr. Smith slid one of the crates into the bed of the F150. Once loaded, they placed several of the garden tools, and bags of compost Akram had been instructed to purchase on top of the crate. The truck looked like one of the hundreds of farmhand vehicles that were always on the road in Texas. As they were finishing loading the crate, Mr. Jones returned carrying a flat package wrapped in what appeared to be a heavy duty black plastic trash bag. Handing the bundle to Akram Mr. Jones said: "Merry Christmas Akram, or whatever you guys say. You've got your SA-20, you know how to use it, there is nothing else we can teach you now. This is the Semtex for the truck. We will help you get it fused, wired, and packed underneath the seat. Then you can be on your way. Do you have any questions, at all, for Mr. Smith or I?" Akram didn't speak, he meekly smiled and shook his head no.

CHAPTER 24

The group that the POTUS had come to refer to as his War Council were again gathered in the White House Situation Room. The Chairman of the Joint Chiefs of Staff had notified the Secretary of Defense that their Pentagon staff had completed revising their North Korean war plan. It would be a massive first strike attack designed to decapitate government and military leadership while simultaneously crippling the DPRK's ability to retaliate. They were ready to brief the President.

Looking around the room, the POTUS opened the briefing. "Before we start I want to say I appreciate the loyalty and dedication everyone in this room have displayed over the past, almost, four years. I also appreciate what I know has been an unbelievable amount of work the SecDef, the JCS, and the men and women at the Pentagon have done in the development of the plan we are about to hear. As I said in our last meeting, we are about to embark on the most perilous voyage our country has ever undertaken. We will either make the world a safer place, or we will destroy it. There is little more I can add to convey the gravity of our situation or the importance of this meeting. Dennis, you have the floor and what I assure you is our undivided attention."

The Chairman of the Joint Chiefs of Staff stood up and pressed the Enter key on the Situation Room's presentation computer. A map of the Korean Peninsula appeared on the screen located at the east end of the room. "Thank you, Mr. President. As you know and as most of you suspected, we have had a North Korean first strike plan for several years; ever since they started their mass destruction weapon build up. We update it on a regular basis using ongoing intelligence assessments of their weapons development progress, troop buildups, and our military capabilities. The plan I will present today took into account the capabilities of their Hwasong-16 and demonstrated cyber warfare capabilities. Equally important, it includes the President's directive to minimize civilian and allied casualties. We also have a trick up our sleeve, metaphorically speaking of course. I will go into more detail on that later. First, it is critical that we understand the way the DPRK plans to wage any future conflict on the Korean peninsula. I will begin by saying unlike the 1950's it will not be a "conflict," it will be an all-out "war."

North Korea's publically stated strategy in the event of a preemptive strike, or any other type of aggression, is total war. They have the military power and the national will to take on the United States, at least on their turf. To put their capabilities into perspective consider the fact that they have over nine hundred thousand soldiers in their active military. That's almost equal to the United States, and we have over ten times the population. And, they have more submarines, tanks, and rocket launchers than we do. They have zero intention of getting bogged down in a drawn-out regional struggle like they did in the fifties or like the United States did in Vietnam and every other conflict since World War Two. That's our enemy folks, that's the environment we are about to enter. If we don't accept it, we lose. And South Korea will cease to exist.

We based our preemptive strike strategy on the facts and assumptions that I have just described. At its highest level, there are three components to our plan, the initial strike, follow-up strikes, and threat mop-up.

Each component will consist of multiple, independent tactical actions. The initial strike and follow-up will occur literally within minutes of one another, a one-two punch so to speak. Our opening, initial strike gambit is that trick up our sleeve I referred to earlier. It's not a "trick" per se. It's something that has been bantered about for decades but never tested in a true military engagement. Something called high altitude electromagnetic pulse or HEMP. This is a short, intensely powerful burst of electromagnetic radiation that occurs any time a fission weapon is detonated. This burst of energy can damage or destroy unprotected electrical circuits.

The result could shut down power grids, destroy aircraft and vehicle control systems, and disrupt or disable virtually any unshielded electrical device. In 2008 a report from the Commission to Assess the Threat to the United States from EMP, better known as the EMP Commission, concluded that a 20 megaton bomb exploded 200 miles above the United States could, theoretically, generate an EMP that could knock out a large portion of the civilian electronic equipment across the entire country. As I said, this is theoretical.

However, in 1962 the United States conducted a test by detonating a 1.5 megaton bomb 240 miles above the Pacific. This, comparatively small explosion damaged electrical equipment in Hawaii, almost 900 miles from the point of detonation. When an above ground detonation occurs, its EMP is generated spherically, like a giant basketball. Most of the energy travels upward and horizontally and diminishes inversely to the center of the detonation. In other words, the further away from the blast the EMP travels the weaker it gets.

It's on the ground, where the basketball flattens out that the charge is at its strongest. That's where the damage to electrical

THE ENEMY OF MY ENEMY

equipment occurs. By estimating the height of our blast, and the size of the bomb we can calculate, well more or less, the area on which we will inflict the most damage. We don't want to shut down the electrical grid in Seoul or Southern China so we will be erring on the safe side. There will most likely be sections of the southern part of the DPRK that will not be affected by the EMP. But almost all of the rest should have their circuits fried.

Within seconds of detonating the EMP weapon, we will deliver a W-78 300 kiloton firecracker to Pyongyang, and smaller 100 kiloton W-76's to military headquarters in Nampo, Chongjin, Toejo Dong, Wosan, Hwangju, Orang, and Taechon.

The Supreme Leader seldom ventures too far away from the capital, so this is intended to be the decapitating blow. But despite his dictatorial, total control of the military, and everything else for that matter, we know we are dealing with a many-headed hydra. Our tactics to deal with remaining leadership will be addressed in the second, follow-up, action. It's important to remember that the first two components of our attack strategy, the initial strike, and the follow-up, occur within the first hour. It may seem like we are spacing these events out but unlike previous wartime scenarios, they are happening almost simultaneously.

The instant the W-78 is detonated over Pyongyang, we initiate the third and fourth elements of the initial strike phase. First, we sever all North Korean internet connections. We know their military has a cyber warfare division and we don't want them wreaking havoc on our digital infrastructure. The United States Cyber Command, USCYBERCOM, headquartered at Fort Mead, Maryland has been preparing for this type of confrontation since 2009.

At the same time, we will begin jamming their radar and communication equipment using, among other things, our carrier-based EA-18G Growler aircraft. Five minutes after the initial strike phase begins the Chang dynasty will have come to an igno-minious end. The country will be isolated from the internet, seventy percent of civilian electronics and some military equipment will be useless, their radar tracking and targeting capability reduced to zero, and the majority of military command and control leadership elim-inated. Now comes the second punch, the follow-up strike phase.

North Korea has eight deepwater ocean ports. In addition to being supply line destinations, several of them serve as a home base for the 76 submarines they have in their navy. It's essential that we neutralize their sub threat at the very beginning for several rea-sons. First some, not all, are capable of retaliating with a subma-rine-launched ballistic missile, SLBM, strike of their own. We aren't sure how many have this capability, but we do know they have suc-cessfully tested an SLBM.

Second, we believe that some of their subs are armed with Russian VA-111 Shkval supercavitating torpedos. Unlike most con-ventional torpedos, these things are capable of sinking one of our aircraft carriers. We can't let that happen.

Finally, our sources tell us that North Korean battle plans call for the insertion of Special Forces, SF, units along the South Korean coast. The DPRK has the largest collection of SF units in the world. Over 130,000 highly trained, combat ready, troops comparable to our SEALS or Green Berets. Although problematic using conven-tional weapons, the fear is that squads of these soldiers could be deposited behind the line of battle and covertly attack civilian tar-gets using anthrax or VX nerve agents. Imagine how easy it would be for some guys in sanitation uniforms to walk around a city wear-ing backpack sprayers. They would appear to be killing roaches or ants but in reality, would be spraying for people. At the first signs of an anthrax outbreak or chemical fatalities, there would be riots and widespread panic in the streets.

At the end of the Cold War, the U.S. started scaling back, at least officially, on its decades-old but effective submarine Sound Surveillance System better known as SOSUS. You might recall the Walker family spy network that was exposed in the late eighties. These traitors more or less crippled SOSUS and our abilities to track and monitor enemy submarines by letting the Russians know where our equipment was located and what our capabilities were. On the bright side, those events coupled with renewed efforts by the Soviets and Chinese to expand their submarine warfare capabilities spurred the Office of Naval Research to upgrade our submarine detection and tracking network.

A few years ago General Dynamics was awarded a contract to develop the Deep Reliable Acoustic Path Exploitation System (DRAPES) to replace SOSUS. DRAPES is just one tool in our submarine warfare toolbox. I say all that to say we have been tracking the DPRK submarine fleet for some time now. We know where most of them are. At least the ones that are at sea. All of their subs are diesel powered, and their ever-present petroleum shortage keeps most of them in anchored near the deepwater ports in their hidden dens. When the follow-up phase of our mission kicks off, we will simultaneously destroy all eight of their deepwater ports using our W-80 150 kiloton submarine-launched cruise missiles, SLCM. These devices are large enough to destroy everything in and around the ports but not so large as to needlessly cause civilian casualties. Or to render them postwar useless.

This action will completely cut off their oil and gas supply lines. The DPRK currently consumes around 15,000 barrels of oil per day, yet they have a production capacity of fewer than 500 barrels per day. And, they have zero oil reserves. You can do the math and see how long their war machine will last once we cut off shipments from Russia and the Middle East. We estimate the destruction of the ports will also eliminate ninety percent of their sub fleet. We will use our Los Angeles and Virginia class attack submarines and our P-8 Posideon aircraft to pick off the remaining subs before they even learn a war has started.

We are positioning two attack boats off both sides of the North Korean coast. Two in the Yellow Sea and two in the Sea of Japan. The P-8's will launch from U.S. Navy Base Sasebo near, ironically, Nagasaki. We will have these components in place before the end of the month. We have to tread lightly to avoid detection by the Chinese.

Yes Bulldog, I know you have assurance from the Chinese that they will sit quietly on the sidelines and not interfere but we aren't taking any chances. Besides, even though these are the fastest subs in our fleet, it still takes time for them to slip unseen across an ocean.

There are two other threats we need to address during our follow-up phase. These are their troop tunnels and artillery. It's a little-known fact that North Korea is the most "tunneled" nation in the world, if I may use "tunnel" as an adjective. We know of twenty tunnels near and deep, deep beneath the DMZ. It is estimated that each one of these tunnels is capable of transporting ten to fifteen thousand troops, and vehicles, per hour underneath the DMZ and into South Korea. In the event of war, they would blast out the last fifty or so meters of the tunnel to create an exit and then start shoving their army thru it and into the south. These tunnels are designed to withstand our thirty thousand pound, GBU-57, bunker buster bombs like we used in Afganistan.

But we have another surprise for them. Two years ago we completed the development of a B61-12 Earth-Penetrating low yield, only two kilotons, nuclear bunker buster. This is a high precision, guided bomb which can be delivered by any of our fighter-bombers.

We will deposit one of these puppies at the entrance to each of their troop tunnels. That will bring a screeching halt to any thoughts of positioning forces behind us. We will also use the B61's to destroy their Sup'ung, Taipingwan, Weiyuan, and Ynfeng hydroelectric dams.

This brings us to the DPRK's massive conventional artillery capability. They have at least thirty artillery brigades equipped with an array of self-propelled cannons, mortars, and multiple-tube rocket launchers. Their big guns are hidden in caves and tunnels strung along the north side of the DMZ. The CIA estimates that the North Koreans could fire ten thousand rockets per minute at Seoul which is only thirty-five miles from the DMZ. Unless we knock them out in the first round of the fight, they could potentially kill three hundred thousand South Koreans, and Americans within a matter of hours. Here is where our cruise missiles come into play. By the end of the month, we will have two carrier groups within striking distance of North Korea. Each group has sixty fighter-bombers and two guided missile destroyers. We will also have two Ohio class submarines prowling off the North Korean coast. Each of these subs carries one hundred and fifty-four Tomahawk cruise missiles. When the opening bell rings for round two, we will unleash four hundred extremely accurate ship, and sub launched Tomahawks on the DPRK rocket launchers, artillery, and airfields. We will follow this barrage up with round-the-clock surgical strikes with our F-18 and F-35 fighter-bombers. The north has almost eight hundred fighters and one hundred bombers. However, for the most part, these are old Russian MIGs and some homemade clones that are no match for our F-22's or F-35's.

Never before, in the history of warfare has so much destructive power been delivered in such a short period. Outside of world war two, and immediately after nine eleven, our country has not been able to muster the political courage that will be necessary to obliterate our enemies' ability to wage war. We plan to do it so fast and so completely that it will be over before our liberal politicians and news media know it has started. Like it or not folks, that's the only way we are going to defeat the DPRK without getting hundreds of thousands of people killed.

On the heels of these follow-up strikes of our "blitzkrieg," we begin what we will refer to as our mop-up operation. We know that the Norks have the most massive stockpile of chemical and biological weapons on the planet. They have eighteen chemical and four biological production and storage facilities. These are scattered across the country disguised as fertilizer or drug manufacturing plants. During the mop-up phase, we go after these and other, conventional, weapon factories, and any still resistant military units, using even more cruise missiles and fighter-bombers. Following the widespread nuclear attacks on the capital, and military headquarters disrupted power and communication, and zero prospect of getting gas, oil, and other supplies we will issue a demand for the immediate and total surrender of all combat forces.

We know that North Korean soldiers are highly motivated and loyal to the Supreme Leader. Hell, they have been brainwashed to the point that they think he and his entire family are divine beings. These soldiers are different than those we have fought over the last few decades. For example, once we blooded their nose, Iraqi troops were surrendering to CNN news crews. We expect them to be more like the Okinawan defense forces in world war two, prepared and willing to fight to the death.

On the other hand, we also know that, with the exception of their Special Forces, they are underfed and incapable of unit level, independent action. No doubt there will be pockets of resistance. We plan to go around those while we establish temporary military governance and allow South Korean led Civil Police to restore and maintain law and order. There is no real animosity among the South Koreans towards the North. It will take years to deprogram the North Korean populace fully but this, along with food and the restoration of fundamental human rights will be a welcome first step. Mr. President, ladies, and gentlemen that concludes my briefing."

The POTUS stood up and motioned for the Chairman of the Joint Chiefs of Staff to return to his seat. "Thank you, Dennis. That was an excellent, albeit chilling, overview of what we can expect once all of our assets are in place and I press the "start a war" button. I want all the pieces on the board by the first week of December. I know, originally I said by the end of November, but I am giving you a little additional time because I know we are behind in B-61 production. And you have convinced me that we can't go scooting another Ohio class sub from its current location to the Yellow Sea without alerting the Russians. I'm not a patient man, but sometimes, especially in this case, a little caution goes a long way. But I want all of our prepositioned assets, and staff, ready to go at an hours notice. Worse comes to worse; we go to war with what we've got. I am not going to open this briefing for the normal round of questions. This was, and is, supposed to be information only. If someone in this room sees a major show stopper speak up now." No one said a word. "In that case, Dennis, you and your team continue to polish up any rough spots. If you need anything from anyone here, say so. You speak for me until this thing is over. Ladies and gentlemen, we are dismissed."

CHAPTER 25

The hotel shuttle drove up the ramp and stopped in front of the Delta sign in front of the departure gate. Cammy, who was sitting in the front passenger seat, opened the door and bounced out of the van as the driver started unloading bags from the rear. She felt like she owned the Denver, Dallas, Jackson route. That route was a new service for Delta who usually required all passengers departing from Jackson to change planes in Atlanta. They had started this route three years ago, and Cammy had been its first Captain. Not just first female Captain, its first Captain. Lonny, her First Officer, had flown with her for the past two years. He was a retired Lieutenant Colonel, LTC, who had flown C-141's and C-17's during his twenty-year career in the Airforce. How he had risen to the rank of LTC was anyone's guess. Lonny had zero ambition. He just liked to fly. Fortunately, he was good at it and was a great co-pilot.

Cammy's long-range goal was to fly Delta's jumbo jets on long haul, overseas, routes. Maybe the non-stop to Austrailia or Paris. But those plans would have to be set aside for a few years, at least until the baby was in preschool. But that was ok, for now, she was more than happy to stick with "her" route. She was only out of town three nights a week and unless there was a delay at one of the airports her daily schedule was as routine as an office job. But today she was beyond excited. She couldn't wait to get home and break the news to Josh.

After grabbing their flight cases and carry-on bags, Cammy and Lonny flashed their badges at the agent guarding the TSA crew entrance, placed their bags on a conveyor belt, and walked thru a metal detector just like every passenger was doing. Delta and the Jackson Medgar Evers Airport management thought it sent a positive message to passengers when they saw airline crew going thru the same security gauntlet that they were required to navigate. After they were on the "five dollars a bottle of water" side of Security, they headed for the flight crew lounge. The Jackson airport wasn't large enough to have a separate Delta lounge like Dallas or Denver. But it was comfortable, had decent coffee, and banks of computers where Cammy could file her flight plan and review weather conditions. At 1035 hours, she and Lonny grabbed their bags and headed for gate four.

Akram folded back the tarp in the bed of his truck and moved the bags of potting soil and garden tools off the top of the wooden crate. Using his battery powered drill, he removed the screws from the lid of the container. He did not remove the lid; he would do that latter. He replaced one of the bags of soil back on the top and folded the tarp back to its original position. Akram then went back to his room and began a long and fervent mid-morning prayer. He felt strangely calm, happy, and at last, at peace. It was 1030 hours.

Cammy noticed that there were hardly any empty seats in the passenger waiting area outside gate four. The sign above the check-in attendants podium read Delta flight 370 Dallas – Denver 11: 30. The few seats that didn't have someone sitting in them was piled with carryon luggage. It never failed. There were always a few self-centered passengers who snatched up the seat next to them for their bags, ignoring the plight of their fellow fliers. This time of year and on this route, there would be a full flight. This pleased Cammy. "Her" route had turned out to be an amazingly successful venture for Delta. Initially it, and similar non-Atlanta connected flights had captured the spillover business from Southwest. Now they were positioning Delta in the lead position on short-haul, one-class, routes.

Flight 370 was a Boeing 737-800 configured to carry 189 passengers and a crew of 6. Cammy knew that today, the day before Thanksgiving, every seat would be booked. There would be a few disappointed stand-by passengers who would vow to book their flight early next time. Cammy and Lonny wound their way thru the crowd toward the check-in counter pulling their small suitcase and flight bag behind them. Seeing the crew boarding the plane was a welcome sight for the throng of impatient passengers. It generally meant their wait, regardless of how short, was almost over and they could begin the boarding process and the fight for overhead storage space.

Cammy waved her badge over the check-in sensor, flashed a cheerful smile, and greeted the Delta gate crew. She recognized all three of the staff and as always called the one at the door by name as she started down the ramp. The Senior Flight Attendant met Cammy and Lonny as they walked thru the door of the plane. Carlos was a slender, thirtyish, fourth generation Hispanic who had clawed his way out of Chicago's south side. "*Buenos Dias*, Captain, it looks like we will be in good hands two days in a row." Carlos was also a regular on this route, and Cammy loved his sense of humor and an insanely high level of energy. "Right back at you Carlos" Cammy replied, "let's get these folks home for Thanksgiving." "I'm on it *Jefa*," Carlos said as he reached for the phone to let the gate crew know they could start the pre-boarding process.

Cammy stowed her suitcase and slid into the left hand Captain's seat. She and Lonny fired up their onboard iPads and started going thru the 737's preflight preparation. Each had a set of tasks they would perform independently. They would then conduct a 737-800 checklist together in what is known as a "challenge and response" format. In their case, using a customized Delta app on their iPads, Lonny, as the First Officer, would read items from the checklist. Cammy would review various switch and computer settings, adjust as necessary, and acknowledge verbally to Lonny's challenge while checking off each item on her iPad. The 737's checklist was exhaustive and Cammy, as with almost all pilots, was a compulsive stickler for its completion. The "before start" checklist was completed at 1100 hours.

Akram closed and locked the door of his apartment. As he walked toward his apartment's designated parking space, he reflected on how silly it was to have secured the door. He wouldn't be coming back, and by now there wasn't anything in his apartment that anyone could steal or even use for that matter. The day before he had put all of his clothes, dishes, TV and every other "worldly" good in the Salvation Army donation box in the Northpark Mall parking lot. Like the old song, "Tobacco Road" went "all he had was hanging on his back." Akram checked the back of his truck making sure the gardening tools and bag of compost was still in place, over the top of the wooden crate. He unlocked the door, got in and checked the plastic-wrapped package underneath his seat. He made sure the blasting caps were firmly inserted in the blocks of Semtex then moved the deadman trigger to the center of the seat where he could easily reach it while driving. Akram started the engine, pulled out of the parking lot, and turned left on Springridge Road. It was 1040 hours.

At 1103 hours Cammy keyed the microphone and pressed a button on her overhead panel which generated two short, distinct, cabin-wide, "dings." This signal told Carlos and the other attendants that it was time to close and lock the front door and to prepare for departure. She then switched to the cabin wide intercom. "Good morning ladies and gentlemen, this is Captain Camile Brooks. On behalf of Delta Airlines, I would like to welcome you to flight 370, Jackson to Dallas with service continuing to the mile-high, in more ways than one, city, Denver, Colorado. It's a beautiful day here, and the weather looks great for the rest of our flight. We are all set for an on-time departure, and it looks like the jet stream Gods are going to give us an early arrival in Dallas. Remember that the next time we have one of those dreaded delayed departures." Camile allowed herself an attempt at humor before takeoff. This practice always seemed to ease what was a passenger's most stressful portion of a flight. However, anytime her flight was below an altitude of 10,000 feet she was all business in the cockpit. There was none of the sophomoric banter and goofing around some of her contemporaries were guilty of. Lonny knew it, the Attendants knew it, and anyone who flew with "Captain Cammy" knew it as soon as the flight deck doors were closed.

After calling the ground crew and instructing them to roll back the loading ramp, Cammy radioed the Jackson Control Tower.

"Clearance, Delta 370, to Denver"

"Delta 370, cleared to Denver via L 2 departure, flight plan route, depart runway 34L, squawk 1-2-0-0"

"Delta 370, cleared to Denver, 34L, 1-2-0-0"

"Delta 370, readback correct, contact 3-1-0-7 for push"

"3-1-0-7 for push, Delta 370"

After receiving flight clearance and permission to have the ground crew push the 737-800 into taxi position, Cammy and Lonny started the planes two massive General Electric engines. Each one of these power plants produced over twenty-six thousand pounds of thrust. As with all commercial aircraft each engine was capable of flying or landing the 737 independently should the other engine fail. At its normal cruising speed and with a full passenger load, in Delta 370's "single class" case that was 189, the 737-800 burned 850 gallons of jet fuel per hour.

The combined flight time from Jackson to Dallas to Denver was roughly 2 hours and 47 minutes which would require a little over 2,365 gallons of fuel. Delta 370 had been loaded with 4,000 gallons in Jackson, well shy of the 737-800's capacity of 6,873 gallons. But far more than enough to complete its mission even if diversion or extended circling should be required. Under normal conditions, the extra fuel provided pilots a comfortable margin of safety. That would not be the case today. It was 1110 hours.

Akram hated driving on the interstate, and he especially hated the section where I-20 intersected I-55 just southwest of Jackson. The locals called it "the stack." He wasn't sure why but he assumed it referred to the way the two highways were built one on top of the other. Or maybe it was because one wreck invariably caused another until there was a string of accidents "stacked" together. He didn't care why. He just knew that the intertwined highway conglomeration made a dangerous situation worse.

But he couldn't avoid the stack today. It lay between him and the airport. So he slowed his truck down to five miles an hour below the speed limit and nervously followed the signs to I-20 south. Finally, he took exit 52 and onto highway 475 north. One redlight later he crossed U.S. Highway 80, drove another quarter mile, then entered a traffic circle at the intersection of Old Brandon Road and International Drive.

Akram knew that today's wind direction would require all flights to take off from runway 34L. He and Khalid had scouted the area several times together and, following Khalid's departure, Akram had made trips to the roads near the airport's two main runways several times each week. He knew exactly which runway would be used depending on wind direction. He also knew that Delta flight 370 was scheduled to take off at 1130 hours. It was 1110.

After starting the 737's engines, Cammy checked its flight controls, ailerons, elevator, and rudder for a response. All systems checked out and they were ready to go.

"Jackson Apron Delta 370 ready for pushback"

"Delta 370 push at your signal, call ready for taxi"

"Delta 370 roger"

"Jackson Apron Delta 370 ready for taxi"

"Delta 370 roger, taxi 34L, hold short, contact Ground on 2, 0, 8"

"Roger hold short, Ground on 2, 0, 8"

Cammy smoothly advanced the 737's throttles to 30 percent to start the giant plane moving then reduced them as she steered toward runway 34L at roughly 12 miles per hour. As she did so, using the intercom, Lonny instructed the Attendants to take their seats and prepare for takeoff. This command sent Carlos and the rest of his team scurrying thru the cabin. They made last-minute seatbelt and tray table checks and ensured all aisles were clear of anything that might trip a passenger should they have an emergency exit.

When they reached the Hold Short Line for runway 34L Cammy stopped the plane and set the brakes as she and Lonny completed their computerized checklist for this position. As Lonny called out the tasks, Cammy set the Autopilot altitude to 10,000, vertical speed to 3,000 feet per minute, and entered their first course heading. She then set the elevator trim and flaps to takeoff and strobes to the "on" position. All of this had been done before taxiing, but these actions served as a re-check immediately before takeoff. It was 1128 hours.

Akram turned right onto Old Brandon Road, drove one hundred yards, and then turned left onto Cooper Road which ran parallel with International Drive toward the airport terminal. He could see the end of runway 34L to his left. After driving another three hundred yards, he pulled his truck off the road to his left and turned the vehicle around so that it now faced south. From this position, he had an unobstructed view of the runway, as well as being off the main road to the airport, International Drive, and was positioned slightly higher than the chain link fence which encircled airport property.

That fence clearance was critical. The missile needed an unobstructed flight path. He was also facing his escape route. After he stopped, Akram got out of the truck, leaving its keys in the ignition. He removed two orange highway cones and placed one near each end of his vehicle. These plus the magnetic sign on his door panels, and the white, nondescript, color of the F150 made him appear to be one of any maintenance or landscape workers that blended into every community in Mississippi. He felt confident that no one would stop to question his presence or what he was doing. If they did, he would kill them.

After positioning his truck, Akram dropped the tailgate, crawled up into the bed and uncovered the wooden crate. As he did so, he looked over his shoulder and saw the 737 taxiing toward the "hold short" line of the runway. Akram pulled the SA-20 out of the wooden crate, got out of the truck, and walked around to the right side. He pulled the caps off of each end of the launch tube and flipped the switch which turned on the SA-20's electrical circuit power. He was at his most vulnerable state now, completely exposed and carrying what any knowledgeable military or law enforcement person would recognize as a weapon. However, the truck blocked anyone on Cooper Road from seeing him, and the Captain and Co-pilot were too far away, and too busy, to distinguish what he had in his arms. The main danger was from someone driving toward the airport on International Drive. But there wasn't that much traffic, and it was almost time. It was 1128 hours.

Cammy pushed the throttles forward enough to start the plane moving then she steered right and into position for takeoff. At precisely 1130 Cammy called the tower and announced that Delta 370 was departing Jackson on runway 34L to the north. Always cautious, she looked around to make sure all was clear then she released the 737's brakes and taxied to the centerline of the runway.

Cammy stopped and set the throttles at 40 percent and made sure the engines stabilized. Then advancing the throttles to 90 percent and applying a gentle down pitch pressure on the yoke, she started the takeoff. The Jackson Medgar Evers airport runway was an ample 8,500 feet long. But as the 90,000-pound plane's ground speed increased from 90, then 100, then 120 knots she invariably recalled an old saying; to a pilot, the three most useless things in the world are "runway behind you, blue sky above you, and fuel on the ground." When the 737's ground speed reached 140 knots, she applied enough back pressure on the yoke to raise the nose 10 degrees and seconds later the plane's altitude was at 300 feet.

Akram shouldered the SA-20 and peered thru its aiming sights at the plane as soon as the 737 started moving down the runway. When it reached what Akram estimated to be the halfway point he pressed the switch which caused the SA-20's missile to start seeking the heat signature of the plane's starboard engine. Two seconds later, just as the 737 lifted off the runway, Akram heard the screeching tone which indicated that the missile was locked on its target and was ready for launch. He squeezed the trigger.

Although he had practiced "dry firing" the SA-20 countless times at the ranch in Texas, Akram was not prepared for the noise and force of the exhaust blast from the SA-20. Compressed nitrogen expelled the missile from its launch tube and shot it forward 5 meters before the warhead's rocket ignited. Despite the "safety distance" the inert gas provided, the exhaust blast still scorched Akram's face. And the noise was deafening.

The missile was moving over twice the speed of sound by the time it had traveled 30 feet. Akram watched the missile scream toward its target for only a couple of seconds. He had been ordered numerous times not to hang around after he had launched the SA-20 and he dutifully complied. He turned to place the empty launch tube in the back of the truck and heard but didn't see, the explosion.

The 737 was approximately 300 feet off the ground when the missile ripped into the center of its starboard engine. Historically, most shoulder-fired surface-to-air weapons had been designed to destroy its target's engines thus only crippling the aircraft. The far more powerful SA-20 took this effect a step further. Its larger warhead was engineered to fly into its target's engine and then explode with a force that would destroy everything within a 5-meter radius. It worked perfectly.

The 737-800's monstrous jet engine was mounted onto and underneath the widest section of the plane's wing. When the warhead exploded, it blew the engine into thousands of ragged chunks of white hot nickel, aluminum, and titanium. It also split the section of wing directly above the engine. When it broke, the wing folded like a knife blade rupturing its fuel bladders and dumping two thousand gallons of flaming jet fuel. This created a massive ball of fire and blew burning liquid into a gaping hole in the 737's fuselage. Passengers in rows eleven thru fourteen on the starboard side were incinerated. They died a quick but agonizing death. In some ways, they were the lucky ones.

Cammy and Lonny were focused on gaining altitude and getting Delta 370 on course when the engine and fuel tanks blew.

The 737-800's onboard computers detected the loss of power from the number two engine and instantly began executing its emergency flight control software algorithms. The software increased the thrust to full power on the number one engine and made adjustments to the elevators, flaps, and rudder to accommodate the loss of an engine.

These adjustments started taking place in less time than it took Cammy and Lonny to realize they had a problem. However, the software did not, and could not, make corrections for the loss of an entire wing. Cammy managed to mutter "holy shit!" just as the 737 careened hard to starboard and started a full power dive nose first toward the field at the end of the runway. Lonny was screaming "mayday, mayday" into his microphone and Cammy was pulling back on the yoke and steering left even as they slammed into the ground at 200 miles per hour. The last thought Cammy would ever have was "oh Josh........."

CHAPTER 26

Akram picked up the two highway cones and threw them into the back of his truck then got inside and started the engine. He turned on the radio hoping to pick up the news as he drove to his next objective. He placed the dead man trigger in his lap, between his legs, then drove the truck across a grassy open space and onto International Drive. In his rearview mirror, Akram could see a huge cloud of oily black smoke and fire raging up past the far end of the runway. He felt not the least bit of remorse even though he had just slaughtered nearly 200 men, women, and children. To him, they were like roaches. He reflected on his utter humiliation during graduation night at Jackson Prep and was overcome with the warm glow of long-awaited, and well-deserved revenge. For the first time in a long time, Akram smiled.

He took the reverse of the route he had followed coming in and got on I-20 heading north. As before he drove cautiously and well below the speed limit, like an old woman in a Buick. This did not sit well with the cars and semi's lining up behind him waiting for an opening in the left-hand lane so they could shoot by, glaring at him and his truck. After once again, and for the last time, negotiating the dreaded stack, Akram took the I-55 exit and headed north. Just as he passed over the bridge crossing the Pearl River an announcement interrupted the "John Boy and Billy" show he had been listening to on his radio. There had been a horrific plane crash at the Jackson airport. "Details are just starting to come in. A sister station news team is on site. Stay tuned for further announcements as soon as we learn more."

As he listened, Akram took the Fortification Street exit just about a mile past the Pearl River bridge. He drove west on Fortification along the fringes of the Belhaven community. An older, once upper-class Jackson neighborhood that had started an inexorable slide into decay. Just as he passed the intersection of Madison and Fortification streets, there was another interruption on the radio. "This just in from WLBT News Now. It has been confirmed that a commercial airliner crashed at Jackson Medgar Evers Airport at approximately 11:35. WLBT has learned that similar crashes have occurred in Atlanta and Chicago. Our sources indicate that there may be others nationwide. Stay tuned to WLBT for additional coverage and updates as they occur."

Akram was a little perplexed. Could there be others with identical missions? Doing Allah's work at the same time? But he didn't have time to dwell on these questions. He was almost at his destination. His courage was starting to fade a bit as he mused, his "final" destination.

He turned right onto North State Street at the corner of the Baptist Medical Center campus. He drove past the Mississippi Children's Heart Clinic, passed under a skywalk which connected two hospital buildings, then turned left into the Emergency Room parking lot entrance. There was a guard shack with a large, red, EMERGENCY sign and a flimsy looking, remotely operated wooden pole gate at the entrance.

Akram turned left into the entrance, stomped on the accelerator, and broke thru the 2" by 4" wooden barrier. He turned sharply to his right and raced around the driveway toward the ambulance entrance as a Security officer ran out of the guard shack toward the truck, shouting and waving his arms. Akram drove past the bollard protected, emergency staff walk-in door and into one of the three ambulance bays in front of a sliding glass gurney entrance. Bollards were also in front of the entrance which prevented him from doing what he ideally wanted to do; drive his truck thru the glass and into the center of the Emergency Room.

He started praying, pressed the dead man trigger, and settled for second best. When the security officer turned the corner and headed for his truck, and when a half-dozen nurses and technicians poured out of the now open entrance, he released the trigger.

The telephone on the Federal Aviation Administration, FAA, Duty Officer's desk rang for the second time at 1210. Not one but two more crashes. Most of the senior management at the FAA's Washington, D.C. headquarters office had taken a vacation day in advance of Thanksgiving. One crash was bad enough, two was a tragedy, but three was a pattern; or worse.

Duty Officer responsibilities rotated among the administrative management staff. Today was Ronald Ledford's, a GS-13 career civil service employee, turn in the barrel. When he received news of the third crash in less than an hour he knew it was time to pull the plug. Knowing that what he was about to do would either make him a hero or get him fired, he decided it was time to shut down U.S airspace. For only the second time in its history, Ron, who as Duty Officer was the de facto Director of the FAA, shut down all commercial traffic over the continental United States. It was 1240 hours. As with the shutdown which occurred immediately following 9/11, only military, law enforcement, or medical aircraft were allowed to take off for the next 48 hours. The FBI and CIA concluded that some terrorist group had perfected a way to get an explosive device past airport security. Then they received another message.

The instant Abdulla heard the news that there had been a crash at one of his designated airports, at the time he had specified, he sent Mustafa, Khalid, and Saad a Dmail he had composed earlier. "Mustafa, we have made our first strike against the Great Satan. Please send the message I have pasted below immediately to the same recipients as our last one. Make sure that you include Reuters, TASS, API and as many other major news agencies that you can without delaying your transmission. Please confirm when completed."

Within minutes Mustafa replied, "I will do so at once Honored One. However, please be aware that Facebook has sutured up the hack we inserted last time. We are scrambling to find another hole in their network. But that could take days or even weeks. Their control network is more secure than the NSA's." Abdulla glowed with pride at Mustafa's reference to him as "Honored One" but was more than a little disappointed in being thwarted by Facebook's technical staff. "I understand Mustafa; please send our message to everyone else on the mailing list." In less than ten minutes another message was transmitted to Mustafa's hacked network recipients.

"The wretchedly evil leaders of the United States government were warned to lift any and all sanctions they have illegally imposed on the peace-loving Democratic People's Republic of Korea and to remove all military forces from the Korean Peninsula, Japan, and Guam. They have failed to do so and have now felt the sting of our invincible military. We can strike at will and with impunity. You now have one week to comply with our demands, or we will again rain our vengeance upon you. Happy Thanksgiving."

"I don't give a fat rat's ass what they're doing. If they are within an hour's drive or copter flight from here I want my War Council in the situation room at 1600."

The POTUS could barely control his roiling fury as he barked orders to his Chief of Staff. "I'm on it, sir! I've already contacted the Chairman JCS, the Secretary of Defense, and Secretary of State. Everyone I talked to was "standing in the door" to use an old Airborne term. As soon as word got out about the latest message they knew it was just a matter of time before you reeled them in."

Khalid drove with a calm caution that would be the envy of any Drivers Education teacher. Heeding Abdulla's order, he had headed north on I-75 the instant he received confirmation of the last strike at Chicago's Midway airport. He was headed toward Sault Ste. Marie, Michigan and the International Bridge that connected the United States and the "twin" city Sault Ste. Marie, Ontario.

Once in Canada, he would head east on Trans-Canada Highway 17 to Montreal. The drive to Montreal would take around eleven hours. He had already been on the road for five and getting thru customs could take at least an hour even if his vehicle wasn't inspected. He decided he would stay the night in Sudbury. After all, he wasn't in a rush; he had completed his mission. He would stay another night in Montreal, check in with Abdulla, and then catch a flight from Montreal to Paris, wait a few more days and then fly to Riyadh.

He would cross the Canadian border using a skillfully forged passport which identified him as a Jordanian citizen. In addition to its financial war chest, the MA had a number of resources which were indispensable to Khalid's line of business. One of which was a staff of unbelievably skilled document forgers. They didn't waste their time on trying to duplicate currency; the Peruvians had that market sewed up. However, they could produce a passport or drivers license that was not only identical to an original; they were also linked to the subject countries databases.

Even though, he never used the same passport for an extended length of time. He would destroy his Jordanian identity once he was in Canada and then become an Israeli citizen for the Montreal to

Paris leg of his journey. Most of the civilized world, outside of the Middle East, had a "hands-off" policy toward Israel.

No one on the President's War Council was late getting to the White House Situation Room. As the Chief of Staff had noted, they had all been "sitting on go" ever since the FAA had learned of the third, and then fourth and fifth crash and had shut down all civilian flights in the U.S.

Everyone stood up when the POTUS entered the room. "Please, take your seats," he snapped as he walked to the head of the conference table. Looking at the Secretary of Defense he ordered: "Dennis, give us a situation report." Without standing the SecDef said "Sir, at approximately 1130 hours this morning we suffered five commercial airline crashes at five geographically dispersed locations; Jackson, MS, Chicago, Atlanta, Dallas, and Denver. Within an hour these were followed by suicide bombings at hospital emergency rooms nearest each of the airports. As you might expect, our investigations are underway, but it is far too early to offer any conclusive, verifiable evidence as to the cause or perpetrators. However, an eyewitness in Dallas swears he saw what appeared to be a missile streaking toward the plane there just before its wing exploded. And the widely broadcast message would imply that the North Koreans are responsible. Or, someone wants us to think they are.

Regardless, U.S. airspace has been shut down, and we are in the process of beefing up airport, and airport parameter security before we open it back up. We are holding at DEFCON 4 and despite these attacks do not recommend we go any further at this point."

"Why is that Dennis?," the POTUS asked. "Sir, every intelligence agency in the world will know if we go to DEFCON 3. There is no way to keep that under wraps and we sure as hell don't want to tip off the Norks until we are ready to cold cock their ass. Besides, we can continue to make just as much progress on our first strike preparations at DEFCON 4 as we could at 3 and do so without show-ing our hand." "OK Dennis, I'm convinced," the POTUS said, "but tell me where we are with getting our assets in place and when we are going to be ready to shoot."

The SecDef's lips pursed and his head slipped just a bit and to the right and shook twice, the universal body language sign of "ah shit."

"Sir, we're dealing with two separate issues that are slowing our preparations for a sucker punch. First, it is taking more time than we anticipated to get our second Ohio-class sub, the USS Louisiana, outfitted, fully armed, and in place. Loading her up with a full complement of 154 Tomahawk missiles and getting her out of Naval Base Kitsap, Washington without being spotted by Russian or Chinese satellites, or ground intelligence, HUMINT, has been, is, virtually impossible. We're almost finished, but then there's that long, sneaky boat ride before it's where we want it off the North Korean coast.

We also ran into production problems with the B61 model 12 bomb. We are pretty much betting the farm on this puppy to oblit-erate the North's troop and equipment carrying tunnel systems. They are dug deep, sometimes eighty meters and hardened with reinforced concrete. All we have to do is snap one, collapse it for a couple of hundred meters, and the road's closed. The B61 can do it, but the boys at Sandia National Laboratories thought it prudent to tweak the earth penetrating fuse a bit before we used the things. It could probably be called a model 13 by now. The 2018 update to the Treaty on the Prohibition of Nuclear Weapons tied one arm behind our backs as far as testing the B61 goes. But all of that, actually a minor change, has been worked out, and stockpiled units are being modified as we speak.

The bottom line for all of this is that we should be fully armed, in place, and ready to proceed by the third week of December." "Change "should be" to "will be," and I won't fire your ass" the POTUS growled.

CHAPTER 27

Kamal Ermias was born in Lansing, Michigan and for the first twenty-six years of his life, he had lived with his parents. He had lived with his father for most of that time. His mother had been struck and killed by a crack-smoking car thief when he was seven. His grieving father had never remarried but had instead had fallen in love with Jim Beam and whatever beer happened to be on sale at the local Seven Eleven.

Kamal's parents had immigrated from Ethiopia the winter before Kamal was born. Native Ethiopians, those who weren't born into Christian or Muslim families, weren't given surnames. Instead, they were just given a name and used their father's or grandfather's first name when additional identification was required. When his father applied for immigration, he listed his father's name, Kamal's grandfather, as his last name, Ermias. Kamal's mother was admitted to McLaren Greater Lansing hospital as Haile Ermias which Kamal subsequently inherited as his Western surname. Kamal's parents listed Pentay as their religion of record on their immigration documents. Pentay is a Christian Protestant denomination practiced by a majority of native Ethiopians in their country and abroad.

It was thru the efforts of a local Pentay congregation that Kamal's parents were able to afford to move to the United States under the sponsorship of a Lansing family. Once he and his wife were somewhat settled in Lansing, Kamal's father applied for a job with the U.S. Postal Service. He listed his race as "black" and thanks to the government's affirmative action programs was hired immediately. He had worked in the local post office ever since and every single day gave thanks that he had escaped the oppressive heat, poverty, and violence that ravaged almost all of Africa.

Kamal had grown up in a lower-middle-class section of town and attended a predominately black high school. So much so that when he entered the ninth grade the only kids in his class that wasn't black were the Rodriquez twins. He learned early on that to survive, much less achieve any degree of popularity he would need to join one of the three gangs that more or less controlled his school.

Inexplicably, considering his home life, Kamal didn't smoke or use drugs and was repulsed by his father's near constant drinking. That probably explained why he gravitated to the Black Mambas, an incredibly tight, all Muslim group of men that had the reputation of being clean living, physically fit, politically vocal and violent. In his Sophomore year Kamal, over his father's objections, converted to Islam. He read the Quran "sura to sura," studied its passages assiduously, and by the time he graduated was known within the Mambas as an authority on Islamic doctrine and social organization. After graduating from high school, Kamal started to grow away from the Mambas but more toward Islam. The more he studied the Quran, and its interruption by fundamentalist factions, the more he became enamored with Al-Qaeda and its terrorist war against the United States and its allies. And the more he secretly wanted to be part of it.

The following year he applied for and was subsequently accepted into, the Lansing Police Academy. After a year of training, he graduated and became one of three Muslim cops in the Lansing Police Department. In May of his twenty-sixth year, the Imam, from the mosque Kamal attended, introduced him to a visitor from Saudi Arabia. His name was Saad.

Kamal was deeply impressed with Saad. Especially his knowledge of world politics and Islam's role, or lack, in shaping that landscape. He was completely blown away when Saad began to share a vision for the future of Islam that Kamal had never once considered. Saad explained that a new leader was emerging from the true holy land. A man by the name of Abdulla Amer Al-Badri. This man had been appointed by Allah to restore Islam to its rightful place as the world's only religion. Abdulla was destined to establish a new world Caliphate and to take his place as its first and all-powerful Caliph. Abdulla Amer Al-Badri had been designated, by God himself, as Muhammad's successor. He would crush the infidels, slaughtering all who opposed Muslim forces, subjugating and enslaving those that were mercifully allowed to live and serve its people in the years to come. There was a fire in Saad's eyes and a passion in his voice that completely consumed Kamal. Then Saad lowered his voice, leaned forward from his waist and staring with white-hot passion told Kamal that he wanted him to play a pivotal role in what was soon to be the greatest struggle in history.

Following their introduction, and Saad's indoctrination spiel, Kamal took two vacation days, and the two of them went apartment shopping. Abdulla had ordered Saad's man in Lansing to begin attending All Saints Episcopal Church. Saad felt it best that they find an apartment as close to the church as possible so that Kamal could begin to be assimilated into the neighborhood. After a relatively short search, they decided on Burcham Apartments which was only a couple of blocks from the church. They were also reasonably close to the Post Office where Kamal worked.

When they applied for an apartment, the Burcham Office Manager said that it would take several days for them to complete a background and credit check. Saad expressed his dismay saying that he needed to return to Chicago the next day. He told the manager that his friend had said that if he mentioned his name, he would be able to get the apartment and move in right away. Saad discreetly took out his wallet as he was speaking. The manager, tilting her head down a bit and wrinkling her brow, said: "now who would go and tell you that?" Taking out five, slightly used, $100 bills and sliding them toward the manager replied: "my dear friend Ben told me." Scooping up the bills and stuffing them into her ample, and somewhat exposed bosom, the manager smiled, actually grinned from one ear to the other, and shot back "if tomorrow's not soon enough, that fine black man can crash at my crib tonight." "Tomorrow will be great," Kamal said smiling, "but thanks for the offer."

Later that same afternoon Saad paid cash for a two-year-old Volvo to be registered in Kamal's name. They also opened a checking account using the alias Kim Sang Duk. The following day, Saad bought a new Lovono laptop computer loaded it with a Mustafa developed security package that would completely erase everything on its hard drive on the 25th of December, rewrite it with ones and zeros then self-destruct its internal code. He showed Kamal how to load and use the Tor browser and Dvideo and set him up with a Dlink email account. When all of these preparations were done, Saad and Kamal discussed, in painstaking detail, when and how he was to attend the All Saints worship and how he should dress and behave while doing so. Things were shaping up as planned in Lansing.

On Sunday, the day before Saad departed for the next city on his target church coordination tour, Kamal started attending the 11:30 Sunday morning worship service at All Saints Episcopal Church. Kamal was pleasantly surprised at the overwhelmingly polite reception he received from everyone he met and especially those sitting next to, in front of, and behind him. They all shook his hand and warmly welcomed him into their midst. Kamal could genuinely sense the love. The congregation was an eclectic mix of whites, blacks, and a sprinkling of Hispanics.

It had been a long time since Kamal had attended a Christian service but the routine and hymns brought back memories from his childhood. They also reminded him of his mother. So much so that he started feeling a little sentimental and melancholic. He had to consciously put out those feelings and did so by focusing on his task at hand. As with most all churches, a registration pad was passed down the aisle before service started. Kamal was careful not to fill out the address and phone number on the form. As Saad had warned, the last thing he needed was a visit from the pastor or the All Saints Welcoming Committee. In the future, once he received checks on the account he and Saad had opened, he would make a twenty-five dollar offering each week in Kim Sang Duk's name.

When the service was over, Kamal left thru one of the two side door exits. He didn't want to stand in line to shake the pastor's hand at the front door or to draw any unnecessary attention to himself by making idle chitchat while waiting to leave. It seemed as though Saad had covered even the most minor detail in preparing him for his mission.

CHAPTER 28

Abdulla was cold. The weather in Washington, D.C. always starting turning cold around the end of November and by late December it had made that turn and waved goodbye to comfortable temps. Today's high was only predicted to be in the mid-forties and for the third day in a row, it was raining. Still, there was a bit of a bounce in Abdulla's step as he walked from his car to his "office," the building with a sign proclaiming it to be Carson Delivery Services.

The five perfectly synchronized airline attacks had gone off without a hitch. And the succeeding emergency room suicide bombings was like a cherry on top of a plate of vanilla ice cream. The combination was horrifically beautiful and spiritually satisfying; to Abdulla. Nearly twelve hundred infidel souls had been sent straight to hell. The entire United States airline industry had been crippled. Literally and totally shut down for two days. It was still clogged up and slowed to a crawl as the FBI, TSA and Homeland Security scurried around looking for non-existent Korean terrorists, explosives, and exotic weapons. Newly implemented boarding procedures made even the Israilies look sloppy. Every bag, checked and carry-on, was physically opened and inspected before boarding. And Americans were terrified. As far as Abdulla was concerned, the sheer panic and the perceived loss of their personal security was worth the expense he and the MA had invested in the attacks. But there was more to come, a lot more.

Saad had been on the road ever since June traveling in a continuous circuit from Columbia, SC, to Jacksonville, FL to Nashville, TN, to Oklahoma, OK, to Lansing, MI. Abdulla had directed him to drive from city to city to avoid any travel pattern analysis by TSA software. He had succeeded in doing so, but he was fast becoming mentally and physically exhausted from the routine. His visits were coordinated to allow him to spend time with each of his, soon to be, martyrs and to be there on Sunday to observe their respective worship services on TV.

During his November rounds, before the attack on the airlines, Saad had presented each one of his men with their martyr vest. They were insanely simple to use. Just remove a safety shield from the dead man assemblage then press and hold the trigger button. The "hold the trigger button" was the important part. Because once you released it…no more martyr. Today would be his last day on the church circuit. Christmas was only four days away. He would watch CNN from his apartment and then two or three days after Christmas when Abdulla felt it was safe for him to travel, he would follow Khalid's path to Riyadh.

As always, the New York Exchange closed on Thanksgiving, the day after the five plane crashes. However, the opening bell on the following Monday brought one of the worst single-day declines in its history, minus 14.03 percent. Although it started to rebound the first week of December, the drop still wiped billions of dollars from individual and corporate investors. And the entire year's earnings of the three target airlines, Delta, Southwest, and American vanished. Equally important, MA moles in the CIA and DoD reported unparalleled increases in the U.S. military's wartime readiness despite an unchanged official DEFCON status.

Things were going just as Abdulla had planned and as had been prophesied by the archangel. But from Abdulla's perspective, the struggle had just begun. Khalid had safely returned to Riyadh and was already at work planning the Caliphate's post-war military strategy against those who would survive the United States-Russia-China slugfest. When the Islamic crusade was over, Abdulla would put Khalid in charge of subjugating Israel and enslaving the surviving inhabitants. He would then name him the new "King of the Jews."

Although still more than a month away, preparations for the presidential inauguration ceremony were well underway all over Washington, D.C. Hotels in the city had been reserved for months. Booked as the "greatest political show on earth," the event and the parties and protests associated with it would draw over a million visitors to the nation's capital. But it was the security surrounding the event that concerned Abdulla the most. Especially after what was going to happen next week.

The Secret Service and hundreds of law enforcement officers from across the country were already converging on the city. Undercover agents were prowling railroad ticket centers, subways, and bus lines looking for the tail-tail behavioral signs terrorists often displayed. FBI sniper hides had been constructed, traffic route changes identified and planned down to the minute, and interviews conducted with everyone living or working along the 1.9-mile parade route. Even the manhole covers along the road had been welded shut.

Although Abdulla was rightfully concerned, he wasn't overly worried. His mortar team had practiced at the Texas training ranch until they could put ten practice rounds in the air in less than thirty-five seconds. And their GPS aiming computer could put all of the projectiles inside a fifteen-meter bullseye or spread every two rounds in widening three-meter increments as was the plan. This would further enlarge the kill zone. There was nothing else for Abdulla and his team to do except to continue to monitor the primary and secondary routes they would be taking and to further refine their knowledge of the GPS tracking and aiming computer. The inauguration attack team was primed and ready.

Eight days after slipping out of its birth at Naval Base Kitsap, Bangor, Washington the USS Louisiana, SSBN-743, reached its launch position. The sub hovered thirty meters under the surface of the Yellow Sea off the coast of North Korea. The Louisiana's complement of Tomahawk missiles could reach any target on either side of the peninsula although that wouldn't be necessary. Its sister ship, another Ohio class sub was also prowling the Sea of Japan off the eastern side of the North Korean coast. This configuration put every square inch of the DPRK within an overlapping fire zone.

As the USS Louisiana was making its way to the Yellow Sea, one half of the United States entire stockpile of the newly modified B-61 nuclear weapons were boxed up and prepared for shipment from their production facility in New Mexico.

Outside of the Pentagon, very few people know that the United States Department of Energy operates an agency known as the Office of Secure Transportation. This organization operates a fleet of specially designed tractor-trailer trucks whose sole mission is to transport nuclear weapons and materials. The B-61's were loaded on to five of the vehicles and dispatched, using different routes, to Barksdale Air Force Base where they were loaded on C-17 cargo planes and flown to Guam and Japan. They were then equally distributed to each of the aircraft carriers positioned in the Sea of Japan. The United States strike force, armed with the most lethal assemblage of weaponry in humanity's history, was cocked and ready.

CHAPTER 29

The Sunday before Christmas, as they were waiting for church to start, Mrs. Simmons told Kamal that he should come early if he as going to the candlelight service. "It's not like our regular service sweetie. It's jam-packed, elbow to elbow. If you don't get here way ahead of time, you won't be able to find a decent seat, especially one near the front. You know this is the time that "twice a year Christians" come to church, Christmas and Easter. And there will be the children. On regular Sundays, they're in Sunday School or the nursery. But during our candlelight service, the whole family stays together."

Mrs. Simmons was a white-haired widow in her mid to late seventies. Every Sunday Kamal arrived at church a good fifteen to twenty minutes early so that he could sit in the same seat on the twelveth row from the front. He had been doing so for almost six months now and at the 11:30 service most regular attendees knew that spot was that "young black man's seat." Most all of the regulars had their favorite seats as well. It was a "church-going thing." When he first started attending some couples would occasionally ask him if he could "scoot down" so they could sit on the end. But Kamal politely deflected such requests saying "he had a bladder issue" and needed to be able to get to the aisle in the event of a flare-up. This always did the trick. Eventually, he had his seat "staked out."

Mrs. Simmons always sat in the same spot but on the bench behind Kamal's seat. She had taken to him from day one, gently tapping his shoulder, scooting forward and introducing herself the first Sunday he attended and chatting every Sunday ever since. She also attended Sunday School, Wednesday night prayer service, and served as Secretary for the Senior Ladies Small Group that met each Friday morning for coffee and Bible study; and gossip.

Mrs. Simmions was one of those generous, kind, people, who didn't have a mean or hateful bone in her body. She always complimented Kamal saying "you look so nice this morning" or "that's a lovely jacket." Now and then she would suggest that Kamal attend an All Saints Small Group Singles meeting as "there are always some nice ladies his age there." He would politely decline by deftly changing the subject. Kamal had grown to like Mrs. Simmons. Now he felt a little twinge of sadness and sympathy for her. But not enough to stop him from doing what he was destined to do.

Kamal stood a little over six feet tall and was a bit on the thin side. As Saad had suggested, he had taken to wearing a long, overly large, black trench coat to church ever since the weather started turning cold. Kamal thought it made him look like a black version of one of those pimply faced misfits responsible for the Columbine massacre years ago. Ironically, it served the same purpose. This evening, it would hide what he was wearing underneath.

At noon, Washington D.C. time, on Christmas Eve, Abdulla sent Mustafa a Dmail message. "Mustafa, please send the following to your "special" mailing list immediately. And now that your team has punched a hole in their firewall's spam filter make sure you include the Facebook accounts from your first hack."

"The American government leaders continue to ignore our demands to lift all sanctions illegally imposed on the DPRK even when we have demonstrated our ability to strike at will and with total impunity. This despite our continued patience and mercy. No more! Today you will once again feel the scorpion's sting. United States citizens, stay in your homes, do not go outside, do not fly your planes, drive your cars, or ride your subways. Do not even breath the air or drink your water without protection. Your government must be taught another lesson. Although our people do not celebrate this silly, superstitious, holiday, we have a special gift for you Americans. Merry Christmas to all, and to all a good night."

Abdulla couldn't resist the insulting salutation at the end of the message. The dark side of his increasingly complex personality was starting to ooze out, manifesting itself in even his most mundane thoughts and actions. Like most people sliding down the spectrum of psychosis, he didn't perceive the changes that had taken place deep inside his brain. In Abdulla's case something, a tumor, a chemical imbalance, a mutating gene sequence, had changed and was continuing to change his inferior frontal gyrus, Broca's area. Outwardly he appeared perfectly normal. Above normal, brilliant. Cheerful. Funny and outgoing. Inside, around the hippocampus, hidden from his consciousness a chemical fire was raging.

That afternoon Kamal had, for the hundredth time, put on the martyr's vest Saad had presented him earlier. It fit perfectly if "fit" was the proper term for the way it snuggled ten blocks of Semtex around his torso. As soon as he slipped it on, he gained nearly thirty pounds and added two inches of bulk to his chest and back. When he put on an extra large Wolverines sweatshirt, he looked like he had been on a year-long Krispy Kream diet. But the trench coat succeeded in disguising his apparent weight gain. Kamal slit the seam on the inside of the coat's left-hand pocket. Before leaving for the candlelight service, he would thread the dead man switch and the wire connecting it to the first blasting cap thru the slit and into the inside of the pocket. He then took off the coat and sweatshirt, removed the vest and laid everything out neatly on his bed.

The Candlelight service was scheduled for 6 p.m., and as Mrs. Simmons had suggested, Kamal wanted to get there plenty early. Although he didn't need to, Kamal undressed and got into the shower. His second shower of the day. He hadn't worked at the Post Office today. He didn't call in sick; he just hadn't gone to work. Saad had cautioned him not to deviate from his normal routine as he got closer to "his time." But for once Kamal didn't heed Saad's advice. He needed a little time to himself. He wanted to meditate and to focus on the task that lay before him. And Kamal wanted to think about his mom. To remember what it was like to be hugged. He couldn't. Too much time had passed and too many other, not so good, memories crowded out his thoughts.

Kamal had driven to a section of East Lansing that had been set aside as a bird sanctuary, the Baker Woodlot. It was thickly timbered and interlaced with walking paths. Not the concrete sidewalks found in most parks but leaf covered trails where you could just walk, and think, and try to remember. He strolled around for well over an hour, maybe two. Over the last couple of weeks, Kamal had begun to question himself, wondering if he would be up to the task. To do what he was ordained to do when the time came. He couldn't remember his mom, and there was a constant stream of thoughts running thru his mind. But he had come to one comforting realization, and that was just how scared he wasn't.

Finally, he decided he was where he needed to be mentally and spiritually. The past was just that, the past. He was not destined to fight with Al-Qaeda. He was who he was for a reason. Allah had given him another role.

Kamal made a detour on his way back from the park and drove to a branch office of the bank where he had his personal savings and checking accounts. He had a balance of $768.32 in his checking account and $3200 in savings. He wrote a check for $748 and withdrew $3180 from savings leaving just enough in each account to keep them active. He collected $3900 in $100 bills and one $20. When he returned to his car, he removed a plain white, security lined envelope from his glove compartment and wrote his father's name and address on the front. He did not include his return address. Kamal put a first-class stamp on the envelope then put 20 of the $100 bills inside. He tore off a sheet of paper from the notepad he kept in his car, wrote "I love you," on the paper and put it inside with the money. He then peeled off the adhesive protector on the flap and sealed the envelope. He would drop it in a postal collection box on his way home.

Next, he took another envelope, put the remaining $100 bills inside and wrote simply "Keneshia, Apt 214" on the address line. Keneshia was a young, twenty-something, single mother who lived two doors down from Kamal. Although he saw her and her little boy, in the hallway or parking lot, two or three times a week, he did not know her last name. She always smiled and spoke, and they sometimes had those short "elevator ride" discussions. He knew she worked her ass off all day then came home for another dose of cleaning and cooking. He didn't know how she, or any single parent, did it. He would slide the envelope in the slot of her apartment mailbox on his way to church. He would keep the $20 just in case, later in the day, he came across someone who looked like they were in need. Mohammad had declared "charity" as being one of the Pillars of Islam.

Kamal decided the clothes he was wearing would be just fine for the candlelight service. He was clean, and the trench coat would cover everything north of his knees. He unrolled his prayer rug, laid it on the floor, and got on his knees facing what he was sure was east, toward Mecca.

Kamal had an app on his iPhone that reminded him, and alerted all those around him, of the five obligatory *"Adhans,"* or call to prayer. It was time for the *Salat al-'asr*, late afternoon prayer. Kamal only spoke a few words in Arabic. He was trying to learn more, but it was slow going. So, like most of the converts in his circle of Muslim friends, when alone he prayed in English. When at his Mosque, he listened to the Imam. As Kamal began to pray he, as was commanded, looked only downward, neither to the left or the right. This was to veil one's gaze from everything but Allah.

Kamal loved the rigidity and respect demanded by Islam. Not at all like the buddy-buddy, loosey-goosey, "talk to Jesus" dialogues the Christians used during prayer. Kamal prayed the four *Rakats Fard* of the *Salat al'-asr* in English but as fervently as even the most devout Imam would have done, especially today, especially at this time. When he was finished, Kamal rolled up his prayer rug and placed it neatly on the back of his couch in his living room. It was time to go.

Kamal put on the canvas vest, tightened it up, then put on his coat. He reached thru the slit in his pocket and pulled the dead-man trigger up thru the opening. He then collected his car keys and the envelope he had prepared for Keneshia and left his apartment. He didn't lock the door, and he didn't look back.

Kamal walked down the steps and stopped at the apartment building's bank of mailboxes. He opened the flap on number 214 and pushed his envelope inside. He felt really good inside as he strolled toward his car. As he slid into the driver's seat, Kamal noticed how awkward he felt behind the wheel. The blocks of Semtex in the vest caused him to sit straight and too close to the wheel. He didn't bother trying to adjust the seat.

It was twenty after five when he pulled into the church parking lot, but there were already people trickling in. Mrs. Simmons had been right. Kamal hurried inside, as always entering thru the side door, avoiding the ubiquitous "official front door greeters."

He was one of the first to arrive for the service but not "the" first. His seat, the entire bench for that matter was vacant, and quickening his step a bit, he walked to it and claimed his spot. According to the clock on his iPhone, it was 5:35. People were starting to stream in, laughing and greeting one another as they too found their regular seats. At 5:40 Mrs. Simmons, entering thru the front door and speaking to everyone she met, slid into the seat behind Kamal. As she did so, she smiled saying "I'm glad you took my advice and got here early. The sanctuary will be full before you know it. Normally the ushers must put out metal folding chairs around the outer aisles for the twice-a-year folks. They aren't very comfortable on us old folks."

After she got settled, she reached into her purse and pulled out a small, gift-wrapped box, about the size of a pack of cigarettes. Handing it to Kamal and smiling from ear to ear she said "I got you a little something for Christmas. Now you can't open it until tomorrow morning. It's not much, but at least you will have a surprise under the tree." Kamal was overwhelmed. Choking back a lump in his throat he told her "thank you so much, Mrs. Simmons, that's one of the nicest things anyone has ever done for me." He slid the gift into the right-hand pocket of his coat. Just then three chimes rang out signaling the brief period for silence and meditation that preceded each worship service.

At 6:01 the Organist began playing a processional hymn, *O Holy Night*. This was also the signal for the congregation to stand and sing as the choir and pastor made their way toward the pulpit and the front of the church. Everyone continued singing until the choir was in the loft and the pastor behind the pulpit. The music ended and raising his arms as if to heaven the pastor said "tonight we worship in the name of the Father, and of the Son, and of the Holy Spirit. Please be seated."

Using a trick he had taught himself after he first started attending these Christian services, Kamal started mentally reciting passages from the Quran in an effort to block out the blasphemous words of the nonbelievers. As the congregation was taking their seats a young family, husband, wife, and two preteen females walked to the front of the church and stood next to a wreath with four burning candles around its outer edge and a single, unlit, candle in the center. It was 6:07.

The husband began reading a passage from the Old Testament, Micah 5:2; "But you, Bethlehem Ephrath, though you are small among the clans of Judah, out of you will come for me one who will be ruler over Israel..." After he finished reading his assigned passage, he passed his bible to his wife. She said, "The story of Jesus' birth continues into the New Testament." As she started reading from Matthew 1:18 Kamal thought to himself "a woman, uncovered, reading in church. These sins will not be forgiven."

When the woman finished reading her passage the youngest child, using one of the burning candles, lit the one in the center of the wreath, the Christ candle. When the Christ candle was burning the Director stood and signaled for the Choir to stand and begin singing the first verse of *Angels We Have Heard On High*. Their voices harmonized with the notes pouring from the massive pipe organ.

Angels we have heard on high
Sweetly singing o'er the plains
And the mountains in reply
Echoing their joyous strains
Angels we have heard on high

Sweetly, sweetly through the night

The Choir Director turned and raised his arms signaling the congregation to stand and join in.

And the mountains in reply
Echoing their brief delight
Gloria, in Excelsis Deo

As the Choir, congregation, and organ combined on this powerful verse, Kamal stood up and stepped into the aisle and began walking toward the front of the church. As he did, he slid his hand into the left pocket of his coat grasped the dead man trigger, flipped off the safety shield, and pressed the arming button.

The Director, standing in the center of the raised loft and busy with the task of leading both the Choir and the congregation, glanced down at the young black man walking up the aisle. Mrs. Simmons stared sympathetically, "poor man, had to leave during the best part of the hymn." Kamal raised his right hand, clenched it into a fist salute, shouted *"Allah Akbar!"* and released the trigger button.

At the corner of Grove Street and Ridge Road, Robert McKinney and his wife had just sat down to dinner when they heard the blast. Robert was a fifty-four-year-old agent with Farm Bureau Insurance. His office was only a block down the street, within an easy walking distance from his house. Although every day, for the past twenty-three years, he drove to work. He used "I never know when I will need to visit a client" as an excuse for this excess. In reality, it was because he was a living icon of a chubby, physically lazy, Insurance Agent. He didn't fool his wife or his fellow workers for a second.

However, that evening when he heard the blast and felt its concussion he jumped up from the table and sprinted out the front door like the running back he never was in school. Looking up

Grove Street, he could see the remnants of white smoke billowing out of the All Saints sanctuary building. Broken glass and smoldering scraps of wood and cloth were everywhere.

Without thinking, he ran up the street and dashed thru what remained of the church's front entrance. Robert stopped dead in his tracks, bent over at the waist, and started throwing up uncontrollably.

CHAPTER 30

The POTUS was sitting in front of the fireplace in the White House Library when he got the call from his Chief of Staff. "Sir, details are just starting to come in. Nothing's confirmed yet, but it looks like there have been at least two, maybe more, church bombings this evening. And we have another one of those "sent to the world" messages allegedly from the DPRK claiming responsibility. It also says that they will attack us again once a week, starting next Friday, until we meet their demands.

But within minutes we get yet another message, this time sent only to our official channels, saying that the DPRK isn't responsible for any of these attacks. Things just got complicated Mr. President." The POTUS, who was well into his third George Dickel, responded "you can't trust those fuckers, Abbie. They're playing us, just like they've been playing us for the last seventy years."

The Chief of Staff broke in, "hold that thought, Mr. President; we just got an update. We are up to four bombings sir, and they are bad. It's all over the news. I'm looking at the one in Columbia, South Carolina right now on CNN."

The POTUS grabbed the remote off the table next to his chair and turned on the TV mounted on the wall to his right. He punched a present channel selector button for CNN. Tufts of smoke and steam could be seen coming from shattered windows and a gaping hole that used to be the front entrance of a church. EMT's came out pushing a gurney toward a waiting ambulance. Sirens wailed as firemen, wearing bulky looking breathing gear, moved in and out of the church. It was semi controlled pandemonium.

As he was watching the news, flipping from CNN to Fox, the POTUS burst out of the brain mist the whiskey was starting to spread. The Fox News anchor, some third string holiday fill in, interrupted the live coverage to read the latest "we warned you" message from the DPRK. He did not mention, at least not during this segment, the other message which proclaimed North Korea's innocence; at least concerning this and the airline attacks.

"Abbie, I know it's Christmas, or soon will be, but I am declaring this a national emergency. Get on the horn to our war council and tell them to have their butts in the Situation Room no later than 0700 tomorrow. I think Major Ferris is the carrier this week. I will let him know that we are in motion."

Major Aron Ferris, USMC, was one of five military aides responsible for carrying what is known as the Nuclear Football for the POTUS. The football is a rather non-descript, black suitcase which contains the launch codes and plans for nuclear war.

Any time the POTUS travels, the football handcuffed to the carrier's wrist is never more than 100 feet away. In fact, there are three footballs, one for the POTUS, one which follows the Vice President in the event the POTUS is killed or incapacitated, and one called the "Spare Tire" which is stored at the White House. There are a set of procedures that will be followed if the POTUS decides that a first, or retaliatory, nuclear strike against an enemy is to be initiated. Below the president, in a submarine, silo, or bomber there is a strict "two-man procedure" required to launch a nuclear weapon; a Commander and the number two in command must concur that any launch code received is valid.

Currently, there are no such restrictions on the POTUS. He or she can initiate an all-out nuclear war at their discretion. The Secretary of Defense, if available, is supposed to verify that the president is in fact, the person giving the order but he or she does not have any veto power. The POTUS does carry a sealed plastic card that contains codes that will be used with a launch order to identify him or her to Pentagon or Ravern Mountain staff that it is indeed the president. This system was designed during the cold war to ensure that a response could be initiated quickly in the event incoming missiles were detected. In theory, U.S. missiles could be in the air in less than ten minutes, and without congressional or any other oversight or approval.

"Clear Sir!" The Chief of Staff replied, "I'm on it." The POTUS ended the call then punched another call button on his desk telephone. The call was answered before the second ring ended. "Major Farris sir." "Major Farris, we just went on high alert. I'm sure you have a news feed on and are getting a good dose of Pentagon alerts. However, just in case you were in the shower, doing whatever Marines do in a shower, we have suffered what appears to be another attack. I need you and your football in the Situation Room at 0700 tomorrow. I am going to try to grab a couple of hours sleep and suggest you do the same." "Yes Mr. President, I'll see you at 0700."

Major Farris knew he needed to rest. He had been awake for over 20 hours. But his brain was giving the "dump adrenalin command," and even though he was physically near exhaustion, he was mentally wide awake. The shit was about to hit the fan.

Abdulla called Saad as soon as the first news reports started coming in. "My loyal friend, you have done well. You will surely reap your earthly reward once our mission is complete. If the news reports I am watching are even remotely accurate, there is unbelievable panic throughout the American heartland. And the hatred and thirst for revenge are even greater than the days after 9/11. Only this time it is directed solely toward the North Koreans rather than our Islamic brothers in the Middle East.

Saad, I trust you will be starting your journey to Riyadh during the next day or so." "Yes, Abdulla I have leased a car and will be traveling to Montreal tomorrow. I will spend the night there and then catch the 1730 flight to Paris the next day. I will follow the same pattern as Khalid, staying a couple of days in Paris and then on to Riyadh. I will keep you informed of my progress via Dmail. I agree with you my Caliph; it appears that we have sorely wounded this paper tiger."

"Once again you are correct Saad" Abdulla replied, glowing in Saad's reference to him as his Caliph. "And on their January twentieth Inauguration Day, the sword of Allah will deliver the final thrust to its heart. Be safe and careful my old friend, *ila al-liqaa.*" Abdulla ended the call, said his evening prayers, and then prepared for bed...and the dreams.

CHAPTER 31

By 0645 Christmas morning, everyone but the POTUS had arrived and were milling around their seats, drinking coffee in the White House Situation Room. The mood was anything but cheerful. Somber, hushed, one-on-one conversations replaced the normal, idle, acquaintance but not friends chit-chat. No one was smiling, and even the occasional "Merry Christmas" greeting was delivered without any hint of sincerity. This was not a day of celebration.

At precisely 0700 the POTUS and the military aide and football carrier, Major Ferris, entered the room. The sight of Major Ferris sent chills up the spines of everyone around the table. The carrier was always within one hundred feet of the President but typically did not accompany him into the Situation Room. His presence and physical proximity to the president could only mean one thing.

As customary, everyone stood up when the POTUS entered the room; the Joint Chiefs snapped to rigid attention. "Take your seat folks; we will dispense with the formalities for the time being. Everyone here is aware of at least most of what happened last night. Christmas fucking Eve for heaven's sake. These heathens have no damn honor or respect."

The president's eyes were red, and his hand trembled ever so slightly. Abbie, sitting to his left near the head of the table couldn't tell if his eyes were the result of crying or a night long bender. She didn't smell alcohol or coverup mouthwash but couldn't be sure he wasn't self-medicating with a few Dickels, his favorite. She remembered hearing stories of Nixon's heavy drinking and subsequent threats to start a nuclear war, during the days before passing the Presidential Seal to Gerald Ford. Another one of those White House legends passed along from Chief of Staff to Chief of Staff. Although unquestionably loyal, Abbie was starting to have serious doubts concerning the president's current state of mind. His sanity for that matter. One thing was for sure; he was pissed.

Turning his attention to the Secretary of Defense the POTUS demanded "Dennis, we need to get everyone on a level playing field. Give us a background summary and current SITREP."

"Mr. President, ladies, and gentlemen, last evening, at approximately 1800 hours central time, five Protestant churches were bombed during their annual candlelight service. They were located in upper-middle-class neighborhoods in Lansing, Michigan, Columbia, South Carolina, Oklahoma City, Oklahoma, Nashville, Tennessee, and Jacksonville, Florida. Immediately following what apparently was the first bombing we, and by we I mean pretty much the entire planet, received another message broadcast over military channels and various social media venues.

This message, apparently originating from North Korea, claimed responsibility and threatened to launch subsequent attacks every week until their previous stated demands were met. Now here's the strange thing. Less than an hour later we, and this time I am referring only to military channels and selective news agencies received another message denying any DPRK culpability. It too appeared to emanate from North Korea."

The Vice President interrupted saying "Dennis, you have used "apparently" and "appeared" while describing these messages.

Does this mean or imply that we don't know where the hell they came from?"

"Mr. Vice President, that means we can't be certain they came from the DPRK. Technically that appears to be their origin, but given the spoofing capabilities that even puss faced sixteen-year-old nerds have at their fingertips these days, we aren't one hundred percent sure, yet. The NSA, CIA, and FBI are all trying to backtrack their source; or whatever the technical jargon is. But that is a tough nut to crack even with amateur hackers. These guys seem to be both sweeping their tracks and laying out false trails. It could take weeks to find out with any degree of certainty.

We are also analyzing the explosive residue from each site. Again, it's way too early to tell, but the explosive does appear to be some form of Semtex. But not from the Czech Republic. The Czech's are, or at least were, the only commercial manufactures of Semtex. Since 1990 the company, Explosia, that makes the stuff has been adding a detection taggant which allows it to be identified even after it has been detonated. None of the residues from any of the churches included this taggant. So no, we don't know who made it or where the explosives originated.

This brings me to the state of our military preparations. Both of our Ohio class subs are now in place and hovering at launch depth, about 50 meters under the ocean. They are essentially playing hide and seek with the North Korean attack subs. But even when they are moving, they are so quiet that the only way the Nork subs, which are all diesel powered, would ever find one would be to run it to it accidentally.

Regardless, they will stay at launch depth until they release their packages or are ordered to move. The problem is that when they are 50 meters underwater two-way communication is impossible. For this reason, every hour, on a constantly moving five-minute sequence, the subs will raise a very low frequency, VLF, antenna which is mounted on a small buoy attached to a long cable. By moving sequence, I mean at 1300 they will raise the antenna, then again at 1405, then 1510 and so on.

It's not inconceivable that a patrol boat or plane could spot the antenna and give away the position of the sub. It's like we are shadow boxing. When the antenna is in place, the sub will listen for a launch, or stand down order for ten minutes. If nothing is received, it will retract the antenna and remain in place until the next sequence.

If a launch order is received, it will contain the codes for a predetermined battle plan and launch times. As I briefed previously, our preliminary strike battle plan calls for near-simultaneous detonations of a HEMP device, a W-78 over Pyongyang and seven W-76's on DPRK military targets. The coordination and timing of these launches are incredibly complex. Especially since they will be coming from four different, geographically separated, submarines and a fighter-bomber who can't communicate with one another or with a command and control facility.

But rest assured, the officers and crew of these boats have practiced this scenario until they can do it in their sleep. If there is a SNAFU, it will not be because our men and women don't know what they are doing or how to do it.

Our carrier groups, radar jamming and attack aircraft, and all other personnel and equipment are in place and are on DEFCON 2 level alert. Although as we discussed previously, we are still officially sitting at DEFCON 4. Mr. President that concludes my situation report."

Except for some nervous paper shuffling the room was silent. The POTUS put his hands on the end of the table, pushed back his chair and stood up. Starting with the Vice President, and moving his gaze slowly and to the left, around the table, he looked every person in the room squarely in the eye. Finally, after what seemed like an eternity, he spoke. His voice was firm, unquivering, and delivered with the assuredness of someone who was clearly in charge and knew it.

"Thank you, Dennis, please be seated. Abbie, start the recorder." The Situation Room was equipped with multiple high definition video and audio recording devices. They were turned on or off at the President's discretion. Some wanted everything that happened inside recorded. Some, like President Clinton, was a lot more selective about what was saved for posterity.

"Folks, not counting today we are only six hundred and twenty-four hours away from having a damn liberal pussy sworn in as the President of the United States of fucking America. The North Koreans have been jerking us around for almost seventy years. And as soon as that guy takes office, they get their ticket punched for at least another four years. They've already started production of a hydrogen bomb, and with the development of their Hwasong-16 ICBM they have the means to park it right here in River City." No one in the room under the age of fifty had ever seen or heard of *The Music Man,* so the President's offhand reference to River City was lost on them. The POTUS was on another one of his rants. This time they knew there was no turning back. He was crossing the Rubicon.

"We I'll be damned if I am going to let that piss ant dictator and his zombie army do it any longer. Major Ferris, it's third and long, time to pass that football, and I mean now!" The silence was broken. Everyone in the room let out the breath they had unconsciously been holding. A disharmonious chorus of expletives, mostly "oh shits," filled the air.

Major Ferris stood up instantly. He unlocked the strap which was handcuffed to his wrist and placed the football on a small table to his right. Then, for all to see, he unbuttoned his jacket and took the safety strap off the .40 caliber revolver hanging from his shoulder holster. The military aides responsible for carrying the football didn't pack the standard Army issue 9mm. They wanted something with a round in the chamber that they could start firing without any preliminaries. It was provided in the unlikely event that someone, even from this august group, may try to prevent the POTUS from getting to the football. The Major was sworn to protect the football with his life. He would not hesitate to use whatever force was necessary to make sure that didn't happen.

"Mr. President if you could please step over to the table." There was a well-defined process that the POTUS and the carrier would follow once a decision was made to use a nuclear weapon. The President would be taken aside so that he and the carrier could confer in at least relative privacy. Normally the second step in this well-rehearsed procedure would be for the carrier to issue a "watch alert" to the Joint Chiefs of Staff. However, since they were sitting less than ten feet away with their eyes glued to the president the formality of this step wasn't necessary.

As the POTUS walked to the table, Major Farris unlocked the football. Contrary to urban legend, there wasn't an elaborate biometric identification mechanism securing the most lethal set of plans and codes in the mankind's history; just a five key combination lock.

Major Farris pulled out a three-ring notebook which contained a plastic laminated sheet of paper referred to as the "Vital Page." This document contained the options for retaliatory strikes or each attack plan. Major Farris and the POTUS, using tones clearly audible throughout the room, selected the recently updated attack plan that had been designed for an offensive strike against North Korea. As soon as the POTUS approved the attack plan Major Farris keyed entered a code into a small one-way communication device inside the football.

Using an ultra highly classified technology, the device transmitted a signal thru an antenna located in the football's handle to the National Military Command Center in the Pentagon. Within minutes the entire United States armed forces went on DEFCON 1, maximum readiness status. Never before had the United States been at this level of readiness. During the Cuban Missile Crisis in 1962, certain units were put on DEFCON 2 alert. But not the entire military and never at DEFCON 1 which indicated that nuclear war was likely or imminent.

All that remained was a launch order from the POTUS. It was 0812 Eastern Standard Time, 2112 Korean Time, or for military operations coordination purposes 1312 Zulu time. Zulu time is the military term for Greenwich Mean Time or GMT. It is used anytime U.S. armed forces are required to coordinate actions involving time zones in multiple geographic locations worldwide. The use of Zulu time, which is five hours earlier than Eastern Standard Time, eliminates the need to convert from one time zone to another when planning military actions or movements.

As the next step in the official process, the carrier had to identify the president positively. Looking at the Secretary of Defense Major Ferris said: "Mr. Secretary if you could join the President and me." The Secretary stood up and walked across the room. When he was approximately five feet from the POTUS and the football Major Ferris put up his hand. "That's close enough sir. Mr. President, please open your biscuit."

The "biscuit" is a plastic envelope containing a card on which a special code is printed. Except for a single incident with President Carter, who accidentally sent his to the cleaners with one of his suits, the biscuit must remain with the POTUS at all times. The President pulled out his wallet, removed his biscuit, broke it open and read the code to Major Ferris who compared it to a code contained in the football. Major Ferris presented both code cards to the Secretary of Defense and asked: "Mr. Secretary, please verify that the codes are identical." The Secretary did so. "Mr. President, we are ready for the launch order."

At this point, the Secretary of State pushed back his chair and stood up. Major Ferris reached into his jacket and grasped, but did not remove his revolver. "Mr. President," the Bulldog pleaded, "I must go on record as saying we aren't positive North Korea is behind these attacks. For Christ's sake, we don't even know if the messages we have been getting came from the DPRK." The POTUS turned his head and glared at the Secretary.

"So noted Bulldog! Major Ferris, execute attack plan delta-mike two one five." As the Secretary of State sank back into his chair, Major Ferris said for all to hear "Sir, I am duty-bound to re-verify that attack plan delta-mike two one five is to be executed." "That is correct Major!" It was 1316 Zulu time.

CHAPTER 32

At 1420 Zulu time the USS Louisiana let out 50 meters of cable attached to the buoy supporting its VLF radio antenna. The Louisiana and the other three subs had been following this same routine at the same times for the last two days. Raise an antenna every hour on a sliding schedule, listen for a coded message for ten minutes, then retract the antenna if nothing is received. Then repeat, over and over again. This time the routine changed.

At 1426 Zulu time the Communications Officer swiveled around in her chair to look at the USS Louisiana's Commanding Officer, CO. "Captain, we are receiving a message." Coded text started to scroll across a computer monitor while simultaneously printing on a paper tape. It was only 150 characters long, a continuous stream of letters, just a little longer than a tweet. It would be the most profound tweet ever transmitted.

When the strip printer stopped, the Captain tore off the coded message, studied it intensely for a few seconds then snatched the microphone from its mount near the main periscope. "Battle stations missile, battle stations missile, this is the Captain speaking. This is not a drill!"

Life on a submarine could be mind-numbingly boring. Hour-by-hour routine is broken up by more of the same. No day or night, no rain no sunshine, no Monday no Friday, just continuous sameness. And then comes the clanging call to battle stations. In an instant, every soul on the sub goes from comatose to near panic. The Captain put the microphone back on its hook, gave the order "Officer of The Deck you have the helm," and headed toward the Weapons Control Room.

The Executive Officer, XO, the sub's second in command, and the Weapons Officer, WO, were already waiting for the Captain when he arrived. While it was alarmingly simple for the President to start a worldwide nuclear war, the procedure to launch an ICBM was strictly controlled and wrapped in checks and double checks. As soon as he entered the Weapons Control Room, the Captain initiated a launch process that he and his officers drilled on at least once every 48 hours. It was 1435 Zulu Time.

CO, "Fire Control, spin up missiles one thru twenty-four."

Fire Control Tech "Sir, spinning up all missiles."

XO, reading a copy of the printed message "we have a properly formatted message, request permission to authenticate."

CO, "Weapons Officer, do you authenticate?"

WO, "Sir, the message authenticates."

CO, "XO, do you authenticate?"

XO, "Sir, the message authenticates."

CO, "I concur that we have an authentic message. XO, you have permission to retrieve the launch code."

XO, "aye Sir, breaking out the launch code."

CO speaking into a Weapons Control Room microphone, "this is the Captain, set conditions to 1SQ, this is not a drill." Condition 1SQ is the highest level of readiness aboard a submarine.

XO speaking into a second Weapons Control Room microphone, "this is the Executive Officer, set conditions to 1SQ, this is not a drill." The crew must recognize the voice of each senior officer before proceeding with launch preparations.

WO, "stand by firing order."

Fire Control Tech, "aye Sir, stand by fire order."

WO, "the firing order will be twenty-four."

Fire Control Tech, "aye Sir, the firing order will be twenty-four."

There are actual "keys" required to launch a sub's missiles. These keys are maintained in physically separate safes in the Weapons Control Room and are retrieved by two of the sub's Officers during the final stage of the launch process.

Once removed from the safe the keys are given to the Captain and Executive Officer for insertion into their respective fire control mechanisms. As part of the, "accidental or rogue launch prevention process," the keys must be inserted and turned simultaneously. Like the launch code safes, the fire control mechanisms are located far enough from one another that it is not possible for a single person to arm both devices.

CO, "XO, the launch order directs that we are to arm and launch tube one at 1455. Hold hover, arm and launch at my command."

In addition to Tomahawk cruise missiles and an array of torpedoes, Ohio class submarines are armed with Trident D5 submarine-launched ballistic missiles (SLBM). Each Trident D5 could be loaded with a multiple independently targetable reentry vehicle (MIRV) which could be configured with one to ten nuclear warheads. The missile in tube one contained one 350 kiloton W-78 and three one hundred kiloton W-76 weapons. The USS Louisiana's sister Ohio class submarine, hovering off the eastern coast of North Korea, was armed with a similar weapons configuration. Both subs had the same launch orders. Neither ship was aware of the exact targets they or their sister sub would be attacking. That information was coded inside each missile warhead based on a specific launch order.

XO, "Aye Sir, hold hover, arm and launch at your command."

CO, "Fire Control, pressurize tube one."

Fire Control Tech, "Aye Sir, pressurizing tube one."

1455 Zulu Time.

CO, "XO, arm for launch command."

XO, "Aye sir, arming for launch command."

The Captain and the Executive Officer inserted their keys into their respective fire control mechanisms.

On the opposite side of the Peninsula, a single F-22 stealth fighter streaked across the North Korean border south of Hongwon heading for the geographic center of the country between Huichon and Tokchon. Despite its ubiquitousness, the North Korean air defense radar network didn't show the slightest blip.

Approximately thirty-five miles northwest of Tokchon, after climbing to an altitude of sixty-five thousand feet, the F-22 opened its bomb doors, executed a verticle half-loop and fired an air-launched missile armed with a 300 kiloton W-80 nuclear warhead. As the F-22 increased its speed to Mach 1.9 and veered east to avoid blast effects the missile climbed to one hundred and ten thousand feet and detonated its nuclear payload. This was the first ever combat test of a high altitude electromagnetic pulse, HEMP, weapon. Its effect exceeded all expectations. It was 1454 Zulu Time.

CO, "Weapons Control, fire tube one."

Fire Control Tech, "Aye Sir, firing tube one."

It was 1455 Zulu Time.

CHAPTER 33

Nighttime satellite images of the Korean peninsula show what appears to be a massive hole between South Korea and China. The simple fact which causes this appearance is that for the most part, the cities, towns, and villages in North Korea don't have their lights on at night. Except for the Supreme Leader's principal residence just north of Pyongyang, colloquially known as the Central Luxury Mansion or one of his dozen or so villas, there practically isn't any civilian electricity at night. For most civilians, power is cut off at 2200 and isn't turned back on until 0500. Unlike almost every other semi-industrialized country on the planet, there is no significant traffic at night. Or anytime, compared to its neighbor to the south. It would be over six hours before most residents of what was soon to be the former DPRK discovered the electricity wouldn't be coming back on. Not for a long time.

Just a little before midnight, North Korean time, the sky was filled with a blinding flash of light. For several seconds it was a hundred times brighter than the sun. An instant later those in the center of the country were awakened by earsplitting thunder, louder than anything they had ever heard. You could feel the concussion caused by the sound waves.

Although startled and jarred awake most people, having missed what would become known as "the night of the light in the heavens," just went back to sleep. There were a few of the more edu-cated, geo-politically aware populace whose first thought was that something had gone horribly wrong at the recently opened nuclear power plant in Yongbyon or that a meteor had slammed into the ionosphere. Even this group dared not imagine what had happened.

There were some advantages to being a backward, technically isolated, country. If the HEMP weapon that detonated over North Korea had exploded over the United States, it would have plunged much of the country into the stone age. The entire electric grid would have had its circuits shorted and shut down. Car and truck electronic ignition and fuel distribution systems would have fried. Airplanes would have dropped from the sky when their avionics and guidance components fused. In an instant, all of this happened in North Korea as well but to a far, far lesser degree.

Civilian and some unshielded military communications were disabled, but only fourteen percent of the population had ever even used a telephone. Electronic medical equipment and physiological monitors stopped working, but hospitals were as scarce as cell tow-ers. The blast of electromagnetic energy was nowhere near as devas-tating as it would have been anywhere else. But it did cripple what little infrastructure the North Koreans had. And its psychological effect, especially among the military, was staggering. They had been brainwashed into believing that no power would ever dare launch an attack on the homeland. Three generations of Supreme Leaders had assured them that the DPRK was invincible. That lineage was seconds away from becoming extinct.

The Supreme Leader snuffed out the last $47.00 a pack Yves Saint Laurent cigarette he would smoke that night. Or ever. He and his wife had just finished watching the third episode of the last sea-son of *Game of Thrones*. This was by far his favorite television series. Like his father, he loved American movies, especially westerns and monster classics. His favorites were *A Fistful of Dollars* and *King Kong vs. Godzilla.*

Although it was illegal for the average North Korean to purchase anything but state-approved DVD's, the Supreme Leader had over 20,000 in his private collection. Many of which, mostly porn, he had inherited from his father. The Supreme Leader's wife, Ri Sol-ju, demurely suggested that it was too late to watch another episode. She was exhausted, and they should go to bed.

Early in 2018, his wife was bestowed the title of "Respected First Lady." This was the first time that title had been officially used since his mother claimed it for herself in 1974. The couple had one son, Chang Ju-ae, a precocious ten-year-old who was never seen in public. Chang Ju-ae would be privately tutored at home until the age of twelve. Then, like his father, he would be sent to the Liebefeld Steinholzli school in Koniz, Switzerland. At least that was the plan.

The Supreme Leader's Central Luxury Mansion lay just a little over nine kilometers northeast of Pyongyang. The sprawling palace was bordered by immaculately groomed forests on three sides and a massive manmade lake on the other. The interior of the mansion was as luxurious as any in Europe. Handwoven Persian carpets covered Belizean recovered sinker mahogany floors. Scores of original paintings hung from virtually every wall, even those in the twenty-two toilets attached to almost every room. These included works by Raphael, Degas, and *The Concert* by Johannes Vermeer. Not all but most of the paintings were stolen, purchased off the black market and never seen again by the public. *The Concert*, which hung in the main hall, is widely considered to be the most valuable painting ever stolen. There was a reported $5,000,000 reward offered for its safe return.

The Supreme Leader was also a vociferous collector of pianos; he owned thirty; cars, he had twelve Mercedes Benz one of which, a specially modified S600, cost over $1,500,000; and a personal collection of wrist watches valued at $7,000,000.

The Supreme Leader, his wife, and one hundred and fifty of their closest friends could also indulge his taste for American movies in a luxurious cinema. His personal theater was outfitted with butter soft goatskin leather MX4D seats which moved in sync with movie effects. It sported a forty-foot screen, a Sony 4K digital projector, and Dolby Surround Sound.

Despite being surrounded by a starving populace, no expense had been spared in building and continuously upgrading the Central Luxury Mansion. It was indeed a marvel of engineering and a testament to the excesses of its current and previous occupants. It was also ground zero for the third but far from last nuclear weapon to be used in war.

The Supreme Leader showed not the slightest remorse when he had a subordinate who had angered him executed in front of an audience of military officers by a specially trained pack of dogs. He had another killed by anti-aircraft machine guns in front of his wife and mother. Yet the Supreme Leader meekly complied when his wife pulled on his arm, stood him up and started guiding him toward the elevator which would take them to their bedroom. "We can watch the next episode tomorrow" she cooed. The omnipresent mansion staff would tidy up the cinema and make sure that his cigarette butts and leftover snacks were incinerated to prevent them from being sold on the black market. Anything the Supreme Leader touched could become a collectible item.

The couple exited the elevator walked down a brightly lit hall and thru the double doors of their unbelievably spacious bedroom. The mansion staff had closed the ornate velvet curtains, turned back their customized California king bed, and laid out silk robes and night clothes for both. The Supreme Leader undressed, put on his pajamas, and then padded over to a bar on his side of the bedroom. His wife walked to where he was standing, bowed slightly then kissed him on the cheek and said "goodnight my love. Sleep well. We will see what evil deeds Cersei Lannister is up to tomorrow night." Cersei and her brother Jaime Lannister were the Supreme Leader's favorite characters in the soon to end series. She walked across the room and quietly slipped into bed. The Supreme Leader wanted his nightly Scotch on the rocks nightcap before going to sleep. He took the lid off the ice bucket sitting in the center of a teak sideboard. The bucket was filled with cubes of ice made from bottled Fiji water, another in a long list of his extravagances. Picking up a pair of sterling silver tongs he dropped first one then another cube of ice into a leaded crystal glass. He never heard the second cube hit bottom.

The W-78 was a 350 kiloton hydrogen bomb. Its explosive power was ten times that of the weapons dropped on Hiroshima and Nagasaki combined. This particular bomb, delivered as one of four in the Trident missile's MIRV warhead launched from the USS Louisiana, was detonated at the height of 500 meters directly above the Central Luxury Mansion. A low-level airburst would reduce radioactive fallout while maximizing the explosive and thermal effects of the weapon. This strategy addressed the POTUS' order to minimize civilian casualties to the extent possible. Even so, there would be over 800,000 fatalities in and around Pyongyang over the next seven days. The fireball from this explosion was nearly two kilometers across and instantly reached a temperature exceeding 150 million degrees Fahrenheit, roughly that of the interior of the sun. In less than an hour, this scenario would repeat itself all across North Korea as the force of the U.S. Navy's nuclear fleet was unleashed.

If the scene in the Supreme Leader's bedroom could have been reduced into ultra slow motion, one would have seen blinding white light streaming thru the windows. This was just the visible sliver of the spectrum, from 700 to 400 nanometers. Invisible x-rays and gamma-rays also burst thru, and for just a millisecond the Supreme Leaders skeleton would have been visible inside his body. In the next millionth of a second the Supreme Leader, his entire family, and everything else within a circle over a mile across was vaporized.

In North Korea people referred to the Chang dynasty as the Mount Plaku heritage. It started in 1948 with Chang Song Il followed by his son Chang Han Un and ended with the simultaneous death of Chang Jong Nam and his son Chang Ju-ae.

In less than sixty minutes after the Commander of the USS Louisiana launched the first missile the most brutal and repressive dictatorship in the twenty-first century ceased to exist. Military headquarters from Nampo to Chongjin were erased from the global map along with every deep-water port north of the Korean Peninsula's 38th parallel. The Americans made every effort to be as surgically precise as possible in their attacks on military targets. Even so by the time the only surviving member of the Central Military Commission of the Workers' Party of Korea was located and signed the unconditional surrender of the DPRK over 2,300,000 people, nearly one-tenth of its population, had died.

The world held its breath. Only a hand full of Chinese, Russian, and American government officials knew of the non-proliferation agreement between the three countries. Not even the South Koreans or Japanese.

David Stakely's idea and the Bulldog's negotiating skills had paid off on a global scale. As could be expected, there was a sharp divide in the United States Congress and the nation in general. More than a few called for the immediate impeachment of the president. Some demanded his arrest and conviction as a war criminal. Most, both conservative and liberal, compared the action to the removal of a malignant tumor. Had this not been done, there was a very real possibility the "host" would have died.

The mood in South Korea was, to put it mildly, celebratory. In the years to come, December 26th would be recognized as an official holiday known as *"geom-eul jegeohan nal"* or day the sword was removed. This was in reference to the fable of Damocles, a courtier in the court of Dionysius. Damocles begged Dionysis to switch places with him for just a day so that he could experience what it was like to be treated like a king. Dionysis honored the request, but that night at a banquet he had a sword suspended by a single hair over Damocles' head. This was to symbolize the constant state of fear Dionysis, and his kingdom had to endure. The South Koreans now referred to only as Koreans, had been living in a far worse state of fear for almost seventy years.

Abdulla was coming unglued. His plans and his dreams of becoming the next Caliph, of reuniting all of Islam into a global Caliphate, a new world order seemed to be crumbling. How could it be? He spoke to the Archangel every single day, almost constantly when he was alone and not talking to someone else. He no longer had to wait for the dreams to receive directions, the voice was always there now. Sometimes whispering sometimes roaring.

It had been a week since the Great Satan had attacked and destroyed the DPRK. Neither the Russians nor Chinese had so much as lifted a finger to interfere. There had been no retaliatory strikes against the Americans. The Chinese had dispatched a contingent of its military to key spots along its southeastern border. This was ostensibly to provide aid and comfort. In reality, it was to stem the flood of would-be refugees into China.

But even worse, news agencies had reported that both Chinese and Russians, along with Japanese, Koreans, and even Swiss were already inspecting former biological and chemical weapons factories. According to one talking head, these would be converted to, or back to, drug and fertilizer production plants. Everything was coming apart.

But there was still the presidential inauguration. He and his team could still inflict unprecedented pain and fear among the American government. Maybe after the new president, and everyone within fifty feet of him was killed they would still lash out at their old enemies. Maybe, just maybe, the Caliphate could still be salvaged. These thoughts along with smoldering anger and fear raged inside Abdulla as he walked to his car. Not fear in the normal sense. It was fear of failure. For Abdulla that was the worse kind.

January was always cold in Washington, D.C. At least it wasn't raining. Or snowing. Snow could really screw up the traffic, and it was going to be bad enough as it was. It was January 2, the day after the Americans celebrated the beginning of a new year. Most were still recovering from their drunken New Years Eve parties. These dates meant nothing to Abdulla or any other Muslim. In Islam, the new year begins on the first day of Muharram, the first month of the Islamic calendar. The Islamic year began in 622 AD when the prophet Muhammad traveled from Mecca to Medina. To Abdullah January 1 was just another day. It held no significance.

Nonetheless, he had given his mortar team time off ever since the Christmas Eve massacre. He wanted them to spend extra time with their families and to prepare themselves mentally and spiritually for the grand finale. The *"coup de grace"* delivered to the nest of infidel snakes that is, soon to be "was," America.

Abdulla pulled into far left "Loading Zone Only" space in front of Carson Deliver Services. A Buick and a Focus belonging to his two team members and the open top panel truck occupied the spaces to his right. He was running a little late this morning, out of character for him, and his team was already here. Probably brewing a pot of tea and smoking their tenth cigarette of the day. No matter, they had become more than proficient in their knowledge and simulated use of the huge mortar and its GPS aiming computer. And they were ready and willing to sacrifice their lives for Islam. Let them smoke. Let them have a plate of bacon for that matter. He smiled at his unspoken blasphemous humor.

Walking to the door, he unconsciously tried turning the handle. It was locked, as it was supposed to be. Abdulla took out his key, unlocked the deadbolt, and then did the same with the lock on the door handle. He opened the door and stepped inside. As he was closing the door, he saw the figure standing behind it. "*Ya ilahi,* Khalid you scared me half to death. What pray tell are you doing here? You are supposed to be in Riyadh! It's no wonder I haven't received a phone call or Dmail from you lately." Khalid was wearing a full-length, dark gray wool overcoat and black, kid leather, gloves. There was a copy of the *Washington Post* in his left hand, folded as if he was going to swat a fly. His right hand was in his coat pocket. It wasn't the least bit cold in the Carson Delivery Service front office, but Abdulla had not had time to evaluate any of his observations yet. His pulse rate was only now beginning to return to normal.

"Abdulla, the Sovereign Council of the *maharib alsamt,* sent me. They are extremely disappointed in the recent turn of events. Disappointed is not the right word. They are outraged. Rather than initiating a war among the infidel superpowers and bringing about the rebirth of the Islamic Caliphate we have made heroes of our most reviled enemy. Heros even among their rivals. We have elevated the Americans even beyond their previous status. And our actions have resulted in eliminating a major thorn in their side. Things are not good Abdulla. I am sorry."

Khalid removed his hand from his pocket revealing a long barrel 22 caliber revolver. Abdulla knew that it would be loaded

THE ENEMY OF MY ENEMY

with rounds of subsonic ammunition. They weren't powerful, but they weren't loud either. And at this range, they were extremely lethal. An assains weapon of choice in close quarters.

"No Khalid, we still have one more….." Two perfectly spaced holes appeared slightly below Abdulla's nose and above his upper lip. The subsonic bullets would not make an exit wound. Instead, they passed thru the medulla oblongata causing what snipers call flaccid paralysis. This resulted in a total and complete loss of muscle control and signals from the brain to the rest of the body. Instant death.

Holding the pistol, Khalid counted to thirty. He didn't want to desecrate Abdulla's body further, but he did want to ensure he was dead. Thin trickles of blood started to ooze from the two holes in Abdulla's face. Khalid put the pistol back into his coat pocket, grasped Abdulla's pants at each ankle and started dragging his body across the office and into a back office.

There, laid neatly next to a wall were the bodies of the other two members of the mortar crew. Khalid positioned Abdulla's body next to his teammates then went to a key box mounted near the office door. He retrieved a set of keys to the Carson Delivery Services truck. Khalid went out the front door, opened up the back of the truck, and for the next twenty minutes worked to pile the mortar tube, its base plate, the ten mortar rounds and bags of propellant onto the bed of the vehicle. He went back inside collected the wallets, cell phones, and two Baek-du San 9mm pistols from the bodies and put them in a plastic Walmart bag.

Khalid moved quickly but thoroughly and with a purpose born from experience. While waiting for Abdulla he had mentally gone over the office layout, his recollection of the weapons and explosives that would be there, and every step he had to take to "sanitize" what would eventually become a crime scene. Although it wouldn't matter, it could be weeks before anyone would come nosing around an obviously closed office. There was always a good possibility a neighborhood "citizen" would break into the building looking for petty cash or office equipment to sell for drug money. They would find the bodies then shit all over themselves trying to get out the door, but they would not call the police.

Kahlid had taken a cab to a church four blocks north of the Carson Delivery Service office and walked the rest of the way. He didn't want to be encumbered by a having to return or dispose of a rental car. After he had finished loading the weaponry into the truck, Khalid made a final sweep of the offices, the three vehicles outside, and the bodies. He found nothing that would, even under FBI scrutiny, link Abdulla and his team to the church massacres or airline attacks. It had been less than an hour since Abdulla had, at last, joined Allah.

After locking the front door, Khalid got in the truck and started heading north toward Baltimore. He would wind his way out of D.C. stopping every few miles at one of the ubiquitous fast food joints along the way. There were several things that every greasy spoon eating establishment had in common besides bad food. They all had easily accessible dumpsters and $11.50 an hour employees who didn't give camel's butt what went inside them. Or who put it there.

He would pull up next to a dumpster, grab a couple of the plastic bag wrapped smaller items he had loaded into the truck, and toss it into the garbage. It would take him several stops and over an hour, but by noon he had disposed of everything but the mortar tube and its base plate. Way too big, heavy, and conspicuous for a dumpster. Driving like a nun, Khalid left the city and headed north on I95. Getting out of the perpetually clogged traffic surrounding Washington he took the Stansfield Road exit and headed west. He wound around the Scotts Cove Recreation Area then turned south on highway 29. A few minutes later he pulled into the breakdown lane on the bridge crossing the Patuxent River. He put on his emergency flashers and opened the rear panel door to shield him from passing southbound traffic. Grabbing first the mortar tube and then its base plate and tossed them one at a time into the river.

Khalid got back into the truck and continued south on highway 29 until he could loop back onto I95. Once on the southeast side of Baltimore, he would exit I95 and drive to Eastern Ave. He would park near the Esperanza Center, leave the truck's keys in the ignition, and catch a cab to the Amtrak terminal. The truck may sit there for a couple of days, but by the end of the week, it would be sitting in some innercity chopshop slowly being converted into spare parts and scrap metal.

Khalid took the train to Pennsylvania Station in New York City and stayed two nights at The New Yorker on 8th Ave. After catching up on his sleep and buying some new traveling clothes Khalid, using a hotel kiosk, purchased a Delta flight from JFK to London Heathrow airport. By 0630 the next morning he was in London, the first leg of his journey back to Riyadh. The Sovereign Council of the maharib alsamt was humiliated at the trust they had placed in Abdulla's vision and devastated that once again the dream of a new Caliphate had been dashed. However, they were more than pleased with Khalid's performance. He was indeed a warrior. As for Khalid, for the first time in a long, long time he felt a twinge of sorrow. He tucked this away and never spoke of it to anyone.

The inauguration of the President of the United States went off without a hitch. There was the Inaugural Parade, and the parties, and ball after ball. No one ever knew how close they had come to yet another slaughter. In time, a surprisingly short period, the horrors of the five plane crashes and the church bombings went away; except for the friends and families of those who were killed or mangled.

It's an odd faculty homo sapiens seem to have. Something that on one day is the most horrific event imaginable, in an amazingly short period that memory fades away. Then, like gazelles on the Serengeti after a lion kills a straggling baby, the herd moves on.

CHAPTER 34

Five years later.

The alarm on Lim Duk's Samsung smartphone went off at 0630. It was Friday, the day set aside for on the job training, OJT, at the recently opened Hyundai plant just outside Yonan. Lim had just turned 17 when Pyongyang was evaporated, and the DPRK ceased to exist. His wife, Min-seo, was in the kitchen of their two-bedroom apartment cooking their morning meal of rice, spicy fish, and bok choy. In the past, it would have been their only meal and then only a third of what she was cooking now. There was never a time during the Chang Jong Nam dynasty when Lim wasn't hungry. Not just hungry but painfully, stomach cramping, hungry. Always teetering on the edge of starvation. But in retrospect that wasn't the worst thing. There was the fear.

Lim was fourteen before he ever saw a television and it was over a year after "the night of the light in the heavens" before he learned about the internet or heard a rock and roll band. Things were wonderfully different now. Hundreds of thousands of soldiers and civilians alike had died that night. Lim didn't feel sympathy or compassion for those who were killed or injured. His capacity for those feelings had been snuffed out before they had a chance to grow. His own pain had inured him to the suffering of others. Psychologists had long known that a child's brain could essentially be prewired to learn a second language if they were exposed to it during the first five years of life. The reverse effect was true as well. Growing up in an environment bereft of empathy for others virtually ensured the absence of that sentiment as an adult. But things were changing.

Unlike the aftermath of previous wars, there were no occupying forces in what had previously been the DPRK. The Charter Member countries of the AIFTU were identified and given the opportunity to buy their allocation of shares in the new venture and to establish its governing board. Each of the suggested member countries leaped at the chance to participate. One year after the destruction of the DPRK corporations were offered the opportunity to submit applications to establish a business presence and become subsidiary elements of the AIFTU. The response was just short of overwhelming.

The AIFTU Charter was, in addition to other concepts, based on an incorporation document developed by the founder of the original Sony Corporation following the end of World War II and Japan's unconditional surrender to the Americans. It was intended to facilitate the rebirth of a nation's business infrastructure and to lift the spirits of a defeated populace. When David Stakely and his team developed the original charter, they did so within a sphere of altruistic governance tenets. The most notable was that the AIFTU would:

Distribute surplus earnings among all citizens in a fair and consistent manner.

Promote the education of science, technology, and the arts among the general public.

Allow unrestricted travel and emigration.

Eliminate censorship and ensure freedom of speech, religion, and political ideology.

The defeat of the DPRK and the subsequent establishment of the AIFTU had unintended and far-reaching positive consequences. The United States, Russia, and China began experiencing unprecedented levels of collaboration and mutual trust. Iran inexplicitly pledged to halt their nuclear weapon development program even going so far as to shutting down their centrifuge facilities and allowing unrestricted access by UN Inspectors. And the global stock markets, after plummeting over seven percent, kicking in circuit breakers and halting trading for three consecutive days, rebounded.

Lim Duk didn't care about all of that. All he knew was that he had plenty of rice to eat, a pretty wife, and he could watch *I live Alone* on his 65" TV without soldiers kicking in his door.

Finally, life was good.

ACKNOWLEDGMENT

I dedicate this book and every good thing I have done or tried to do, to my wife. She is the source of my strength and encouragement. She comforts me when I am down in the dumps and kicks me in the butt when I need to be motivated. I love you, Trisha!

AUTHOR'S NOTE

The Enemy of My Enemy is a work of fiction. All characters are fictional, and any similarity to people living or dead is a product of my imagination.